Unexpected Findings

a novel

by Jenifer Rowe

ACKNOWLEDGMENTS

Thank you to my friends and to my family, and also to the following:

My associates at the Sacramento branch of the California Writers Club, for their encouragement, referrals, and shared experiences.

My talented editor Ernesto Mestre, whose insightful criticism helped me to move this book from a third draft to a finished product.

Gerald Ward at I Street Press, for his assistance with formatting and production of Advanced Reader Copies.

Women United, a chapter of United Way Sacramento, for their tireless work on behalf of fostered teens.

Cathy Amundsen Vincent, for recounting her experience of post-traumatic amnesia.

Orin Bennett, Colleen Tamaru, and Garth Youngs for their helpful responses to first readings.

Linda Furst, who spent three days scouting locations in Pittsburgh with me.

Finally, great thanks to my partner Richard Haugh, whose creative ideas, support and encouragement were priceless.

Chapter 1

On a wet June morning, Tess shivered as she tried to edge closer to her mother's warm body in their shared bed, only to find that her mother wasn't there. Startled fully awake by the drops of water landing on her face, she squirmed further under the play structure in Arsenal Park that only half-sheltered her from the rain. She froze when a hand grabbed her ankle. Looking over her shoulder, she saw a young man squatting next to her and backed slowly out of her leaky nest. He flashed her a silver-toothed grin from beneath the hood of his black rain poncho.

"SloMo, leave me alone, for God's sake," she said. "I'm tired of you always comin' after me. What do you want, anyways?" She tried to hide her fear and play for time although she knew the answer. Sitting up in a crouch, she got her feet under her in hopes of a chance to sprint away.

"Same as always, girlfriend. I want my share of your take from yesterday," he said as he moved a toothpick from one corner of his mouth to the other.

"I didn't do nothin' yesterday. I don't have any money."

"You sure about that?" He pushed her onto her back and swung his leg over her, pinning her down while he jammed his hands into her pants pockets and up under her bra. She twisted under his assault and tried to spit at him but missed.

"Well, now, that's a shame," he said as he released her. "Nothin' there. What're you gonna eat today?"

She scowled as she tugged her shirt down, trying to look tough. "I don't know yet, but I'm hoping it won't be some pimply kid's pecker."

"Oh, now, life ain't all that bad. You got to survive somehow, and I got me a business to run."

"My mama didn't raise me to be no 'ho," she said angrily.

He stood and nudged her with the toe of his boot. "Girl, your mama's gone and you're squattin' in my 'hood, so you better think about Plan B. I'll check in with you later," he said calmly as he sauntered away.

She waited until he was gone before she retrieved a hooded sweatshirt from a small duffle bag and pulled it on over her damp clothing. Taking everything with her, she set off across the playground to the women's restroom. While she was in a stall, she could hear voices from outside the wall. The words were muffled, but there was obviously a drug deal going down. She waited silently until the voices moved off before she flushed and opened the stall door. *No good getting in the middle of anything,* she thought. It was a rule she had observed daily since taking up refuge in the park two weeks earlier.

The rain had stopped. She spotted a bench drying in a patch of sunlight and sat down on it to warm up. It was a lucky thing SloMo hadn't checked her shoes for money. The twenty dollar bill she'd earned yesterday off of some fifteen-year-old would buy her breakfast at the drive-in down the street. She'd rather hold onto it for a while, though. It was the last money she had until she was forced to degrade herself yet again.

She sat in the sun waiting for her clothes to dry. None of this situation was good, but it was no worse than what she'd run away from. Not just once, either. Each time she ran, she'd been caught and returned almost immediately, because she'd

2

made mistakes. This time she was determined not to repeat those mistakes, and so far she'd been on the streets for about a month without being turned in. She had moved from one place to another – parks, alleys, and one night on the front steps of a church - in an effort to evade SloMo, but he always found her. She stayed on her guard, watching out for the police, keeping out of sight of the drunks, the druggies and the crazies who were her fellow campers. She had once resorted to chasing pigeons off of a discarded sandwich so she could eat it herself. The effort of staying alive was exhausting.

Thinking about food, her stomach started growling, so she stood and began a thorough search of the trash cans in the picnic area. After half an hour, she'd come up with nothing but greasy paper napkins and take-out cups. She rinsed her hands at the drinking fountain, wiping them on her pants, and then made a decision. She had to get away from SloMo. How was she going to find her missing mother when she was spending all of her energy just to survive?

The park trash was picked clean daily by a regular crew of homeless gleaners. She thought about trying to camp in a more upscale neighborhood. Surely she could find better leftovers in a waste bin behind someone's kitchen, and maybe better shelter in a thick hedge or under a tree in someone's yard. She was pretty good at staying out of people's sight. She feared she might face an upset dog from time to time, but that seemed better than being shaken down by SloMo every day.

Arsenal Park had once held some good memories for her. Her mother had brought her to the playground many times when she was younger, and she remembered Mama explaining to her the civilian tragedy behind its Civil War memorial. Tess's mother was pretty and smart. She always dressed neatly, and she watched carefully over Tess, teaching the girl to take care with both her appearance and her manners. Tess had loved to visit the park with her strong, confident mother. Now, though, the park had become just a sketchy refuge for a homeless girl. It seemed dirty and dangerous, and she thought that pretty well described her current life. It was time to move on.

So after packing her bag, she headed down 40th Street, planning to slip in the back door of a bus on Penn Avenue and travel east. She was small and quick. If anyone noticed her "crashing" the rear door of the bus as several passengers got off at Penn and 42nd, no one called her on it. She rode for a while, peering through a window, and left the bus at a stop near several restaurants. She walked until she found an alley cutting through the middle of the block and followed it until she came upon several dumpsters behind the restaurants she'd spotted.

When she started climbing into the nearest one, the smell of rotting fish overwhelmed her. She looked up to read the sign over the restaurant's back door, proclaiming that it was a Japanese sushi bar. She dropped to the ground and surveyed the other two choices, settling on the bin behind a Mexican restaurant. Tacos and enchiladas, covered paper cups containing nachos, an entire salad that looked untouched in its take-out carton, all were scattered among the usual garbage. This, she decided, would work for her.

She wondered why she didn't have any competition from the usual street crowd. These were much better pickings than anything she'd found in the trash cans at the park. Then she realized that it was early morning and they were all probably still sleeping off whatever helped them through the night.

The amount of food that people threw away amazed her. She filled her stomach with what she deemed to be reasonably healthy food and then crammed an entire package of tortillas, along with several still-wrapped pats of butter, into her bag for later. She felt a lot better once she had eaten well without having to break the twenty-dollar bill in her shoe. With the whole day ahead of her, she hopped another bus, intending to scope out the scenery along the route and get off when a location suited her.

In a city like Pittsburgh, made up of distinct neighborhoods each with its own culture and history, it mattered where a person lived. Tess had been born and raised in Lawrenceville, a solid working-class neighborhood with an industrial past. She had learned in the fourth grade that it was named for Captain James Lawrence, a hero of the War of 1812, whose dying words were, "Don't give up the ship!" Her mother had told her those were good words to live by. The neighborhood had been changing in recent years with the addition of hip new businesses and an influx of young people, but a lot of it had stayed the same – the tattoo parlor, the Arsenal Bowl, the hair and nail salons, the coffee shops, the bail bond offices.

A first-floor apartment in a divided row house was home for Tess and her mother Rose - until the day when Rose disappeared and Tess's whole world fell apart. While they were never anywhere near well-off, it seemed like the two of them had been doing okay on their own until Gram died. Tess didn't understand all of the details, but she remembered that her mother had a hard time paying the bills after Gram was no longer there to help out. She didn't think Rose would have let Antwon move in otherwise. A sharp pang of sorrow struck her when she thought about her grandmother's sudden death.

Now, riding the bus away from that familiar neighborhood, she felt tears burning in her eyes, threatening to roll down her cheeks and start a keening that she might not be able to stop. She shoved her fist into her mouth and bit down on the knuckles, willing herself through the pain to regain control. She could not draw attention to herself. Survival depended, for now, on staying under the radar. *Don't give up the ship*, she reminded herself.

The stop and start motion of the bus, the jostling of passengers against each other, and her careful reconnaissance of the various streets that passed by, all helped to calm and focus her. The bus turned down Friendship Avenue, taking her into Bloomfield. Its row houses looked a lot like where she'd grown up, only they didn't have so many cars parked out front, and the lawns looked greener. As the route continued on Friendship, passing into the Shadyside neighborhood, the shops disappeared while the houses grew in both size and grandeur. She didn't see too many people walking around, and the only ones she saw that had brown faces were the gardeners. She figured she'd better get off and back-track into Bloomfield, since it looked a little more down-home and less ritzy.

She got off the bus and started walking in the opposite direction. Gardeners were out trimming hedges and watering flowers. Some of them looked her way, peering under their hat brims, but no one waved or greeted her. She had the feeling that she stuck out like a raisin on a bed of rice, and she didn't like the sensation. She walked on for another mile or more, until things got less posh and businesses appeared on the street again.

After backtracking several blocks, she found herself in a long, narrow sliver of park that she'd seen from the bus. She decided to rest a while and laid herself down under a tree with her duffle beneath her head. A full stomach and relief at being out of danger (for the moment) washed over her, and she slept for much of the afternoon.

She awoke when a soccer ball rolled into her side and a boy of about six came running to retrieve it. Deep brown eyes stared at her for just a moment from a face framed with nappy black curls, then he snatched up the ball and ran off again.

Sitting up, she looked around. The late afternoon crowd of mothers and children, and just a few fathers, were enjoying some sunshine before going home to fix dinner. Women in hijabs, others in workout clothing, grandmothers, people in business suits, what Tess thought of as a normal neighborhood was what she saw. She felt like she could camp somewhere in this area without attracting suspicion. The trick would be to stay out of sight while she continued her search for her mother. She hoped desperately that she'd left SloMo behind her for good.

Chapter 2

Irv had been sitting peacefully in his recliner, reading by lamplight in the slanted rays of a late June afternoon. Fat, buzzing flies knocked repeatedly against the window screens. An ambulance siren wailed somewhere, probably headed off to Pittsburgh General, the sound fading as it raced away. Just as he was beginning a new chapter, a clatter in the alley followed by rustling paper and clinking tin cans caused him to lay aside his book.

"I am very weary of those wandering mongrels spreading my trash all over the yard," he said to the cat on his lap. He evicted the cat and rose, stretching his stiff legs and moving to the closet where he grabbed a shotgun. It was the second time this month that he'd had to chase a pack of dogs off with gunfire.

Opening the kitchen door, Irv shot off a blast somewhere in the direction of the trash bin but high enough not to put holes in his garage wall. As the smoke cleared, he lowered his gun and saw not a stray dog but a human face peering at him from behind his overturned can.

"Who in the hell are you? What are you doing prowling around my back yard?"

"I'm not makin' any trouble, just lookin' for food."

"Well, then go home and eat."

"Screw you, old man. I got no home, or I'd'a already had a nice dinner with my dear family by now."

"Come out where I can see you."

After a few beats, a young girl edged out from behind the bin and stood near the door to the garage. She wore a dirty red T-shirt and jeans, and she held her thin brown arms away from her sides.

"Anybody out there with you?"

"Naw, just me. You gonna shoot me?"

The words hung in the air for a moment.

"Not likely," he said. "That would just bring all kinds of trouble down on me. Get yourself in here and wait while I call the authorities." *Damnation. The last thing I want is the police barging in here, giving my son another reason to interfere.* "I suppose I ought to turn you in," he said.

"No you don't got to, far as I'm concerned. Besides, since when is lookin' for food a crime?" But she went through the back door, since Irv was still holding the gun. On her way to the front room, she let out a low whistle.

"You got enough boxes in here to build you another house." She passed by piles of envelopes heaped on a bench. "Don't you ever open any of your mail?" Glancing around, she wrinkled her nose and said, "This place smells like a dumpster. Lookit all the take-out bags and pizza boxes."

Irv followed her, using the gun as a cane. He lowered himself into a chair and nodded to her to sit as well. Except for the gun, she didn't feel particularly threatened. He was just a frail old white guy with patches on his sweater elbows and scuffed slippers on his feet. Once he put the gun down, she'd be out the door.

"How old are you, young lady? And what is your name, so that I may properly address you?" Irv watched her closely, wondering whether she was going to try anything funny.

9

"My name's La'Teesha Baxter. I go by Tess. I'm thirteen, and I know plenty, so don't go treatin' me like some kid." Her eyes began to tear in response to the ammonia fumes of cat urine, and she blinked, trying to refocus so she could see him more clearly.

"All right, Tess. My name is Dr. Irving Gladstone, and I am a retired professor of history. Now that we have introduced ourselves, let us turn to the task of escorting you off my property."

Tess continued to look around the room, her gaze darting back to him frequently as she examined it. It wasn't dirty, really, just crowded with stuff. She glanced toward the front door, counting two locks and a chain.

"What's your deal, Irv? Looks to me like you're hidin' away in here an' you don't know shit about the outside world anymore." She stared at him boldly.

"Where do you live, Tess?" he asked, trying to keep his voice neutral. He reached for a phonebook from the side table without taking his eyes off her.

"I'm on my own." She lifted her chin defiantly. "I rather be dead than go back to that last foster home. I get by okay doin' what I need to do on the streets. 'Least I get paid for it, and I don't get beat up like before."

Irv's glasses slipped down his nose a bit as he closed the telephone book. He didn't want to ponder what she might have been getting paid for. Should he call someone about this? Looking around, he shuddered at the thought of law enforcement or a county agency coming into his home. One of his cats jumped up on a pile of boxes and stared at him while another rubbed his pants leg. Three more cats were lounging on a rumpled bedspread in the corner. He wasn't sure where the other two were hiding, but he figured the health department would probably take his cats if they were ever alerted.

Watching her, he considered his alternatives. He could just toss her out the door and tell her not to come back. He could do that, if he was sure she wouldn't report the gun or make up some damning story. Irv did not like contact with authorities. The thought struck him that he hadn't had contact with anyone, really, for quite some time. No one, that is, other than his once-a-month housekeeper and his twice-a month son. Still, a homeless black teenager was an unexpected visitor.

The girl looked around. "You live alone? How many bedrooms you got here?"

"Since you ask, the first floor of this house includes two bedrooms, one full bathroom, a kitchen and a front room," he said. "The second floor is not in use at this time. What you see is more than sufficient for my needs."

Irv opened the phonebook again and started thumbing through the government pages. As the hour struck, no fewer than six clocks started chiming in various tones. The noise excited the cats, and they started wailing for their dinner. Tess watched Irv closely before speaking.

"How's about you letting me sleep in your garage for the night?" she asked finally.

He looked up in surprise. "And why would I do that?"

"I dunno, maybe 'cause you feel sorry for a poor homeless kid like me?" She lowered her head and looked up at him under her lashes. "Maybe I could even do some odd jobs for you in the morning."

"I am not in the habit of sheltering runaway minors. I could get in a lot of trouble for that."

"Who's gonna know? You prob'ly don't talk to nobody from one day to the next. It could even work out good for you."

"What are you talking about?"

"I'm sayin' maybe I should stay here," she said, growing more excited. "We can cut a deal, and I can do stuff for you. I know how it is with you. You're scared to go out. We had a neighbor like that when I was little. He nearly burnt his place down when a spark jumped off the stove. He was right there to put it out, but all those newspapers and pizza boxes 'most got past him."

Irv turned to face her, lifting a cat off his lap and readjusting his glasses. "Are you suggesting that you would like to room here? And why should I consider such a wild proposal?"

"So here's the plan: I work for you, see? You let me sleep here. I go where you don't wanna go, then I bring back whatever you need. It works for both of us. You down with that?"

"Why would I think that if I give you money, you'll come back here with anything?"

"Cause I wanna sleep with a roof over my head and a toilet to pee in and nobody messin' with me, that's why. All you gotta do is try me one time. If I run off with the grocery money, you're not losin' much, is how I see it. But I'm thinkin' I'd be stupid to run off, since we got a chance at a good deal. And I'm not stupid. Whadda you think about it, old man?"

"I think you make great presumptions, young lady."

"Yeah, whatever. Jes' tell me whether you're in on this deal."

Someone knocked at the door, and Tess ducked into the kitchen. Irv slowly got up to make his way the few short steps toward the entryway, leaning on the gun for support. The knocking grew louder.

Irv cleared his throat and yelled, "Hold your horses. Give me a chance to get there." Reaching the door, he undid two locks, cracked the door for a look, and then spoke through the chain. "Yes?"

A youngish man Irv didn't recognize stood there. "Hi. I live in the house next door. I thought I heard another gunshot, second time this month. Is everything okay here? Do I need to call the police?"

"Everything is just fine. I suspected some dogs were into my trash again, but I was mistaken. Thank you for your concern." Closing the door in the man's face, he turned around to see Tess with a grin on her face.

"I didn't think you was stupid neither, old man."

The cats renewed their clamoring to be fed, which reminded Irv that he hadn't eaten yet. Ignoring Tess for the moment, he moved past her to the kitchen. She stayed out of his way, watching what would happen next.

Rummaging through the refrigerator, Irv found a KFC carton shoved in the back. He pulled it out and sniffed at the contents. He couldn't remember when he'd purchased it, but it smelled okay.

Tess watched him set a couple of drumsticks and a half-empty carton of coleslaw on the table. She jumped up to grab a couple of plates from the dishrack and plunked them down.

"Inviting yourself to dinner, eh?" Irv said. "All right then, for the time being. But go and wash your filthy hands first."

She ran off to find the bathroom. What was he going to do about her? He wondered whether the neighbor would call the police to report that he'd been firing a gun. Above all else, Irv valued his privacy, which was dependent upon him maintaining his independence. Which seemed to be getting harder every day.

He turned to the cats mewling around his feet and shuffled between them to retrieve the sack of kibbles from the counter. Bending over to pour it into their bowls, he grunted and grabbed the counter. The girl came back to see him unable to straighten up. She put her hands on his shoulders and her knee in his lower back and pulled. He gasped and fell back into a chair.

"We gonna eat this cold?" she asked as she sat.

"The microwave doesn't work. Take it or leave it."

"I'm down with that." She snatched a drumstick and took a big bite, wiping her mouth with the back of her hand. She ate rapidly, her arms circled around her plate in a protective pose. Irv tried not to look at her as he cut his chicken with a knife and fork, but her smacking noises got on his nerves. At last he spoke.

"I'm not going to turn you back onto the streets this evening. It'll be dark soon. You can stay here tonight, but tomorrow first thing you'll have to make some other plan. You may use my phone to call your case worker or whomever in the morning."

She snorted and rolled her eyes. "My case worker's the one got me where I am now. She don't know what she's doing, and she gets smooth-talked by every con wants to get paid to starve some foster kid."

Irv raised his eyebrows. "You sound quite bitter. Surely the adults running the foster system are more professional about their work than you portray."

Tess looked at him, considering what to say and what to keep to herself. Finally, she decided to school him with a little bit of her recent history.

"Listen up, Irv. The first foster mom had a fancy house in a fancy neighborhood, four other girls besides me, but she beat us when we didn't clean hard enough for her. Hardwood floors everywhere, and she flipped out when she saw footprints. The fridge had a padlock on it so we couldn't get at any of the food when she wasn't home. We was hungry all the time. At dinner she'd cozy up to one girl and treat her like a favorite, give her extra food and such. Then when her back was turned the rest of them girls would whale on the favorite. Next time it was someone else. Wasn't worth the extra food, believe me."

"Did you report this to the case worker?" he asked.

"Oh, yeah. That just solved all my problems. Lorraine — that's my case worker - she stuck me in another home where the lady's son got me cornered in the basement and did what he pleased. He showed me a knife an' said he'd kill me if I told."

Her anger burned now, thinking about it. The boy must have been about seventeen. He'd pushed her to the floor on top of an old blanket, pulled down her pants, and clapped a hand over her mouth. He thrust into her and made fairly quick work of the whole ordeal. She remembered that it had hurt. A lot. The blanket showed blood stains, and he balled it up and took it away. She pushed the shame way down inside.

15

Irv wondered what the boy had actually done. Was Tess being truthful or was she was just fabricating accusations? If she was making it up, what might that mean for Irv? His concern grew that he could get into real trouble here.

Tess shoved a forkful of coleslaw in her mouth and continued talking. "Anyways, I was only twelve and I didn't know much, so I believed him about cuttin' me and kept quiet about it. I tried to run off, but the cops found me right away and brought me back. After a while, though, the old lady got suspicious every time her son was around starin' at me, so she sent me back to Lorraine."

Tess tucked back into her coleslaw. The ticking clocks filled the silence.

Irv had laid down his fork and now sat with his hands lying still on the table, looking at her as his cheeks twitched slightly. He was obviously unacquainted with the inner workings of the foster system.

"Well, then, where were you placed after that? It had to have been better, yet you ran away again. And now here you are."

She stared at him while she chewed, sizing him up.

"I'm not gonna tell you exactly where I was. How do I know you won't just send me back there? But that house wasn't any better, that's for sure. That lady – Dolores was her name – she made the five of us girls clean all the time whenever we wasn't at school. I guess I was used to that from those other foster homes, but she also had a creepy boyfriend name of Carl hangin' around the house all the time. And all we got to eat every single day was rice and beans."

"That doesn't sound pleasant, but surely it was better than living on the streets."

16

Tess could have told him what wasn't better than living on the streets, but she didn't want to make it real by talking about it. She fell silent, remembering.

Irv wanted to know more, though, and he interrupted her thoughts with another question. "Where are your parents? What happened to them?"

In response, her face hardened and her eyes took on a guarded look. She pulled the last bit of meat off the bone she held and pushed back her chair.

"I got to get my stuff from out back, seein' as how I can stay here tonight. And don't be lockin' the door behind me, 'cause I'll just climb in a window if you do. A deal's a deal." She ran out the kitchen door and reappeared in under thirty seconds with a duffle over her shoulder. Moving to the front room, she dropped the bundle and began pulling things out.

"Hold on there, young miss. You can put your things in that first bedroom, I don't want them all over the floor."

"Oh, yeah. Sorry to mess up your tidy place an' all." She stuffed the items back in the bag and stood.

Irv glared at her. "You may not approve of my décor, but I know where everything is, and I like to keep it that way." He indicated the piles of newspapers lining one wall. "Those periodicals, for example, are a history of selected current events for the past five years. I may need to refer to a specific article at any time, should a question arise."

"Yeah, like, who's gonna axe you about somethin'?" she said under her breath. She dropped her bag in the designated room, then locked herself in the bathroom. He heard the tub fill and felt grateful that she would emerge without the coating of street dirt that had come in with her.

Turning to the mail that had come through the slot in his front door, he examined every envelope carefully. An offer for life insurance, coupons for pizza and haircuts, a request for a donation to the Peace Officers' Association, and a utility bill. He tossed the donation request – Irv never donated to anything – and placed the utility bill on top of a pile of older bills sitting on the side table at his elbow. The account was set to auto-pay, but he liked to keep a paper record of everything.

What should he do about the rest of it? He might want more life insurance. His son had said that no, at his age he did not need more life insurance, but what did his son know? He'd better keep the flier, just in case. It never paid to waste an opportunity.

Pizza was an easy decision. Of course, he would want pizza, he ate it three nights out of seven. He would add it to the stack of coupons in the kitchen, on the bottom: first in, first out was his motto. Sometimes he would put on his extra strong readers and look at the expiration dates, but he didn't really like to discard any of them. There was always a chance that the pizza delivery person would accept an expired coupon, thereby allowing him to save the good ones for future use.

The haircut coupon was a tougher matter. He considered it carefully. The top of Irv's head was as smooth as an egg, but he had some lingering fringes around his ears and neck. When these grew long enough to start tickling him, he generally used a nail scissors to trim them as best he could. He couldn't really imagine himself ever going to a hair salon, and yet the discount for first-time customers was tempting. He laid it on the table beside him and sighed with the satisfaction of a difficult job well done.

Thinking about what Tess had told him at dinner, he wondered whether he could believe her. She was probably just conning him as she had no doubt conned others. He knew from his faithful newspaper reading that people were out to get you in this world. Yet she did seem convincingly like just a young girl who had met with great misfortune. Tomorrow he would turn the whole matter over to the foster system. In the meantime, she had gotten nothing more out of him than KFC leftovers.

"Well, kitties, I think I've done enough for today. I'll brew a cup of herb tea and be off to bed soon. We'll figure out what's to be done about that girl tomorrow."

Chapter 3

Tess emerged from the bathroom thirty minutes later and scrambled into the front bedroom. She shut the door firmly behind her and looked around. A blanket printed with cowboys riding horses and swinging lassoes covered a twin-sized bed. A small table sat under the window next to it, holding a lamp with a Daniel Boon-themed shade and a graduation tassel for a pull-cord. She switched on the lamp, and it threw dim light across the bed. A desk against one wall was buried under a scattering of paperback books, three-ring binders, pencil stubs and pens. Between the door and the closet stood a narrow dresser covered with cheap soccer awards and scraps of paper.

She dragged the dresser over to one side until it blocked the door. The scraping noise alerted Irv, and he called out from the next room.

"What are you doing in there? Are you rearranging things? I won't stand for that."

She chose to ignore his comment. He seemed pretty old for mischief, but so had the boyfriend of her last foster mother. She'd been lucky to get out of that house through a window with her meager belongings in tow. She trusted no one. Remembering the ordeal at dinner had sharpened her sense of danger.

+++

At first glance, the well-kept home in the stately Squirrel Hill neighborhood, with its beautiful rugs and furniture, looked promising. Tess sat in the front room while female faces in varying shades of brown peeked silently around door frames. The interview went just fine, with Dolores – the house mother – answering all of the social worker's questions straightforwardly, in a soft voice reeking with humility about the sacrifice she was making to house these poor girls. Tess could smell chicken roasting in the oven, and her stomach rumbled in response.

The rules were laid down as soon as the social worker left with the completed paperwork. Dolores ran a tight ship. Tess was one of five girls sharing two rooms in the house, and she was made to understand that she and the others would be cleaning this fine house any time they were not supposed to be in school. Her first day being a Saturday, the front door had barely shut when Dolores whirled on her with a list of chores. The girls all scrambled to their stations and began scrubbing, dusting, polishing, vacuuming – whatever they'd been assigned for the day. When they were finally called to dinner, it turned out that the chicken Tess had smelled roasting was to be eaten only by Dolores and her teenaged daughter Joy. The rest of the girls got rice and beans, which proved to be their diet day after day after day. When they complained, Dolores wasn't shy about smacking them with a broad hand.

Tess went off to the bus stop that first Monday morning along with the rest of the girls, but they pulled her to the side when the bus came. They convinced her to keep going with them to a nearby park, where they started to pass a joint around. Tess had never smoked, and she wasn't sure she wanted to then, but she did want to be able to co-exist with these older girls who'd been stealing food off her plate every chance they got. So she smoked. It felt weird and unpleasant at first, but after a few days she got used to it and started to copy the other girls' speech, swearing and laughing along with the rest of them.

It turned out that school hours were the only ones they had unaccounted for in their daily lives, almost the only time Dolores wasn't watching them or controlling them. It felt good to be away from her slaps and kicks, her derisive words about their skin color, her task lists, and Carl, her boyfriend.

Carl was older than Dolores, a whitey like her, with thinning brown hair and a tiny mustache on his upper lip. He came around a lot after school hours, claiming that he was in sales and that's why his schedule was so flexible. Tess started to notice that he liked to be there when Dolores was out for one of her many salon appointments, or shopping – her other favorite activity. He'd stick around until she got back and then ask her to fix him something to eat, which she always did. She seemed stuck on him, although Tess couldn't figure out what the attraction was.

When the weather turned cold, Dolores took the girls to a thrift shop to dig among the piles of discarded sweaters, jackets and boots until they had each found a few necessities that fit. The gold bracelets on her wrists jangled as she pawed around in her purse, pretending she couldn't find the fifty-dollar bill she planned to pay with. After making a big scene about how tight her money was, she hauled out the fifty for the bored clerk, telling the girls in a loud voice that the clothing would be their Christmas present as it was all she could afford.

Tess pretended that year that it wasn't really Christmas. She told herself that she had been kidnapped and taken to another planet where they only had a sort of imitation

Christmas, and she would celebrate the real one when she returned to Earth and rejoined her mother. She spent a lot of time making up stories in her head as the months went by. Some of them, like the one about Christmas, she wrote in the spiral notebook that she kept under her mattress, in which she recorded every day's events with a flashlight after the other girls had fallen asleep.

As the days grew warmer and April turned to early May, Tess began avoiding school more than ever, hanging out at the park with the girls until they saw the bus go by and headed back to Dolores's house. Tess was mostly getting along okay with the others, but she was tired of always being surrounded by them. One morning when she was in the bathroom, she overheard Dolores on the other side of the wall, making an early afternoon hair appointment on the phone. Tess decided that she'd go to school that day and then walk home during the lunch period so she could have the house to herself for a change. None of the girls had keys, of course, but they all knew how to take the screen off of one of the bedroom windows and sneak back into the house. So she got on the bus as planned, waving off the others, and then went home at noon.

As she climbed through the window and replaced the screen, she was feeling good about the prospect of some time alone. She froze when she heard a sound in the living room. Could Dolores have changed her plans? Tess crept out of the bedroom into the hallway where Carl stood in front of her in his shirtsleeves and boxer shorts. Her eyes widened at the sight of his boxers covering an obvious stiffy, and her heart beat wildly. He smiled and backed her into the room she'd just left. He held a glass of water in one hand, and with the other he pushed her down onto the bed.

"I got something for you that'll make this real fun," he said as he held out a pill. "This here is what Dolores loves, and I think you will, too."

He laid on top of her, his bulk making it impossible for the slight girl to escape. She began to yell, so he stuffed her mouth with a corner of the bedclothes until she thought she would suffocate. Stripping her clothing off her as he pinned her down, he began to slide his hands over every part of her body in a way that made her shiver with fear and disgust. He pulled the cloth out of her mouth and quickly pushed the pill in, pouring water after it until she had to swallow or drown. It didn't take long for the drug to kick in.

She saw the ceiling open up into a strange space filled with laughing faces. She saw her mother's face there, laughing along with the others. A voice in her head told her that she was a slut and a whore. Or maybe it was a voice outside her head. How would she know? She lay immobilized, all of her muscles reduced to dead weight, unable to move or speak. Whatever Carl did to her, it didn't seem to hurt as much as the first time. She finally passed out, and when she woke up, he was gone.

She got off the bed and struggled to pull on her clothing. After stuffing her few belongings into her duffle, she removed the window screen and set off. She vowed that this time she would not be caught and returned.

+++

Now she sat on the twin bed and emptied the contents of her small duffle onto the cowboy blanket. Digging around, she found her comb and set to work getting the tangles out of her hair. It felt real nice to have clean hair again, and she had found some toothpaste lying on the sink edge as well. She was careful not to lose her toothbrush, but she didn't always have a tube of Colgate to go with it. All in all, she felt pretty good. She wasn't sure what she would do in the morning, but she'd figure it out somehow. She had learned in her wandering days that there's more than one way to work things out.

That was what she called this time in her life - her wandering days. She didn't know if she would ever see her mother again, but she wanted to stick around just in case. Life on the streets was hard, though. Picking up a locket, she opened it and ran a finger around the edge of the tiny photo inside. After gazing at it a moment, her face went blank. She snapped the locket shut and tossed it back in the bag.

Next she grabbed a beat-up wallet and placed into it the twenty dollar bill that had been riding in her shoe. That was all she had, until and unless she gave another blow job to some kid in the park and picked up another twenty. She had decided from the beginning that she would try to avoid the more high-paying but also more dangerous gigs. SloMo, the monster in her nightmares, was always after her to put herself out there for more money. Tess had other ideas, number one being to stay away from SloMo. She just needed some time to think about her options.

"I'm turning out the lights now, young lady," called Irv through the door. "I rise early, and I'll expect you to have other plans when you are up and dressed."

In response, Tess shoved her bag and its contents on the floor with a clatter.

"I told you already, my name is not 'young lady'. It's Tess."

Shaking out her still-damp curls, she pulled back the blanket and fell across the bed. When was the last time she'd laid her head on a pillow? She was going to have to find a way to stay here for a while. Maybe she should start by acting a little less surly.

"'Night, old man. I mean, Irv. And thanks." After taking a last look at the dresser standing firmly in front of the door, she reached out to the little lamp and switched it off.

+++

Daylight was just starting to brighten her window when Tess woke to the sound of Irv's voice coming from the kitchen, accompanied by a chorus of meows.

"Yes, yes," he was crooning in a soft voice. "I know you're all hungry. Let me get your kibbles." A bag rattled, stirring the cats into frantic vocalizations. "Here we go. What shall we do today, kitties?"

He continued talking to the cats while Tess drifted back to sleep. The whistle of a tea kettle woke her a little while later, and she sat up in bed.

I better figure out a plan, or I'll be out the door. Running her hands through her tangled hair, she thought about the Three Main Things that her mother had stressed to her once she grew old enough to be out alone during the daytime.

First off, be polite – always and with everyone, but especially with white folks, and most of all with old white folks. Some of them aren't used to you having a voice at all, she had said. *I got a voice, and I'm not scared to use it.* Maybe not scared enough.

Second, try to be useful, but never to the point where you give up your dignity. Find something you can do that's worth

26

paying you for. *I guess I been useful, Mama, but I sure gave up my dignity along the way. Maybe now I got me a second chance.*

Third, be prepared to run fast if you get yourself in a bad situation. *That I am good at, Mama, you would be proud to see how fast I can disappear.*

Irv knocked on her door. "Are you awake in there, young lady? You'd best be up soon, my son is coming today. I want this situation taken care of before he gets here."

"I told you, my name is Tess," she said. Then, "Yes, sir." Didn't pay to be sassy, certainly not from where she sat right now. After pushing the dresser aside, she took her turn in the bathroom and then wandered into the kitchen with her hair braided down her back.

Irv sat at the table with a cup of tea and a piece of unbuttered toast. She saw that another piece of toast lay on a saucer in front of the other chair.

"Do I get that piece?" she asked.

"You may have it if you wish," he answered, "but you'll have to pour your own tea."

"You got any eggs? Or maybe some peanut butter?"

"I'm afraid not. Today is grocery shopping day, which is why my son is coming. He drives into the city every other Saturday to purchase what I need and bring it here."

"Irv. There's an Aldi around the corner. You can walk, I seen you do it. Why you wanna wait two weeks, runnin' out of food, waitin' for your twice-a-month shopping boy to deliver?"

"I dare say there is much you don't know about me. I do not feel a compulsion to enlighten you, however. Have you made your plans for the day?"

27

"Lorraine only works a half day on Saturdays. I can't get her till noon. But I got an idea what I can do in the meantime."

"And what would that be?"

"I seen out back where you got a big trash bucket fulla' smashed cans. I could drag it to the recycle center behind the Aldi and bring back the cash."

Irv looked at her sternly over his bifocals. "I am saving those cans until the price of aluminum has topped out. Then I'll be able to sell them to Schnagel's scrap yard for a decent price."

"What? Say what? You might die before that happens. And how you know what the top price will be? Why not cash 'em in now while you got 'em? You could make some space at the same time."

He opened his mouth to reply, but just then the phone in the living room began to ring. Irv scraped back his chair and pushed to a stand. He stood for a moment to regain his footing, then shuffled off to answer it. When he was through the door, Tess darted to the refrigerator and searched for something more to eat. Coming up with a carton of yogurt, she tore off the lid, found a spoon, and dug in.

Irv's voice came through from the other room, and she stopped eating to listen.

"Well, I know you want to be supportive of him, but what am I supposed to do? .... Yes, yes, I understand, but it's been two weeks and I am out of provisions....What? Next weekend? I suppose that will have to suffice. But I am disappointed, Joseph, I must tell you. ... All right, then. Goodbye."

Irv returned to the kitchen, where Tess had already disposed of the empty yogurt carton. He sat down at the table with a heavy sigh.

"It appears that my son is unable to come into the city for our bimonthly shopping trip. His girlfriend's son is playing in a soccer tournament, and he feels he must attend. It will be slim pickings from now until the next weekend, I fear."

"What? He only comes to see you twice a month?"

Irv considered his reply. The girl didn't need to know every detail about his relationship with his son. Joseph's latest girlfriend – Mary Ann, or something like that – she already sounded jealous of the time he spent dealing with his father's needs, and Irv wasn't interested in fanning the flames. To be honest with himself, he was afraid that Joseph would manage to put him in some God-forsaken 'assisted living' situation, where he would most certainly die of chagrin.

"Twice a month is usually sufficient. This time, however, the cupboard is unusually bare."

"Irv, I got you. I can do the shopping. Just make a list and give me some cash, and I'll do it."

"I hope I have made it clear that I see no reason to trust you with my money. You are a stranger to me."

She looked at him, considering her next move. Sometimes her mother spoke to her in words as audible as the noise the clocks were making, but Tess knew that only she could hear it.

"My mama used to tell me a saying that Gram had. Sometimes when you invite strangers in, you're really entertaining angels. Just pretend I'm an angel, Irv. I know I ain't no angel, but we both got to eat, and this is one way to work it."

Irv looked down at his hands. His knotty fingers knitted themselves in and out, in and out until he unclasped them. Taking off his glasses, he drew out his handkerchief and polished the lenses. Finally, clearing his throat, he spoke.

"I guess that's what we'll do for now," he said quietly.

Tess smiled and reached down to stroke the cat next to her chair.

"I will give you enough money for a carton of eggs, a stick of butter, and a loaf of bread. If you return, and if none of the eggs are broken, I'll fix us a real breakfast. If you fail, you will not get a second chance and I will have to call the authorities." He had no intention of calling any authorities – he didn't want them anywhere near him - but he thought he'd at least try to scare her with the threat.

"How 'bout enough for some bacon, too?" she asked hopefully.

"Don't press your luck."

+++

Tess was determined to complete this simple task and earn Irv's trust, but he was acting like it was some kind of war game. He must have told her four or five times not to give anyone his address. She could tell he didn't want anyone to trace her back to him. *Like the grocery clerk cares where I'm going.* He wouldn't give her a house key, just told her to ring the bell and shout, "It's Tess," real loud. Plus, she couldn't come straight back to the house, she had to walk around the backside of the block and make it a circle. If she thought she was being followed, she had to double back and repeat the loop again. Those were his rules.

It all seemed pretty ridiculous to her, but she wanted those fried eggs at the end of the performance, and it sure wasn't the hardest thing she'd ever done for a meal. She took his carefully counted money and stuffed it in her pocket, then walked out the door hearing the click of the lock behind her.

She'd gone about halfway down the block when she saw a figure that froze her in her tracks. He was tall and broad-shouldered, wearing a hoodie pulled up over a baseball cap, the sleeves pushed up to his elbows. The tats on both of his forearms, even at a distance, were unmistakable: diamondback rattlers climbing up from his wrists and disappearing under the sleeves. He walked with a rolling motion, owning the sidewalk as though it were his uncontested territory. As indeed, it was.

"Hey, girl. Where you goin'?" he called out. He grinned and spat off to the side as he approached.

He'd found her. She thought about turning back and hammering on Irv's door to let her in, but she didn't want to reveal her exact location. She considered running into the nearest backyard and hiding behind the trash cans. She briefly entertained the notion of screaming for help. *Like that ever did me any good.* As she stood paralyzed with indecision and fear, he caught up to her and took away all of her choices.

"Hey, Slomo. 'Sup?" She tried to sound casual as her heart hammered in her chest. On no account did she want him to snatch Irv's grocery money and doom her plan.

"You are, girl. I been missin' you, so I had my boys keep track of where you was. The other ladies been pullin' the freight without you, and that ain't right. Now it's time you stepped up."

"I already told you - you ain't my pimp. I don't work for you, I don't need you, and I don't want none of your

31

protection. I can get by on my own." She stared at him with fierce eyes, trying not to let her voice quaver.

"You think so, but maybe it's me you need protection from. Ever consider that?"

"What you gonna do, haul me off the sidewalk right here? I can scream real loud, and seein' as how it's broad daylight, somebody just might notice."

"Not here and not now, I won't. But watch your back. Me and my boys been keepin' an eye on you, and I can always find you." He smiled and walked away slowly.

She could feel him watching her over his shoulder. Tossing her head, she put one foot in front of the other and kept walking toward the Aldi, knees trembling, left hand clutching the money in her pocket as her right hand swung evenly at her side. When she turned the corner, she kept on going past the grocery store and followed a driveway leading to an alley. Moving from one alley to the next, she traversed about two miles of increasingly beat-up neighborhoods until she looped around and headed back to the Aldi, keeping a lookout up and down the blocks all the way. She was pretty sure Slomo was long gone when she entered the store.

Mixing in with the mothers pushing children in shopping carts, and the occasional fathers asking their kids what they never got to eat at their mom's house, she was anonymous – just the way she liked it. There were plenty of faces of all hues here, and she felt less obvious than she had in the last all-white neighborhood where Lorraine had parked her.

She found the things she needed and took them up to the express register. They rang up to a dollar and twenty-eight cents more than Irv had given her. She couldn't purchase part of a dozen eggs, so she hauled out her twenty-dollar bill and held it out. She hated to do it, but she figured it was kind of a business deal. Irv had paid for most of the breakfast, and she would find a way to make a profit in the end.

Chapter 4

Irv shuffled through the papers lying on the side table one more time. He was looking for a coupon that he was sure he had saved, offering fifty cents off a loaf of whole wheat bread. He regretted not having sent it along with Tess, but by now he figured that the girl was long gone anyway. When the clocks struck noon, he cursed himself for entrusting her with the grocery money.

Once an old fool, always an old fool, he thought bitterly. This situation was all his son's fault. At least Irv wouldn't have to deal with the girl or her social worker, and that was some relief. He would just have to keep ordering pizza and drinking tea until the next time Joseph could shop for him. It had felt curiously pleasant, though, to share a meal with someone.

A loud banging on the door startled him.

"It's Tess," the girl called out. "Let me in."

Pushing himself to his feet, he shuffled over and unlocked the two deadbolts. After checking to make sure it was her, he drew off the chain and opened the door about a foot. She turned sideways, clasping her grocery bag, and sidled in. Heading straight for the kitchen, she deposited the bag and pulled the receipt out of her pocket.

"You owe me $1.28. I had to put some of my money in," she stated in a flat voice.

"Is that so?" he said. "Did you plan to eat some of this food yourself? And where, if I may ask, have you been with my grocery money for the past three hours?"

"I ran into a situation. I had to take *evasive action* so's I wasn't followed, just like you told me to do. Anyways I followed your instructions, and here I am with the food. Are you gonna cook some of it?" She met his gaze until he looked away.

Damn. The girl was still here, and he was hungry, so he moved to the kitchen with a scowl on his face. He got out a pan, melted some butter in it, and added four eggs. Bread in the toaster, kettle on for more tea. That was the extent of Irving's kitchen skills. Thank God for take-out and canned goods. These days, as ever, mealtime was when he missed Joseph's mother the most.

Irving salted the eggs and grabbed the toast that had popped up. The tea kettle was screaming at him, so he turned off the burner and poured boiling water into the two cups he'd set out with tea bags. He had a sudden feeling of déjà vu, realizing that, other than canned soup, breakfast was the only meal he had ever served his wife.

Helen was so frail toward the end. He would sit on the edge of her bed, holding her hand and gazing at her until she told him to go away. He took her temperature twice a day, bathed her with a soft cloth dipped into warm water, changed her diapers, replaced her sheets with the utmost of care – rolling her weightless form first to one side of the bed and then the other, just as he had been taught by the hospice nurses. Grimly unwilling to let her go, he talked to her every day about politics and teaching and her favorite television shows until it was obvious that she was asleep. When she finally left him for good, the foundation underneath him shifted. He had no use for the outside world.

Now he shook himself to clear his head and shed the memories. The eggs were cooked, and it was time to eat before everything was cold.

"Alright then, I've cooked the eggs and toast that you brought home," he said to the air. He shuffled off to find the girl. She was sitting on the bed, wedged against the wall into a corner of the room he had assigned to her, writing in a notebook. When he appeared in the doorway, she jumped slightly.

"What?" she said, looking up with wide eyes.

"Our meal is ready, such as it is," he answered.

She scrambled up off the bed faster than he expected and tore off to the kitchen. He had a hard time keeping up, with his cane and all, but they both sat down at the tiny kitchen table and looked at one another.

"Oh. I guess I should get the plates," she said, jumping up.

"That's fine," he answered, "but if you think you're going to earn the right to stay here by performing a few routine tasks, you are very much mistaken. I still mean for you to call your social worker after our meal."

"You got it, Irv." She fetched the plates, filled them with the eggs and toast, and sat down. She had to think fast to figure out a way to buy some time. She knew very well that as soon as she called Lorraine, the social worker would send CPS to pick her up and stick her in a group home until another Grade-A Loving Foster Mother could be located. After fourteen months of this, she was having none of it.

They ate in silence, cats brushing up against their shins, forks scraping against plates. Afterwards, Tess cleared the table and did the washing up. Irv was content to make use of this temporary situation and hobbled off to his chair in the front room. The thought occurred to him that he could get used to having some company around the place, but he reminded himself that he didn't know beans about this girl. When Tess emerged from the kitchen, he insisted that she go to the phone and call this social worker Lorraine, or Lou Ann, or whatever her name was.

Tess picked up the phone and punched in the number for the correct time.

"Hello? Yes, my name is La'Teesha Baxter, and I want to talk to my social worker Lorraine." A brief silence. "B-a-x-t-e-r." She glanced at Irving and continued. "Her name is Lorraine McMasters, and she told me she works on Saturday afternoons. Oh. Okay. When's she gonna be back in the office?" The girl played with a strand of her hair. "What am I s'posed to do in the meantime?" She peeked again to see whether Irv was listening. "I guess I can do that. Thanks." She hung up the phone and sat in the chair opposite Irving.

"Well?" He looked at her expectantly and laid his paper aside.

"No luck, Irv. Lorraine went on a vacation, and she won't be back for another week. They told me to stay with a friend 'til Monday. 'Cept I don't have any friends around here." She tucked her chin, looked up at him and smiled. "I guess you could qualify."

"Now just a moment, young lady. This situation will not stand."

"Well, what are you gonna do, Irv? Call the police? Cuz before you do that, just remember that I can be your hands and feet out there 'til your son comes around again. Besides that, do you really want the cops snooping around here?"

He shifted uncomfortably in his chair. She had him there. He looked at the ceiling and blew out a long breath. He guessed he could stand her presence for two more days, and he was out of ideas as to what else he could do. Tomorrow he would call his son and consult with him about it. What a mess.

"Fine, then. We will resolve the matter on Monday when business hours resume. In the meantime, you will stay out of my way. Is that understood?"

"Yup. I got things to do anyways," she said as she went to her room.

Irv turned to the newspaper lying on his lap and resumed his reading. He was particularly interested in anything related to taxes, stock market forecasts, political wrongdoings, and the "collectibles" ads in the personal columns. From time to time, he would pick up the scissors lying on the side table and cut something out, sighing gently as he added it to the pile sitting on top of the table.

Tess emerged from the room that had been assigned to her around three o'clock and stood in front of Irv. "This isn't so bad, right?" she said. "We can make this work, you and me. If we want to." Irv said nothing, and after a few minutes of silence, she retreated to her borrowed room.

Clocks ticked, cats slept, and the afternoon passed with only the occasional reminder of his inconvenient roommate when she made use of the bathroom or got a drink of water. He cleared his throat as if to speak to her on one of her appearances but thought better of it. The sunlight moved to the other side of the house, and Irv switched on a lamp so that he could continue to pore over the paper.

One time when Tess came out of her room, she noticed that Irv wasn't sitting in his chair. Moving to the kitchen for a glass of water, she heard his gravelly voice talking somewhere above her head. She listened closely, fearing that he was secretly plotting to turn her in, and then she heard him exclaim loudly, "Oh, Helen, what shall I do?" A shiver ran down her back as though she had seen a ghost, and she scampered back to her room.

As the multiple timepieces struck six, the cats began to yowl, mutter, purr and wind themselves around Irv's feet. He rose, stretched, and shuffled off with his cane, all seven cats following after him. Tess, roused by the activity, peeped out of her room and joined the procession to the kitchen. She waited until he had accomplished the distribution of kibbles and then spoke up.

"So. What we gonna eat tonight?" she asked, eyeing him in an attempt to gauge his grumpiness.

He looked up from watching the cats enjoy their meal.

"Well, I suppose that 'we' are going to order a pepperoni pizza, as usual. Do you have an opinion about that choice?"

"Nope. Sounds good to me. 'Cept my Mama woulda wanted me to eat some vegetables with it."

"Perhaps we could ask for some olives on top. Would that do?"

"Irv." She looked disapprovingly at him. "Olives don't hardly count as vegetables. Who taught you how to eat, anyhow? What about some broccoli and onions and peppers and mushrooms, that's what I'm talkin' about."

"That sounds like overkill. I'll order one half with the extra toppings and eat my portion plain, the way I like it."

He rummaged on the countertop, pushing aside piles of unopened bulk mail until he found a stack of coupons that were clipped together. Removing the top slip of paper, he picked up the wall phone receiver and dialed.

While he was talking to the pizza parlor, Tess wandered back into the front room. She started absently poking into the tops of some of the boxes lining the walls. Out of one box she pulled a Ninja Turtle action figure, tossed it back, found another one and threw it in on top. The box next to it was covered by a foot-tall stack of magazines. She riffled through them and found that not one was less than four years old. Three faded sofa cushions lay piled on the floor, partly covered by several afghan throws that were covered in cat hair. She sneezed, then turned when Irv cleared his throat behind her.

"I will thank you not to go through my things," he said.

"You play with Ninja Turtles? I'd'a thought you was a little old for that."

He glared at her. "They belong to my son. Or I should say, they were his when he was younger. I am safeguarding them for him until such time as he may find a use for them, although he thinks that's foolish."

"Why don't you just let him keep his stuff himself?"

"Joseph moves around a lot, from one place to another and one girlfriend to another, and he doesn't have storage space. He's been fairly rootless since his mother died. I have about given up on him starting his own family. Still, these items may appreciate in value as time passes. They're worth holding onto."

"Yeah, I know just what you mean. My junk gets more valuable every day. My hairbrush, f'r instance, it's practically priceless by now."

Irv didn't reply, just raised his eyebrows and turned back to his chair. He was about to sit when the doorbell rang. Tess disappeared into her room and shut the door. She heard Irv mumble something, and the delivery boy responded.

"Dude, this coupon is way expired. You owe me three more dollars."

More mumbling, feet shuffling off to the kitchen and back again.

"Okay, I'll take that one. Now you can afford to tip me, right?" She heard the front door slam.

He was cheap, that's for sure, but she wasn't going to point it out to him. Not while she was eating for free. She came out and headed for the kitchen, thinking how the pizza smelled a whole lot better than anything she'd found in dumpsters the past few days.

Again they ate silently for a time, Irv carefully cutting his piece with a knife and fork while Tess took huge bites from the slice she held in her hand. He tried not to look at her, but when she burped loudly, he raised his head.

"The pizza isn't going anywhere. You needn't behave as though you're competing with a pack of jackals for it," he said, peering down at her through his bifocals.

"Sorry. Where I been livin', you eat fast or you don't get to eat. I'll try to slow it down."

After another couple of minutes, he looked up again.

"Where did you say your parents are?" he asked.

"I didn't. Cuz I don't got a father and I don't know where my mother is. All's I know is I woke up in the hospital and they told me she was gone. A week later, they popped me into a group home, and I had nothin' to say about it." She looked at her pizza while her words hung in the air, then tucked back into it. She chewed and swallowed before adding, "But I been lookin' for her."

"Well," he said after a pause. "Perhaps your social worker can help to locate her."

She stared at him for a moment before answering.

"Mama and me was mostly doing fine on our own, and my Gram was helping some. Then one day Mama's friend Janelle hooked her up with this dude called Antwon, and they started dating. But a few months after Gram died, Mama said Antwon had to move in with us to help pay the rent. Things were okay for a while, and then they weren't so okay. Anyways, Mama and Antwon are gone now."

"What happened to them? Where did they go?"

"I don't *know*, that's what I got to *find out*." Her voice became almost shrill in her frustration. "I can't remember what happened just before I got conked on the head."

"Had your mother ever taken off like that before?"

"No. Never! My social worker says she gone and left me, and if the police find her, she'll be arrested for child abandonment. They said it happens all the time with druggies and such. But Mama wasn't no druggie, and I know she didn't leave me on purpose. It's been fourteen months, and the cops aren't even looking for her anymore, that's what she said. She says my Mama's prob'ly dead. I don't believe it."

Tess threw down her half-eaten slice and covered her face. Tears dripped off her chin. Pushing back her chair, she retreated to the bedroom and shut the door. Irv could hear her blowing her nose. He continued to eat in silence, pondering what he would say to Joseph when he called tomorrow.

Chapter 5

On the third day, Sunday, Tess was awakened by a dog barking frantically in the alley behind Irv's garage. The sun wasn't quite up yet, nor was Irv, judging from the steady snores that followed the dog's outburst. She lay there for a few more minutes, then rose and scrabbled in her duffle for her flashlight. Switching it on, she crept out the bedroom door and into the front room.

The house seemed familiar to her, resembling a larger version of the divided row house that she and her mother had lived in. This neighborhood was a lot nicer, though. In the front room, bay windows looked out beyond the porch onto a tree-lined street. A small brick fireplace sat along one wall, looking as though it had never been lit. Tess remembered how she and her mother had used their fireplace all winter for heat. Rose bought boxes of wood at the grocery store, and Tess collected newspapers from the curbside recycle bins to use for kindling.

Built-in bookshelves sat on either side of the fireplace, and these were stuffed to overflowing. Leather-bound books shared shelf space with tattered paperbacks, stacks of old vinyl record albums, framed photographs, diplomas, knick-knacks, clocks, cat toys, Christmas cards and piles of old catalogs. A door to the rear led to the kitchen, from which the back door led to a small, weedy lawn and then to the garage which sat on an alley.

Tess's bedroom was in the front of the house, to the left of the living room. She figured she must be bunking in what had been Joseph's room, decorated with frontier themes and cowboys, still sporting the detritus of a teenager who had long crossed into adulthood. Irv's room was in the back.

Although a full bath separated the two bedrooms, Irv's snores carried clearly across the gap. The bathroom had no shower, just a tub surrounded by tiles with tiny violets painted around the edges. Tess loved the tiles with their detailed artwork. She was pretty sure that was the kind of tiles that rich people would have in their bathrooms. The mildew growing on the grout between the tiles did not cool her enthusiasm. From the first night when she had filled the tub with hot water and scrubbed away the street grime from her skin, she determined that this was the most perfect bathroom ever.

A closed door to the right of the kitchen must lead to a stairway, since this was a two-story house. She was consumed with curiosity. What could be upstairs? She advanced on tiptoes, trying not to wake that grumpy old man in the next room.

With a sweaty hand, her heart beating fast and her eyes darting to Irv's still-closed bedroom door, she turned the handle and began to climb the stairs. A tread creaked, and she froze, listening hard for footsteps but hearing only snores. She turned at the landing and followed a hallway made narrow by the slope of the roof at the top of the wall. A small bathroom stood at the end where the hallway turned to the left. She could see straight ahead into the room at the end of the hall, but it was empty. A door to her right was closed, and she opened it carefully.

Her breath caught as she flipped on the wall switch. A daybed sat along the inside wall. A table with a sewing machine and a lamp stood opposite, under a window. To the right of the table, shelves lined the wall from floor to ceiling. On them lay neatly folded fabrics of varying patterns, grouped according to color and blending from one shade to the next, like the color wheel that Tess had loved to study in art class at school. She was looking at a rainbow that was complicated and enriched by the details of the designs and prints in each color.

On the left-hand wall hung various tools that looked familiar. A rubber mat printed with a grid marked off in inches hung from one hook, and a piece of plastic scored with slits hung next to it. Smaller squares, yardsticks, string, scissors, tape measures and cutting wheels dangled from other hooks. A basket on the floor held partially completed blocks of fabric ready to add to a larger design. Tess felt a stab of nostalgia as she recognized these quilting tools and their similarity to her grandmother's sewing collection. Suddenly one particular quilt flashed into her mind. She felt a jolt like a kick in the gut, and her legs weakened. The image in her mind was that of her own quilt, the one her Gram had made for her the Christmas before she died. Now it was lost, just like her home and her mother. She sank to her knees, unable to account for the feeling of panic that was washing over her.

She knelt on the floor, head bowed forward, unwilling to move, as daylight stole through the window. She was back in her mother's bedroom, hiding under the quilt; it was pulled up over her. She heard yells, glass shattering on the floor, something heavy hitting her in the head and landing on the rug next to her. Warm liquid was pooling around her. Then blackness. She didn't hear Irv as he approached and stood over her.

"How dare you sneak into my wife's sewing room like a spy?" he said in a low voice.

She jerked and sat up. "It's not like that, Irv, I swear," she said. "I woke up early and I just...I just...okay, I was snooping. But I didn't mean any harm. I was thinking about my Gram, and how much I miss her. And then I remembered something. I just don't know for sure what I remembered."

"Well, you can remember it somewhere else. You are never to enter this room again. Is that understood?" His old limbs were trembling, and the veins stood out on his neck. "I don't even know why you're here. What brought you to my doorstep?" he asked, mostly to himself, as he wrung his hands. He fell into the chair in front of the sewing table.

"I'm sorry, I'm sorry, I'm so sorry," she said as she pushed the hair out of her face and curled her legs around crosswise. "Listen, Irv, I'll go make you a cup of hot tea, okay?" Rising to her feet, she looked at him for a moment. Getting no response, she walked down the stairs and on to the kitchen with a trail of cats following her. Irv made his way downstairs after her eventually.

After the two of them had shared some tea and toast, she was back in her bedroom with the door closed, scribbling in her notebook, when she heard the doorbell ring.

"Dad, it's me, open up," someone yelled.

She could hear Irv shuffle to the door and pull back the deadbolt.

"Joseph. This is a surprise. I thought you were at a soccer tournament all weekend," he said as he unhooked the chain. "I was planning on calling you later."

46

"Dylan's team lost yesterday, and they're out of the running. I had the day free, so I thought I'd better check on you. Let's take a look at the fridge, shall we?"

They moved off out of earshot. She wished she could hear what Irv was saying and strained to catch her name being mentioned, but she heard only mumbles from the kitchen. She turned back to her writing, trying not to rustle the paper.

She'd been focused on keeping a record of every little thing that had happened to her since the death of her grandmother. She felt sure that somewhere in those events she would discover what had happened to her mother. She had "seen" her 12-year-old self taking refuge under her quilt, and the shock convinced her that other clues would lead her to remember what had happened that day. Her last clear memory was of coming home from middle school, looking forward to the week of spring vacation ahead, and finding her Mama throwing Antwon's clothing into a suitcase.

"Baby, we're gonna get rid of that man Antwon," her mother was saying. "I have had it with his drinking and his drugs and his sketchy friends. It's just gonna be you and me again, girlfriend. Rose and Tess, we don't need anybody else."

Tess had asked if that meant she could go back to sleeping in the big bed with her Mama again. Ever since Antwon had moved in, she had been sleeping on a cot behind a curtain in the living room. She had taped posters of her favorite boy bands on the wall over the cot, and she had a little nightstand to hold her books. Even with her few belongings arranged around her, though, she mostly felt temporary there, like she was just waiting for a real room.

Now, trying to bring that day back into focus, she couldn't remember whether or nor her mother had answered her question. She dug into her duffle and came up with an older notebook, the one that she'd managed to grab from the apartment when the police brought her back to collect her clothing.

+++

Her tiny family had never included a man. She knew that her grandfather had died when Rose was in high school. Rose used to tell her stories at bedtime about Gramps' work at the railyards and all the jokes he used to play on his friends. Gram's apartment was a short bus ride away, and Tess spent a lot of time there while her mother worked at a nearby bakery shop. Gram just pressed her lips together and looked away whenever Tess asked about her own father. Mama told Tess only that her daddy was a jazz musician, and that his life was on the road, not home with a family. So she stopped asking – stopped caring, in fact. The girl felt loved and secure within the small circle of females that defined "family" to her.

Tess knew that Rose had always had boyfriends, none of whom lasted very long, but she had never had any of them over to the apartment. She only went out on Saturday nights when her upstairs neighbor Janelle could come and sit with Tess. On Sundays, Rose and Janelle sometimes took the girl along window shopping, treating themselves to lunch at the Shine, a diner where Janelle waited tables part-time.

One Sunday in July of Tess's tenth year, the three of them were sitting in the diner when a man walked up to greet Janelle. She introduced Rose to Antwon, explaining that he was an assistant cook. He was a tall, muscular man with a droopy left eye on account of a scar. In spite of the scar, though, Tess thought he was handsome and wondered whether her own father had been as good-looking. Rose

48

seemed impressed as well, and she agreed to give Antwon her phone number.

Of course, he called. Rose was very pretty, and Tess could see that men found her attractive. He would come by the apartment after his shift sometimes, and Rose would give him a piece from a day-old cake that she had brought home from the shop. At first, he was jolly with Tess, teasing her lightly and calling her "Li'l Stuff." He would tell her riddles and try to stump her. Soon he and Rose started going out on Saturday nights when Janelle could come by. After Tess turned 11 that September, Rose told her she was old enough to stay home alone. That felt both important and scary to the girl, and she always stayed up until her Mama got home.

Around that time, the bakery shop closed down. Rose got a job at the bakery department in the Aldi two bus stops down from their apartment, but Tess heard her mother complaining that the pay wasn't as good, and she couldn't get enough hours. Rose sometimes had to ask Gram for help paying bills. Tess knew this because Gram would come over and fuss about the receipts that Rose laid out before her on the kitchen table.

"Why can't you spend less, Rose? You're always thinking somebody's going to help you. What will you do when I'm gone? Think about it, girl," her Gram would say.

Rose and Gram had a hard time with each other, that was clear enough. Tess knew her mother loved Gram, but somehow, they always rubbed each other wrong, and the girl could certainly see it. She had overheard enough to know that Gram had not been happy about Rose's "wild days" after Gramps was killed in a railyard accident. Rose had been seventeen when Tess was born, still living at home, but she managed to get her high school diploma, a job in a bakery, and eventually a small apartment for herself and Tess. She was proud to be independent and raising her child on her own.

When Gram died suddenly of an aneurysm just after Christmas, Tess didn't know what to do with her own grief nor how to comfort her mother. Rose was clearly broken-hearted. She cried a lot, and she even stopped going out with Antwon. He called all the time for three weeks, begging Tess to put her mother on the phone, but Rose wouldn't talk to him.

One evening he just showed up at the door. Tess let him in, and Rose came out to the kitchen in her bathrobe. Rose and Antwon sat at the table and talked for a long time while the girl sat in the bedroom trying not to listen. Still, she could hear enough.

"Rose, I can't get along without you," she heard Antwon say. "Y'all are my family. I got no other, I left them a long time ago. My own daddy, that son of a bitch, he used to beat me bloody – how you think I got this scar over my eye?"

"Antwon, I've got my own girl to think of, I can't be your family all of a sudden," Rose said.

"I can help with the bills," was the quiet response. At that point they lowered their voices and Tess couldn't hear any more. He left after quite a while, and Rose came in to sit on the bed next to Tess.

"Baby, how would you like it if Antwon moved in here with us?" asked Rose. "Just for a while, till I get my feet under me again. Money's real tight, and I could use some help with paying the bills."

"I guess it'd be okay, Mama. But maybe could I help instead? I could babysit the neighbor kids or collect cans for recycling. Something."

"That's real good of you to say, Tess, and I'm grateful. But we need more than that. My hours got cut again, and now that Gram is gone, she can't be helping us anymore. I know it's always just been you and me, but I'm going to try it out with him."

So that's how Tess wound up sleeping behind a curtain in the living room. The cot wasn't as comfy as the big bed with her mother, and yet she had her own private space for the first time in her life. That was when she started writing every day in a spiral notebook, on whose cover she had written MY DIARY across the top in black Sharpie, with magazine photos of her idols pasted under the words.

Life didn't change much for Tess at first. Rose was working the early shift, and most days when she got home from school, her mother was already there fixing something for dinner. The two of them ate together, chattering about the day. Once the table was cleared, Tess would cover it with her schoolbooks and tuck into her homework. Tess always felt better when it was just her Mama and her.

Antwon's key in the lock woke her late every night. She would lie still and pretend to be asleep, listening to him stumble into chairs on his way to the bedroom. Some nights he woke Rose as he fell into the bed, and Tess could hear her mother's hissing, angry whispers. He never responded with anything but a snore.

After Gram was gone, Tess feared that she would have nowhere in particular to go during the summer vacation while her mother was at work. She felt better when Mama found her

51

a day-camp program at the YMCA where she could swim and do crafts on weekdays. She thought she was a bit old for it, but on the other hand, she didn't want to hang around the house with Antwon while he waited for his evening shift to begin. He had made it clear to her that she was to stay out of his way as much as possible. Also, she was not to go into her mother's bedroom. Ever.

Tess started the seventh grade that fall. Rose was working a later shift, so she approved when Tess got a job taking care of the next-door neighbor's kids after school some days. Tess didn't like babysitting all that much, but she did like the money that she could spend on CD's, earrings or the occasional T-shirt. Rose figured that by now, Tess could take care of herself after school.

She had become an adolescent, and Antwon started treating her differently. He no longer called her "Li'l Stuff" or told her riddles. She often caught him staring at her, then looking away when she met his gaze. She once told her mother that it kind of gave her the creeps, but Rose laughed it off and said not to worry about it.

Mondays were Antwon's day off. Tess usually got out of school before her mother was off work, so when she wasn't scheduled to babysit, she was supposed to go to the library until it closed at five. When she got home, her mother would often be chasing Antwon's men friends out, telling them to go on home to their dinners. The air would be thick with cigar and marijuana smoke, and the table was always covered with empty bottles and sticky playing cards.

One Monday in March, Tess came home from the library at closing time, but Rose wasn't there yet. The poker group was snockered, as far as she could tell. A couple of the guys were cat-calling her as she walked in, so she went straight to her mother's bedroom, turning the button lock on the doorknob and hoping that Rose would be home from work real soon. She said a prayer, begging God to protect her as she lay curled under a blanket. She heard the men's rough laughter and caught her name in the flow of talk. After a while, she could hear the guys leaving one by one, and her spirits lifted a little. Then she heard plodding footsteps approach the bedroom door, and she cowered further under the covers. The rest of the apartment was silent. Her terror rose as she peeked out, watching the doorknob turn. She didn't know what to do or where to go.

She stared, frozen, as the knob shook and finally gave. She watched in horror as Antwon pushed himself into the room. He stumbled his way forward, fell onto the bed and grabbed her, pressing her further down onto the mattress. He stripped off her pants, then fumbled around groping her.

"Rose," he slurred. "Rose! Why you got to be so cold to me all the time? Can't you see I'm crazy over you?"

Tess was too desperately afraid to argue with a crazed drunk. She struggled, but he outweighed her at least three to one. Unable to move, she closed her eyes and imagined herself to be somewhere else. In the end, he was just too damn drunk to hurt her. He finally gave up and passed out on the bed next to her. She pulled her pants back on and slipped out of the apartment, running shaking up the stairs to Janelle's door.

Chapter 6

Joseph opened the refrigerator and stared at the contents. He began tossing out small plastic containers of leftovers as his father objected.

"Dad, these little dishes were all in here the last time I was over, two weeks ago. You've got to throw things out after a while or you'll poison yourself," he said.

"I don't eat that much at one sitting, so I save the rest. There's nothing wrong with any of that stuff. I'm not made of money, you know, and I don't approve of wastefulness." Irv scowled as he spoke, but his shifting eyes had the look of a boy caught misbehaving.

Joseph continued his excavation, pulling out a small square of cheese that was covered with green fuzz and dropping it into the trash bin.

"Just a minute, there." Irv grabbed the morsel out of the bin. "Cheese is made with mold, so what's wrong with this?"

Joseph shrugged and closed the refrigerator door.

"Fine, Dad. Go ahead and eat rotten food. I can't stop you. In fact, I'm tired of trying."

"What's that supposed to mean?"

Joseph sat down at the table and pushed his glasses up his nose. "I'm saying that I can't take care of you if you won't accept my help. I've asked you over and over if you wouldn't like to move in with me and Marian, but you won't do it. I'm getting tired of managing two households when I could manage just one instead." He rested his head in his hands.

Irv wondered what Tess was doing in her room. He fervently hoped that she wouldn't come wandering out while Joseph was there.

"I like it here just fine," said Irv. "I have all of my important papers and research materials right where I can get at them. I couldn't continue my work if I let you clear it all away and take me somewhere else."

Joseph looked up. "What work, Dad? You're a retired history professor, and you last taught in 1998. We're living in the 21st century now."

"Secrets remain to be uncovered. Do you know for certain exactly how Stalin died?"

"No, and I really don't care."

"You see? That's exactly the problem," Irv said with a note of triumph in his voice. He folded his arms across his chest, leaned back on the counter, and cocked one eyebrow at his son. "And while we're on the subject, if you like living with Marian so much, why don't you marry her?"

Joseph sighed. "Because as I've told you before, if we stay single, she keeps on getting her alimony and child support checks. We split the rent and the groceries. The arrangement works nicely for both of us. She's starting to complain about me being here so much on weekends, though."

"I have met Marian, and she strikes me as a very strong-willed woman. I'm not at all sure she'd like me competing with her for domestic rights. Besides, I prefer the mobility options of city dwelling to the dependence on automobiles that life in the suburbs fosters."

Joseph shook his head. "Okay, Professor. You want me to go to the grocery store? What's on your list?"

"I can manage, thank you. Since I didn't expect you this weekend, I've made other arrangements."

"Other arrangements. Sure. I don't even want to ask." He pushed back his chair and stood. "Take care, Dad, I'll see you in a couple weeks. Call me if you need anything. And think about my offer." He gave his father a brief man-hug and turned to leave.

As soon as she heard the deadbolt shoot into place and the chain rattle across the front door, Tess came out of her room. She glared at Irv, her mouth set in a line and her hands clenched into fists, ready for an argument.

"What's he gonna do about me?" she asked.

Irv was standing at the door, peeking out through the spyhole. At the sound of her voice, he looked around at her. "Do? He won't do anything about you, because I didn't tell him about you. It's none of his damn business," he replied. He looked back at the street. "Just like it's none of his damn business what my research is about."

She shoved a cat off a chair and sat down. In the quiet that filled the room, she unclenched her fists and took a deep breath. The myriad clocks ticked. She gazed at a pile of pizza boxes stacked along the wall beneath the bookcase. A plastic milk crate in the fireplace was heaped with crumpled papers, cereal boxes, egg cartons, catalogs – recyclables, it looked like, or else kindling. Her eyes travelled to the three-foot tower of neatly folded paper grocery bags that lay next to the fireplace. On top of the bags rested a miscellaneous pile of what looked like junk mail. Next to that, some metal parts that she couldn't identify were lying in a heap.

"Irv, this place is a fire trap," she said. He didn't answer. She looked down at her hands and sat in silence.

"So anyways," she started. She cleared her throat. "I got to find out what happened to my mother. And I need a place to live while I do that. I can bring home the groceries and take out the trash and do whatever else, long as you promise to stay out of my room. You down for that?"

He turned from the door and dropped into his recliner. Rubbing his chin, he sucked on his teeth as he stared at her for several minutes. Fidgeting under his scrutiny, she reached down to pick up the recently evicted cat.

"I never had me a pet. Does this one bite?" she asked. She concentrated her attention on the cat as she stroked its back.

At last he spoke. "In my opinion, your status as a runaway from the foster system does not give you many bargaining chips." *And I must be insane to consider taking you in.* "However, I can see some benefits from this arrangement for both of us in the short term. I will give you lodgings for ten weeks, on a trial basis. After that, school will start up and you will need to find a more permanent address. But there are conditions."

"What 'conditions'?" She tensed her jaw and narrowed her eyes at him.

"Obviously, you must tell no one where you live, as this is clearly not a legally sanctioned arrangement." *Joseph would have a fit if he knew the risk I'm taking.* "You will bring no one home with you, and you will be home by five o'clock without fail on a daily basis. You will stay out of my late wife's room at all times. You will also stay out of sight should anyone – most especially my son – come to the door. I will entrust you with a limited amount of cash and a grocery list, in trade for which you will put away the food and give me the change and the receipt. And if you should steal so much as a dollar from me, you will be out the door without a moment's notice."

"That it?" she asked.

"That is all for now. Other conditions may arise during the course of this experiment."

"Where you gonna get this grocery money, seein' as how you don't like to leave the house?"

"Obviously, I have need to go out from time to time. I call the OPT for a ride when I visit my doctor every three months and my dentist once a year, and also when I need to withdraw cash at the ATM on Liberty Avenue. My son helped me to set up the rest of my banking with automatic deposits and bill payments. Supermarkets, however, give me panic attacks." He looked at her. "That is not an uncommon affliction, by the way."

"Hm."

"Oh, one more thing: I will want you to do my laundry. It's getting too difficult for me to stoop in front of the washer and drier, moving things about. The machines are out back in the garage. You may, of course, wash your own clothes and linens as well."

Tess started to speak, but something stopped her. Pressing her lips together tightly, she nodded once. She paused to take in a big breath before she responded.

"Well, Irv, I think we got ourselves a plan. And I do want to thank you kindly. Life on the streets is pretty hard, that goes without saying. But sometimes life can be even worse off the streets, if you know what I mean."

"I think you will find that we can stay out of each other's way. I'll be glad to be less reliant on Joseph. A bit more independent, perhaps, eh?" He chuckled softly and pushed himself to his feet. "And now it's time for my Sunday nap. I'll put my laundry in the hallway outside my door."

He grabbed his cane and headed off.

+++

Tess sat still, absently petting the cat on her lap and considering. Life had certainly sucked so far in her young life, ever since losing her mother. At least here she had a roof, a bed and a bathroom. Irv didn't look like he was going to scam her – so far. Things were looking up. Maybe now she'd be able to figure out what had happened to Mama.

She heard something in the hallway hit the floor with a thump. A door clicked shut, and she figured Irv's laundry was ready for her to deal with. Lifting the cat off her lap, she went down the hallway, picked up a faded canvas sack, and took it to her room. She pulled open each dresser drawer, rummaging among the cast-off items until she found a T-shirt and a pair of gym shorts that she figured would fit okay. Peeling off her dirty clothes and adding them to the sack, she immediately felt better. She stuck the few remaining items of clothing from her duffle in with the rest of the dirty laundry and swung the bag over her shoulder.

The door to the garage wasn't locked, as the hasp had rusted through and was hanging loosely from its hinge. She pushed the door open and flicked on the light switch. The weak fluorescent bulb over her head cast a weak glow, so she waited for her eyes to adjust to the dimness. When she could see her surroundings better, she gasped. Except for some passageways through the clutter, the room was filled floor to ceiling with cardboard boxes, books, old magazines, rusty radio parts complete with vacuum tubes, paint cans, broken toys, piles of rags, wooden fruit crates, roller skates, glass jars full of screws, nails and nuts, the back seat of a car with ripped upholstery, bags of cat sand, a bed frame, lawn chairs, worn out shoes and boots in a jumble, and God knew what-else. Spider webs and dust lay thick upon all surfaces. Irv had obviously given up trying to stay on top of the situation.

Tess edged her way over to the far wall where she could see a washing machine and a drier. A shelf nailed above the machines held a few open bottles of detergent and bleach, and over the shelf was a window letting in what little additional light there was. She emptied the sack into the washer and pushed the contents down, adding liquid from one of the bottles. She'd helped her mother at the laundromat plenty of times, but this was the first time she didn't have to put coins in to start the machine. Despite the almighty mess piled around her, she felt kind of privileged as she mentally added free laundry to the list of benefits she'd be getting out of this deal.

While the washer chugged away, she looked around a bit more. Spotting a trunk in a corner with some rugs piled on top, she pushed the rugs off and raised the lid. A jacket and some overalls with a green and brown pattern all over them lay folded inside. Next to the clothing were a canteen, a pair of binoculars, a billed cap, and some kind of maps like she hadn't seen before. She spent quite some time examining the maps, trying to figure out what all of the semi-circular squiggles meant.

Giving up on the maps at last, she picked up the binoculars and pointed them out the grimy glass pane. The upstairs window of a house came into her view, and a figure passed in front of it. She hastily put the pair down, remembering her mother's warnings "not to go spying on people." When she tossed the glasses back into the trunk,

60

they knocked the billed cap over, and she saw what lay beneath - a knife with its blade stuck into a leather sheath.

Tess looked at it. She had never tried to use a knife for anything but cooking, and she wasn't planning to start now. On the other hand, she figured there's a first time for everything. Might not hurt to take it with her. As she reached toward it, the washer's spin cycle kicked in with a clatter. She jumped back and whirled around, the lid of the trunk slamming shut behind her.

Just then the fluorescent lighting above the laundry shelf winked on, and she heard Irv making his way into the room, his cane bumping into boxes as he progressed. When he saw Tess staring back at him with wide eyes, he stopped and peered closely at her.

"What's wrong with you, girl? You looked frightened out of your wits," he said.

She sat down on the trunk and made an effort to calm herself.

"I'm just fine," she answered. "The washer spooked me with all its rattling, that's all."

"I came out to make sure you got the load started alright. Sometimes you have to jiggle the knob to get it going. Looks like you're handling it, so I'll leave you to it," he said. He turned and shuffled back to the door, taking what seemed like forever to Tess. When she heard the kitchen door slam shut, her breathing slowed.

The washer finally shuddered to a halt. Tess loaded everything into the drier and started it up. Slowly, she turned back to the trunk. She paused for only a moment before opening it, grasping the knife, and shoving it into the waistband of her gym shorts. Pulling her shirt down over it, she closed the trunk and walked across the empty yard to the house.

Chapter 7

Tess walked in like there was nothing unusual going on. She passed by Irv, sitting in his usual spot in the recliner with his eyes closed, and moved on to her room. Closing the door, she leaned against it and thought hard. Where could she hide the knife so that Irv wouldn't find it if he decided to snoop through her things?

She decided that the best plan was to slip it between the mattress and the box spring. The old guy's back was so bad that she couldn't picture him lifting the mattress in an all-out search of her room. Sliding the knife, still in its leather sheath, to about the middle of the twin bed, she breathed more easily. *See? That wasn't so bad. Screw SloMo, I can take care of myself.*

Feeling better about her general security, she went to get a slice of cold pizza. Taking it back to her room, she flopped onto the bed, and pulled out her spiral notebook. Carefully, she wrote down the day's events. She needed to record every detail of her surroundings - she didn't know why for sure, but it was a compulsion with her. Ever since Gram died and Antwon moved in, creating a big ripple in her universe, she had felt strongly the need to capture everything that happened in her life.

After writing for about an hour, Tess realized that she needed to fetch the clothing from the drier. She'd been trained in laundromat rules almost since she could walk, and the concern that someone would steal your clothing (worst) or just throw it on the floor (not as bad) when they wanted your drier kept her vigilant.

On her way to the garage, she passed by Irv and noticed that he was asleep in his recliner again. She crept up to him to check if he was still breathing. He was older than anyone she'd ever known, even older than Gram, and she expected he could go at any moment. His soft fluttering breath reassured her, and she continued out the back door. *Still got me a meal ticket — so far.*

She collected the clothing from the drier and stuffed it into the canvas sack. Before she left the garage, though, she thought she'd take a better look around, now that all the lights were on. Moving between the stacks of debris, she kept her eye out for anything that might be useful to her. When she got to the roll-up door, she managed to release the bolt-lock at the bottom and hoist it up about half-way, letting in a lot more of the late afternoon light.

The sight that greeted her was even more chaotic than what she'd been able to make out earlier in the dimly lit gloom. Lidless boxes stacked higgledy-piggledy were stuffed with old clothing, even infant outfits. Other boxes held broken parts of toys and torn comic books. Piles of rusted scrap metal lay heaped against a couple of dented file cabinets. Tess pulled open one drawer to reveal yellowed file folders with dates on the tabs, some of which stretched back thirty years, all packed tightly with papers. She counted three battered and grass-stained lawn mowers among other gardening tools and buckets.

For the next hour, she became engrossed in poking through the piles of junk that filled the space from the floor almost to the ceiling. She didn't find anything she wanted to keep. She mostly wanted to know what-all a person could accumulate and hold onto over a span of three decades. The discovery process made her wonder why Irv couldn't seem to let go of anything, even when it was broken and useless. She hoped that the junk had been confined to the garage while Irv's wife was alive and his son was growing up with them.

Tess had never been too snobby to pass up a good opportunity that was lying in someone's junk pile. She and Mama had been dumpster-picking since way back. They were choosy, though. They didn't take outright trash, and they had come away with a few nice lamps, some serviceable chairs, unbroken coffee mugs – stuff like that. Tess had no trouble with the idea of gleaning. Her Gram had taught her that word, it was straight out of the Bible. What she saw here was strange and a bit frightening, like the uncontrolled growth of an alien jungle that could bury a person alive.

Picking her way past the debris, she came upon two dirt-encrusted bicycle frames leaning against a tool cabinet. One of them had no tires, and the seat was torn up pretty badly, by mice it looked like, but the other one seemed to still have most or all of its parts. The possibility got her excited.

Now that she had a chance to actively search for her mother, the problem of how to get around town remained. She'd been thinking that since she had almost no money, the bus was out of reach. She didn't like to hitch rides; the police could spot her and turn her in to the county foster agency. It had happened before. The agency would send her straight back to the hell from which she had escaped a month ago. She felt encouraged by this new discovery. *Seems like I got me a ride, if I can get this bike fixed up.*

She knew that she'd need Irv's help to fix the bike, and she knew also that he was still far from comfortable with their arrangement. So she figured she'd have to be extra useful in order to swing the deal. Carefully pulling down the roll-up door and bolting it shut, she retraced her steps and picked up the laundry sack. She decided that she would not only wash his clothes but fold them for him as well. After turning off the light, she pulled the door shut and headed back to the house with a kind of a plan in mind.

The heat of the late June afternoon pressed down on her as she left the garage and stepped into the sunshine. When she walked into the kitchen, though, she noticed for the first time how much cooler the house was. The dim lighting in the house had creeped her out at first, but she began to consider it from other angles. Maybe Irv's habit of leaving the drapes closed wasn't just paranoia. Mama had been all about sunlight, they'd had no curtains or other blinds on their windows. Up till now, Tess had been feeling pretty closed in at Irv's place. Now she appreciated the coolness.

Shutting the kitchen door behind her, she turned – and stopped dead in her tracks.

"Irv! What the hell's the matter with you?"

The old man lay thrashing on the floor. Tess didn't have a clue what was going on, and she briefly considered bolting out the door. Instead, she knelt down next to him and gripped his shoulders. His head was hitting the floor with every spasm that ran through him, and she pushed the laundry bag under him to try to cushion the blows. Straining with the effort, she turned him over so he wouldn't knock himself out. After a couple of minutes, he quieted and seemed to be asleep. Or unconscious, she didn't know which. She noticed that he'd peed himself. He was too heavy for her to move, so she just sat there waiting for him to come around. After a few minutes, he did so.

"Unngh." He spat and rolled onto his back.

"You're a sight, Irv," she said.

He didn't try to speak. He just raised his arms like a baby, waiting for her to help him sit upright. When he got his knees under him, she slung his arm around her shoulders and hauled him to his feet. Together they shuffle-stepped down the hall to his room, where she peeled off his wet pants. He tried to stop her, but he was far too frail to be effective.

"Irv, quit fussin' at me. I already seen all that man junk, and it's nothin' special in my opinion. You're gonna catch a chill in those wet clothes. Now get under that blanket."

Obediently, he fell back and pulled the covers over himself.

"What happened?" he whispered, hoping that she didn't know what a seizure looked like.

"I'm not sure. All's I know is Mama always treated anything wrong with me by cooking me up something to eat. Unless I had a fever - then she'd just wait for me to sweat it out. Or if I was hurling. A person doesn't eat when they're hurling." She said all of this mostly to herself, ticking off possible maladies on her fingers. She looked at him. "You don't have a fever that I can tell, and you're not hurling, so I guess I'll just feed you."

As she went out the bedroom door, all of the clocks began to strike six, sending up a general wailing from the assembled cats. A parade of tails followed her down the hallway to the kitchen.

Once the kibbles were dished out and the floor was mopped up, Tess began to search the cupboards. She found some provisions that Joseph had no doubt supplied. Irving, cooking-challenged as he was, had never noticed them nor tried to put them to use. She located a small bag of rice, a can of tuna, some condensed cream of mushroom soup, and even a few spices – onion flakes, garlic powder, salt and pepper. She found a can of green beans that looked like it'd been there for a while, but firmly believing that beggars can't be choosers, she plucked it from the shelf, along with some canned peaches.

Tess had learned how to make a decent tuna casserole in about the fourth grade. She found a pot that she could use for the rice and set it to simmering. When it was done, she pulled out a casserole dish that said "oven-proof" on the bottom, mixed everything together, and stuck it in the oven. It wasn't fancy, but it would do. Damn if it wouldn't feel good to eat real food again, instead of that slop that she was forever being fed at the last foster home. Even McDonald's trash was heartier than what she and the other kids in that house had been getting.

She put the green beans on the stove to heat and poured the peach slices into a cereal bowl. While she worked, she heard the sound of water filling the tub down the hall. A while later, Irv appeared in clean pajamas and a robe, lowering himself with a grunt onto a chair at the table.

He looked up at the ceiling and began to speak. "Thank you for your assistance. I deeply regret that you had to see me in such unfortunate circumstances," he said without smiling. His little speech reminded Tess of the kids back in her fifth-grade class trying to recite poetry from memory, as though the words were written there on the ceiling for them to read. She almost laughed, but she choked it back with a cough.

"Yeah, well, that's cool," she said. "I don't know much about doctoring, and I sure don't know what all else is wrong with you, but what I figure is you haven't been eating right. Not like my Mama taught me, that's for sure. Nothin' but fried chicken and pizza have got to be taking a toll on you. So I made us some real dinner."

He cleared his throat but said nothing more. Tess filled two plates, brought them to the table, and sat down. As they ate, she thought carefully about how to get what she wanted without making the old man suspicious. She sure didn't want him tracking all of her comings and goings the way they'd started out this deal. Finally she spoke up.

"How about I make a grocery list, a real one that's got some meat and fruit and veggies on it? Then you can look it over and figure how much money to give me. I can go to the Aldi tomorrow."

"That sounds like an acceptable plan, provided you know how to cook the groceries that you purchase. Sadly, my wife had all of the kitchen arts while I have none."

It was an encouraging response, so far. She wanted more.

"But here's the thing. I want to go in and out of the kitchen door here, so's I can put the groceries down and get to work organizing them. I don't wanna stand out on the front porch hollering till you open up. It doesn't look right, and it might attract attention, you know what I mean?"

Silence ensued. She was wise enough not to rush him. He finally looked up from his plate.

"Yes, I see your point."

"So, Irv, how 'bout you give me a key to the kitchen door? I can hang it on a hook right there next to the mugs when I'm not using it, and you'll always know where it is."

He gazed at a spot somewhere over her head as he continued to chew. She waited, already knowing that to push him was fruitless. The clocks ticked, the cats wound around their feet, their forks scraped their plates, the moments went by, and she tried not to fidget. She had almost given up hope when he spoke.

"Very well. I am in agreement with your plan. Give me your grocery list this evening, and I will provide you with a key and some money tomorrow morning."

Hallelujah! She was going to make herself useful. Maybe this arrangement would work out for both of them after all.

Chapter 8

Tess woke up feeling hopeful. She'd given her grocery list to Irv before going off to her room the night before. The provisions she had written down were nothing fancy, but they sure beat take-out every night. She wouldn't mind eating decent meals as a regular occurrence, and clearly Irv needed some nutrition as well. Also, she was counting on getting her hands on that house key to further her plans.

Now she heard the cats yowling and the tea kettle whistling. She pulled the locket out of her duffle and opened it. *Today I'm going to be real useful, Mama.* She gazed at it for a moment and then, snapping it shut, she started to get ready for the day.

After washing up in the bathroom, she came back to her room, pulled on her now-clean jeans and a T-shirt, and began to attack her hair. It hadn't been cut in quite a while, and the thick black curls were always a challenge. Usually she just braided it. Today she took extra time so she wouldn't look like some street kid when she dealt with the folks at the Aldi. After making a single fat braid in back, she wound it in a circle and fastened it in a bun with a second rubber band so it would look tidy. Feeling ready for the challenge that the day presented, and pretty grown-up as well, she made her way to the kitchen.

"Good morning, Irving." She thought she'd better greet him extra politely on this important occasion.

He grunted in response. He was still in his bathrobe, sipping at his tea, not seeming quite his usual superior self. He

71

looked, in fact, like an embarrassed schoolboy. Tess was surprised to realize that she was also still kind of shaken by yesterday's incident, which seemed to have sapped some of Irv's "spit and vinegar," as her Gram would have said.

She pulled out the eggs and butter from the refrigerator and set to work making something they both could eat. He didn't offer to help, and she was just as glad to have his old self tucked out of the way. Putting some bread in the toaster, she wondered what she should say first.

While she cooked, she opened up the subject that was top of mind: groceries. Which would lead to a related topic: a key.

"Did you look at my grocery list?" she asked without looking at him. She was trying to breathe normally so she wouldn't seem nervous.

"I did. Unfortunately, I have no idea what some of those items on your list cost. Joseph normally does my shopping. I reimburse him for the total, but I don't examine the receipt in detail. Also, you are asking for things I normally wouldn't buy. All of those vegetables, for example. What's wrong with canned peas?"

"Canned food is what I got day in and day out at the group home where they stuck me after the first time I ran away. I hate it. Tastes like mush. And then at the next house, all's I got every meal was rice and beans. Period. You could learn to eat some greens, cooked or not."

"I don't know how to prepare those things. That's what I like about take-out."

She put a plate of eggs and toast in front of him and sat down.

"You want to wind up havin' a fit on the floor again, Irv? You need to start eating right. I'll cook for the both of us, my

72

mama taught me enough. I been sayin' I can do for you, long as you let me live here. And I can't live here if you end up dead."

He offered no answer. He was busy mopping up egg yolk with his toast and washing it down with tea.

"Just give me eighty bucks. That oughta be enough, and if it's too much, I'll bring back what's left. Listen, I'll leave all my stuff here, so that way you know I'll be back. I'd never take off without my duffle, there's some real important things in there. Just please trust me."

She tried to keep the urgency out of her voice, and at the same time she wondered whether she could trust him not to go nosing around in her belongings. In fact, the duffle itself was a prize she had found in a dumpster. Most all of the other foster kids dragged their belongings from house to house in trash bags.

Irv finished wiping his plate and set his empty teacup in its saucer. Sighing, he looked at her with rheumy eyes. She realized she was holding her breath, and she breathed out slowly. Didn't he know how much she was risking in trusting this man that she'd met only three days ago? She'd never known any really old people before, that is, older than Gram. He looked as though a strong breeze could knock him clear to the ground. Since yesterday's situation, she felt a sense almost of responsibility that was new to her, and she didn't like the feeling at all. She didn't want to be responsible for anyone, she just wanted to find out what had happened to her mother.

"I'll give you eighty dollars in cash," he said. "And a key to the kitchen door. I'll be here waiting for you when you return." Tess grinned.

73

After clearing up the breakfast dishes, Tess realized she had another problem. How was she supposed to get the multiple bags of groceries home from the store? Her mother had had a fold-up cart that the two of them used when they went to the Save-Mart six blocks away from their apartment. The Aldi was about four longish blocks from Irv's house, and she didn't think she could lug all the food on her list home by herself. She mentioned the difficulty to Irv, and he led her out to the garage.

Flicking on the light, he began to tap his way around the piles, using his cane to search for open passages.

"I'm sure it's right around here," he said, without explaining what he was looking for.

Tess followed along behind him, brushing cobwebs from her face and trying not to sneeze. Almost everything she saw was in far worse shape than anything she or her mother had ever considered "liberating" from a dumpster.

Finally, he stopped in front of a stack of old record albums that was resting on a packing blanket that, in turn, covered up the shape beneath it. He pointed to the stack and indicated with a head wag that she was to move the records. She piled them on the floor and stood waiting. He pulled off the blanket to reveal a faded red wagon with a slightly bent handle and the words "Radio Flyer" painted on the side.

"You can use this," he said, and turned to go. Clearly, it was up to Tess to extricate the wagon from the mess and maneuver it to the store. She looked down at it and smiled. *Problem solved, girl.*

Once she had the wagon out the garage side door and wiped down with a rag, she went back into the house to reckon with Irv. She stood in front of his recliner, rocking from one foot to the other. She was half-afraid he'd change his mind any minute and refuse to give her the money or the key.

Instead, he held out her list and eighty dollars, which she hastily stuffed into her pants pocket. Then, pulling open a drawer in his side table, he rummaged around among note scraps, rubber bands, paper clips, a few pairs of reading glasses, a bottle opener, several stray playing cards, and whatever other claptrap lay in there. At last he laid his fingers on a key bound to a cheap keyring advertising Schlitz beer. He handed it to her with a stern warning.

"I do not make a habit of coming and going through the kitchen door. This is the only key that I have left, so take care not to lose it. From now on, when I have not given you permission to roam about, the key must hang from a hook over the kitchen counter, so that I can keep the house secure."

"You got it, Irv. I guess I'll be off then." She took the key and was out the back door before he'd even picked up the newspaper lying on his lap.

Tess grabbed the wagon handle and pulled it into the alley. The day was warm and pleasant, not as humid as so many summer days are in Pittsburgh. She felt buoyant, as though her feet might just lift her off the pavement. It was the same feeling she'd had whenever she and her mother set out on Saturdays together. It didn't matter what their errands were: groceries, laundromat, discount store or dumpster-diving. The two of them were together, a strong woman and a lively child. Tess had felt invincible on those days, full of excitement for what the future would bring.

The past fourteen months had been one nightmare after another, starting the day her mother disappeared: beatings, rape, abuse, a constant feeling of hunger, and the hopelessness of being found and returned every time she ran away. Today was different. She'd found a safe (so far) place to regroup and make her plans. No one in charge had ever believed, or else they chose not to believe, her experiences in the foster system. Having learned not to trust authorities, she was determined to find her mother on her own.

When she got to the Aldi, she pulled the wagon inside with her. Almost immediately she was challenged by a man wearing a name tag that identified him as *Alan – Store Manager*. He wore a pressed white shirt and khaki pants, heavy black shoes, and silver-rimmed glasses that gave his face a severe appearance. Strands of reddish-brown hair were pulled back over his bald spot, and he had a tiny brown mustache sitting under his nose.

"I'm sorry, miss, but you can't bring that wagon inside the store," he said. "You'll have to leave it outside and use a shopping cart like the rest of our customers."

Tess straightened up and looked directly into Alan's eyes, meeting his clear disapproval of her head-on. She had been taught to be polite to adults. She was also unwilling to give up her plan without a major struggle.

"Well, sir, here's the problem," she replied. "While I'm in here shopping, somebody likely as not will take off with my wagon. Then how am I supposed to get all my groceries home?"

He looked unimpressed and was about to answer when a bagger moved closer to the conversation.

"'Scuse me, sir, I'm about to take my break. Seein' as how it's so nice out today, I thought I'd just go on outside with my coffee. I can watch the wagon."

The manager looked from the young man to the girl standing in front of him. She was blushing furiously, but she refused to avert her gaze. The bagger grinned.

"All right, Rasheed. If that suits the young lady, I have no objection." Alan Store Manager moved off to attend to other matters, and Rasheed turned to Tess.

"Let's get your wagon on out the door so's you can shop. My break is s'posed to be fifteen minutes long, but I might be able to stretch it to twenty. I get an extra smoke that way."

Tess was fully aware that this cute boy was flirting with her. She was also determined to get her groceries, so she smiled her brightest and passed the wagon handle to him. Then she grabbed a cart and dashed into the store.

Her first stop was the home hardware aisle, where she flagged down a clerk and asked him to make two copies of the key she held out to him. From there, she pushed her cart down each aisle, following her list exactly so Irv couldn't challenge her about any "unauthorized purchases." The ever-present recorded pop music played in the background as she moved from the meat counter to the produce section, choosing her items carefully and quickly.

After less than ten minutes, she returned to pick up the keys and paid for them with her own dwindling cash supply. After counting the remaining money that she could call her own, she stuffed it into the pocket that did not contain Irv's eighty dollars. She figured there wasn't much time left in Rasheed's break, so she wheeled off to the cereal aisle. As she was searching for Cheerios, the sound system began playing Stevie Wonder's tune, "Isn't She Lovely."

She froze in place, then sank to her knees. What was happening? She closed her eyes, and she was suddenly back in her mother's bedroom, only now she wasn't under the quilt. Her mother's iPod was playing this same song as she filled the suitcase lying open on the bed. Tess was dancing and twirling to the music when the door opened, and Antwon walked in. The look on his face stopped her cold. Then she saw the gun in his hand.

Tess stayed on her knees in that grocery store, shaking, with her hands over her head. A buzzing noise rose around her, and the P.A. system was announcing something. Suddenly a pair of strong brown arms lifted her up and led her off to a side room. She was lowered into a molded plastic chair, and someone handed her a glass of water. She sat blinking, looking at a kind-faced woman wearing an Aldi nametag.

"You okay, Sugar?" the woman asked in a deep, soft voice. "I think you need a minute to rest yourself."

"I'm okay. I just – remembered something, is all."

"Seems like what you remembered was nothing good. You want me to call someone to come get you?"

"No," said Tess, standing. "No. I got to buy my groceries and get on home with them. Plus, there's somebody watching my wagon, and he can't stay out there all day. I got to go."

She looked at the woman whose name tag, she could now see, said Ruth. She was still shaking, waiting for her legs to steady under her.

"You don't look so good to me. Let me call your mama." Ruth's eyes were bright with concern, but Tess wanted no more prying. She had to leave, and fast.

"Th-thank you, Ruth," she said, stammering. "Thanks for helping me. I surely am grateful." Then she spun and bolted out of there, pushing her cart through the check-out line in a desperate attempt to reclaim her wagon in time. She paid for her purchase, grabbed the receipt, and raced out the door pushing the cart in front of her.

The wagon was still there. So was Rasheed. He smiled at her as he ground out his cigarette with his shoe.

"All done? Here's your wagon, safe and sound."

She looked at him warily, ready to fly if he even looked like he was going to try to follow her home. She figured his break was over, though, and he'd have to go back in. He moved her bags from the cart to the wagon and inclined his head slightly.

"Thanks," she said, then added, "I don't like smoking." She turned and headed off, towing her wagonload of groceries behind her.

Chapter 9

Tess glanced back a few times on the way home to make sure Rasheed hadn't decided to follow her after all. She took care to look like she was just checking that a bag hadn't fallen off the wagon. Her mother had told her often enough that if she acted fearful on the street, the predators would mark her as prey. Early on she had adopted a bold, sassy demeanor meant to show courage. She figured that pose had gotten her out of a few tight corners already in her young life.

She turned up a side street before the block where Irv's house sat and towed the wagon down the alley. Coming around the garage with it, she pulled the original key out of her pocket and opened the kitchen door.

"Irv! I'm home," she shouted. Hearing no reply, she started unloading the grocery bags onto the table. When the wagon was empty, she pushed it back into the garage and returned to close and lock the kitchen door. Remembering Irv's instructions, she took a cup off of its hook over the counter, and in its place the key now dangled from its Schlitz keyring.

She looked at that key and realized that it was her proof that she wasn't gone. If the key was there, then so was Tess. Irv sure didn't need to know about the two duplicates in her pants pocket.

While she was unpacking and sorting out the groceries, Irv shuffled into the kitchen and sat down. Without saying a word, he laid his hand on the tabletop, palm open. Into it she carefully placed the receipt and the change. She continued putting things away as he examined everything, counting out the money, wiping his glasses with a handkerchief and squinting at the tiny print on the receipt.

After several minutes he cleared his throat and looked up at her.

"It seems that all is in order with regard to the money. Now it remains to be seen whether we will eat a decent meal with what you've brought home. As I've said before, you cannot look to me for assistance on that matter. Let me be clear that I am not in favor of waste, so you will have to make good use of these supplies."

Tess ducked her head into the fridge and grinned. *Looks like I passed the first test. I better cook something he'll eat tonight, or I might flunk the second one.* Straightening up, she turned to him.

"You sure talk a lot of words at me, Irv. Let's see if you can eat those fancy words. Now fix your own lunch, if you please. There's some canned soup and soda crackers on the shelf. I got to think you can open a can of soup. I'll take charge of supper."

After eating a quick peanut butter sandwich, Tess went out to the garage and searched around until she found the two bike cadavers. Pulling out the one that still had two tires, she looked more carefully at it. She'd never had a bike of her own - Mama couldn't afford to buy her one - but she'd tried out a neighbor kid's bike a few times. It seemed like this one had all of the parts she remembered from those wobbly attempts to ride.

She tried to roll the bike out the door to the back yard to examine it in the daylight, but the wheels wouldn't turn. Both tires were flat, and it had a lot of leaves and grass and cobwebs stuck in the spokes. She dragged it outside and picked the debris out as best she could. Looking around the tiny yard, she spotted a hose coiled beneath a faucet and turned on the water. While spraying the dirt off the bike, she considered how she might fix the tires. She came up with nothing. At least now that the spokes were cleared, the wheels turned. Sort of. Sighing, she took it into the garage and went back in the house.

Later that afternoon, Tess looked up from her notebook to find Irv standing in her bedroom doorway.

"What's up?" she asked, sliding the notebook under her pillow.

"I've come to request that you go to the hardware store for me," he said. "One of my metal file drawers seems to be stuck shut, and it contains some reference materials that I need. A lubricant of some kind should take care of it. Probably WD-40."

"Where's this hardware store at?"

"It's the True Value over on Liberty Avenue. I would estimate that it's about a mile and a half from here. Do you know your way around the neighborhood?"

"I can go. But it'd be a lot faster if I could bike over there."

He raised his eyebrows. "I didn't realize that you have a bicycle."

"I don't," she said. "You do. I found it in the garage and cleaned it up some, but it has two flat tires."

"I see. Well, then, I suppose you'll just have to walk."

"So you're sayin' you don't know how to fix that bike? I'm surprised, Irv." She looked up at him in wide-eyed innocence. "I would've thought you was pretty handy, bein' a homeowner and all that."

82

"I never said I couldn't fix it. There's a hand pump out there somewhere, but I can't take the time away from my research to inflate bicycle tires."

"Supper's gonna be pretty late if I spend my time walking all that way and back. Why don't you just show me how to fill the tires?" She knew she was expecting something from him outside the bounds of their agreement, but it didn't hurt to ask.

Irv folded his arms and scowled. He wondered how much more she was going to try to get from their arrangement, and he was wary of giving in too easily.

"Look, Irv, this here is what I call a trade-off. You help me with the bike, and I go get your stuff. Or else I go tomorrow on foot, take your choice."

He sighed and turned to go, beckoning her to follow him.

After at least twenty minutes of poking around in the garage, the two of them found the tire pump. They took it outside with the bike, and Irv showed her how to connect it, then straightened up with a grunt and dusted off his hands. He reached into his pocket and pulled out a few dollars.

"I'd like a twelve-ounce bottle of WD-40. I'll expect the correct change." He went back in the house, leaving Tess to judge how much air to pump into the tires. When she figured they were inflated enough, she got on the bike and started to pedal slowly around the grassy patch. She fell off it a few times, then finally got it to go in a circle. She kept pedaling, gradually losing momentum and tilting further like a spinning dime, until she and the bike collapsed sideways. She didn't notice Irv watching her from the kitchen window.

Next, she took it out in the alley and practiced riding up and down past the row of garages, feeling more confident with every lap she took. She glanced around as she went, to make sure SloMo was nowhere in sight, and at last she rode out onto the street with a loud whoop. She had wheels, and with them came mobility, freedom, and power.

She was back in less than an hour with her purchase. Riding through the South Bloomfield neighborhood had given her a much better idea of her surroundings. Everybody knew 5th Avenue, it ran right through her old Lawrenceville neighborhood as well. Following it east, farther away from the area where she'd grown up, she got to explore a bit. The houses weren't all as grand as the last foster home she'd been in, but they were generally well-kept, and most of them had a few trees out front. As well, Tess had learned through bitter experience that a nice house didn't guarantee nice people living in it.

Irv was waiting for her in the front room, seated at his wooden desk with papers spread out in front of him. She delivered the can of WD-40 to him, along with the receipt and change, and headed to the kitchen to start supper. She felt better than she had in a long time, and as she started some onions frying, she hummed an old Aretha Franklin tune to herself. The song made her think of what had happened at the Aldi that morning. Rather than casting a pall over her mood, the thought stiffened her determination to figure out what had happened to her mother.

She decided that she needed to track down Antwon, since he was the last one to see Rose, but her mother had never even told her his last name. She knew someone who could help her, though. Tomorrow she would pay Janelle a visit.

As the clocks struck six, the cats started up their usual frantic vocalizations. Tess was determined to work around them without letting them trip her as she moved around the small kitchen. She called to Irv, letting him know that those were *his* cats and she hadn't signed on to tend to *his* cats.

He appeared in the doorway, leaning on his cane.

"I'd like to remind you," he said, "that I am providing both food and shelter to you – on a temporary basis, of course – and you, in turn, have offered to assist me with those activities that no longer come easily to me."

"So?"

"I am finding it increasingly difficult to bend over far enough to dole out kibbles to my beautiful companions. I would like you to take on that task henceforth."

Tess looked down at the cats, who were still hollering at her. "Even in the morning?"

"Even in the morning." He shifted his weight on his cane and huffed out some air. "Additionally, the litter boxes need tending to, as you can probably tell."

"You got that right. This place stinks. It sure would be nice if my eyes weren't watering all the time. But I'll only go so far. I got my dignity to think of, and before you start adding on jobs every time they occur to you, I think you and me need to have a sit-down."

"You and *I*," he said automatically. Then he added, "A sit-down?"

"Yeah, a little chat about who does what around here, you know what I'm saying? I'm square about helping you out in exchange for room and board, but you got to define my jobs. As I recall, slavery went out a long time ago. You can't just keep adding to my chores any old time you feel like it."

"Or you'll do what?" he asked.

"Oh, I don't know, maybe call the city health department and tell them about an old guy that's got a whole bunch of cats and enough paper lying around to catch the block on fire?"

He stared at her and tightened his jaw. Wiping his forehead with a large white handkerchief, he said, "We'll talk after dinner."

"I'm good with that," she said, and she dug into the kibble bag with a scoop.

When dinner was ready, she called him to the table. She had tried to stay pretty bland with the first meal that she had planned from start to finish: hamburger stew with onions, garlic, potatoes, celery and carrots. She was planning to ease her way toward more adventurous fare, such as collard greens, for after she'd trained him up some and earned his trust. Tonight she noticed that he ate steadily, after dosing his plate with a serious shake of salt and pepper and pouring a blob of catsup off to the side.

"How do you like it?" she asked after he'd taken several bites.

"It's pretty good," he said. "Who taught you to cook?"

She thought for a minute, wondering how much to tell him. "Well, first it was my Gram. I'd go over to her house every day during school vacations while Mama worked. Gram figured I better learn how to take care of myself early, so she got me started. But Mama made sure I learned about proper nutrition."

When they had finished, he moved off to his recliner in the front room, leaving her to clean up the kitchen. As she worked, she thought about chore divisions – what she could do, what he couldn't, where they'd have to broker a deal, and so forth. After her foster family experiences, she had become accustomed to being used as an unpaid maid service. She wanted something better here if she could work it, and she was confident that she could.

Leaving the kitchen behind, she grabbed her notebook and a pen from her room and joined Irv.

"So. I'm ready to make a list," she said.

"A list of what?"

"What I'm s'posed to do around the place so I can keep on living here. Let's start with what you and me - I mean you and *I* - each want. I'll go first: I wanna stay off the streets while I figure out what to do next." She said nothing about her mother. He didn't need to know too many details.

"Yes, you made that clear when you first appeared in my back yard," he said. "Against my better judgment, and hearing more about what you'd recently been through, and – eh – accepting your request for temporary assistance, I have agreed to house you through the summer months."

"Okay, so we made a deal. I told you I could help you out, and you let me move in. Now, I can't swear it, but I'm thinkin' your son is up in your business, and you don't like it. Why you didn't tell him about me, that's for you to know. And if you don't want him around, then I'm supposed to do what he used to do for you. Is that about right?"

"My son seems to think it would be preferable if I lived with him in his God-forsaken suburb. I disagree with his opinion. So I suppose your conclusions are not far off the mark."

"Jesus, Irv, let's just make a damn chore list and cut out the formal shit, okay?"

They argued back and forth for another half hour and came up with an agreement that Tess could live with. She was to handle grocery shopping, dinner preparation and clean-up, laundry, and cat maintenance. Irv would provide food, shelter and $30 per week in allowance. They were each responsible for their own breakfast and lunch, and they would stay out of each other's bedrooms at all times.

Tess wrote up the details on a sheet of notebook paper that she insisted they each sign. Then she stuck her hand out. Irv looked at it for a long half minute before he briefly shook with her. They had reached an understanding. At least for now.

Chapter 10

Irv didn't sleep well that night. He kept having what he liked to call "struggle dreams," where he was constantly fighting impediments. Driving a car in which his feet didn't quite reach the pedals. Trying to swim while wearing a heavy overcoat that dragged him down. Walking a large dog that he couldn't control and being dragged down the street behind the beast. Repeatedly he woke up in a sweat, his breath coming fast and his heart beating strongly. In the dark pre-dawn hours, he finally woke for good and lay there wondering what he'd gotten himself into with that young girl.

Tess, on the other hand, slept soundly. Both she and her clothing were cleaner than they'd been in at least a month. Her head lay on a pillow rather than on a scrunched-up duffle set down on the grass under some park bench. She had eaten the best dinner she'd had since she could remember. She had transportation. And she had a plan for the next day.

When the early morning sun began to brighten her room, she was up and moving. She washed and dressed so fast that she beat Irv to the kitchen. The cats swarmed around her, and she loaded their bowls before putting a teakettle full of water on a burner. Two sandboxes sat under what had probably once been intended as a phone counter. Turds were piled high in each of them, and the rest of the litter looked solid with absorbed cat piss.

She opened all of the drawers, one by one, until she found a box of plastic trash bags. *Merry Christmas! I can't live with this smell. That shit has got to go.* She took the litter boxes outside, dumped the contents into a bag and heaved it into the trash. Using the hose, she sprayed out the boxes and tipped them upside down to drain. She found drying rags and a large bag of cat litter in the garage, and finally she had two clean litter boxes where once had sat two containers of raw sewage. She even swept up the stray litter and crumbs off the kitchen floor.

By the time the kettle was whistling, she had scrubbed her hands and set out two mugs with a teabag in each. She could hear Irv moving about, so she poured the water to steep the tea. Then she sank down at the table and laid her hands out in front of her. She sat silently for a couple of minutes, until her thoughts began to speak up.

God, or whoever, I'm not used to talking to you. My Gram used to go to church, and sometimes she took me along, but Mama didn't like it and wouldn't go. She said everybody was just tryin' to pass the buck off to you and not take responsibility for their own shit. I don't know about that, but I could use some help if you're in the mood. I need to talk to Janelle, so I can find Antwon, so I can find out about Mama. She might be dead, or she would've come for me by now, but I still need to know. She raised her chin and looked around the kitchen. *That's all.*

She could hear the cane thump-thumping down the hall. Irv came in wearing creased trousers and a worn tweed jacket over a collared shirt. He lowered himself into his chair and paid attention first to his teacup, adding sugar and stirring it a few times before he looked up.

"Good morning," he greeted her. "I want to thank you for taking care of my dear kitties. It was a great relief this morning not to have to bend over the kibble bag while they tried to knock me off my balance."

"You're welcome. I guess I like not havin' to smell cat pee, so it works for both of us."

"Yes, well. I have an appointment this morning with my doctor. I've already called the OPT, and a driver will be picking me up at nine o'clock. I should be home by noon, and I expect that you will be here watching things while I am away."

"No, Irv, we talked about that last night. Before I got here, you used to just lock up your house and away you went. It's no different now that I'm here. You didn't add "guard the house" to my list of chores, and I'm not takin' it on." She looked at him straight on. "I got things to do today, too."

"But how will I know that you're safe?" he asked. "And how will I be sure that you've locked the door behind you?" He furrowed his brow.

"Look. Why do you wanna bother about how safe I am? It's not like you invited me in here in the first place." She scoffed gently, but inwardly she warmed at the thought that someone cared about her well-being. "And if the key on the cup hook is gone, then I must've locked the door behind me. I got stuff I don't want to go missing, too, you know. 'Course I'll lock the door."

With that, she got up to make herself some oatmeal in a pot on the stove. Almost without thinking, she asked Irv if he wanted her to make a double portion. Damn. Now she was making breakfast for the both of them as well. Truth was, it was easier to make a batch for two than it was to clean up after the mess he'd make on his own.

His ride arrived shortly before nine, as he expected, and he made his way out the door – not without a worried look behind him as Tess handed him over to the driver.

"She's my homecare helper," he said to the man helping him into the van. The driver just grunted and climbed behind the wheel.

Tess breathed a sigh of relief when she saw the van pull away. She went straight to her room, where she unloaded the contents of her duffle into an empty dresser drawer and stuffed her small wad of cash into her pants pocket. Heading to the back door, she felt elation at the idea that she could actually cruise the streets of Pittsburgh on her own. Straight to Lawrenceville was her goal.

The sites started to look familiar as she pedaled east. Once she crossed Robinson, she saw the houses become shabbier and the trees thin out. Factories and warehouses replaced the small shops that lined the streets in Irv's neighborhood. The change of scenery didn't bother Tess; in fact, she felt a wave of nostalgia as she passed tiny Kennard Park, where her mother used to take her on Sundays when she was small. A stab of sadness hit her as she remembered Mama sitting on a bench, watching her climb the play structures.

Rose had taught the girl to recite her address and telephone number when she was very small, putting the names and numbers into a singsong to make them easier to remember. She found their old apartment house without any trouble and tossed her bike under some scraggly bushes to keep it out of sight. She walked up the front steps and examined the mailboxes.

The house resembled a shabbier version of the ones in Irv's neighborhood, and it had long been divided into two apartments. Tess and her mother had lived on the ground floor, and Janelle was upstairs. The first mailbox showed the name L. Eastman where once the label had said R. Baxter. The label had long ago peeled (or been torn) off the second box, and Tess could only assume that Janelle still lived there.

But maybe that had change as well, along with everything else in the past year. Tess turned away and started down the steps, her courage failing for a moment. Then she stopped, squeezing her fists and taking a deep breath. Spinning around, she marched back to the door. She rang the bell and waited for what felt like long enough, then rang it again. Still nothing.

Tess wondered whether Janelle was still waiting tables at the Shine Café. It didn't open until eleven in the morning, and most usually she worked the dinner shift, so she wasn't likely to be at work yet. Growing tense with anticipation, Tess leaned on the bell for a good ten seconds. She let off when she heard footsteps on the stairs and a voice shouting, "Y'all better not be sellin' nothin' or you'll wish you wasn't here." The door flew open, and Janelle stood there clutching a robe around her waist with one hand, holding a burning cigarette in the other, hair jutting out around her face at odd angles, dark circles under her glaring eyes. Seeing Tess, she squinted and then her eyes widened.

"Baby girl! Where you been? What happened to you?"

She threw her cigarette down on the cement and ground it out with the toe of her slipper, then gathered Tess into her arms. Without quite knowing why, Tess began to cry. After a long moment, Janelle spoke softly while she stroked the girl's head.

"Hush, girl, it's okay. I got to hear what's been happening with you. I can't ask you in 'cause I got a visitor upstairs, but you just sit down here on the porch step while I go up and put some clothes on. Then we'll go get us a bite and you can tell me all about it."

When Janelle reappeared in jeans and a striped top, she'd tied up her hair in a raggedy knot and she wore a bit of makeup that mostly hid the dark circles. She smiled and held out her hand to pull Tess up from her seat. They walked around the corner together in silence, holding hands while Tess wiped at her eyes with her other sleeve. They found a table at the coffee shop down the block, where Janelle ordered a Danish for Tess and a coffee for herself.

"Now, tell me what all's happened. Last I knew, the police were asking me questions about 'my neighbor Rose,' on account of she'd gone missing. I never heard no more about it after they left. I was about crazy with worry at first, but time passed, and I decided Rose just up and went. People do that sometimes. I was hurt in the beginning 'cause she didn't tell me, but after a while I let it go."

"No, it wasn't like that," Tess said, and she told Janelle as much as she could remember about the first few days surrounding her disappearance. Janelle sat smoking and sipping her coffee while she listened.

Tess had woken up in a hospital bed with her head wrapped in bandages. The first day was a blur, with people in green uniforms coming and going, poking and prodding her with thermometers and blood pressure cuffs and what-not. No one wanted to answer her questions.

They told her to try not to speak. She was in a double room, but the person in the other bed just slept all the time. Tess didn't want to eat the Jello they brought her. She threw up once, when she tried to sit up and it made her dizzy. At night they left a light on all the time over her bed. She was forced to pee in a bedpan, because she had tubes connecting her to a pole with bags on it, and she wasn't allowed to get up. She hated the bedpan.

The next day they left her alone for longer periods, and she slept a lot. In the afternoon, a policeman and a woman who said she was a social worker came to talk to her. She asked them where her mother was, and they replied that they were looking for her and needed Tess to tell them what had happened two days before, when she came home from school. The only thing Tess could remember was that her mother had been packing a suitcase. Then nothing.

"Your mama was packing?" asked Janelle.

"Yeah, she was throwin' Antwon's stuff into a suitcase. She said it was gonna be just me and her from now on. She said she didn't want him around."

Janelle stubbed out her cigarette and lit another one. Her hands shook slightly as she drew on the match. Tess watched her, but Janelle didn't meet her gaze, just stared at her coffee cup instead.

"Janelle, my mama never told me what Antwon's last name is. But you worked with him, so you must know. Does he still work at the Shine? I got to find him."

"Naw, girl, he quit prob'ly a week or two before y'all went missing, is what I remember. Just walked out in the middle of a shift. I don't know where he went after that."

"But you know his last name, right?"

"I'm not sure. Jones or Johnson, somethin' like that." She took another drag and blew out the smoke slowly. "The cops said you were in the hospital, but they weren't allowing nobody to come see you. What happened after you got better?"

"That social worker lady came and got me discharged from the hospital. Then her and another policeman took me back to the apartment in the middle of the day so I could get some of my clothes and a toothbrush and such. They didn't let me take much, but I grabbed my notebook and stuffed it in the plastic bag they gave me before anyone saw.

"Then the social worker took and put me in a group home to wait until they could find a 'placement' for me. That's what she called it. Come to find out that means until some sorryass foster family could take me in. The other kids in the group home explained it all to me. That is, when they wasn't busy stealing my food off'a my plate while the house mother was in the kitchen. And you don't even want to know where all I been since then."

"Okay, but where are you now?" Janelle asked. "I heard some bad stories about some of them foster homes. Are you good right now?"

"Yes. I'm okay for now. But I got to find Antwon. I feel like I remembered a couple of things since Mama disappeared, but I don't know if they're real or if I'm making them up." She started to tear up, but she bit her cheeks and willed herself to stop.

Janelle looked at her closely without speaking. Then she took out a pen and wrote something on a napkin.

"Here," she said, pushing the napkin toward Tess. "Here's my cell number. I'm sorry I can't help you more, Sugar, but if you run into trouble, you can call me any time."

"Thanks," Tess said, folding the napkin carefully and putting it in her pocket. Somehow, she had hoped for more of a response from Janelle, she didn't know what exactly, but she had learned not to count on much of anything.

Janelle paid the bill and tipped the server. The two of them walked out, rounding the corner back to the house. Janelle gave Tess a tight hug before walking up the steps to her door. Tess pulled the bike out from under the bushes and pedaled off toward the Shine, more questions than answers occupying her thoughts.

Chapter 11

Sundays when Tess got to go along window shopping with Rose and Janelle were some of the best days she could remember. They pretended they were going to buy the rings they saw in the jeweler's window. They laughed at the hats on the mannequins' heads in the vintage clothing shop's display. Tess would pick out her favorite dress in the department store window and then insist that it wasn't fine enough for her after all. Hooting and giggling, they had themselves a fine time for an hour or two without spending a penny. They always ended their outing at the Shine Café, where they treated themselves to soup and half-sandwiches.

The last time the three of them went "shopping" together was the day that Rose had met Antwon. Now, pedaling away from Janelle's place, Tess thought about how much had changed, and not for the better, after that day. She wasn't happy that Janelle didn't try harder to get in touch with her after her stint in the hospital. And how come Janelle didn't know that Rose was planning to toss Antwon out? Things just didn't add up.

She rode her bike up to the door of the café and saw the "Closed" sign still showing. Workers were moving around inside, getting ready to open, so Tess leaned her bike against the wall of the building next door and sat down cross-legged next to it to wait.

She was looking down at the napkin Janelle had given her when a shadow loomed over her, blocking the sun.

"Ho, what you doin' back in my neighborhood?" said a voice that sent chills down her spine. "I don't remember givin' you my permission."

She looked up. SloMo had a couple of his homies with him this time, and that wasn't good. He'd want to play up his toughness in front of them. His pals were already snickering and jabbing each other with their elbows.

"Don't mess with me, dude. I'm just mindin' my business, waitin' for this lunch place to open." She wouldn't show fear. If he wanted a staring contest, she'd give him one.

Reaching down and grabbing her shirt, he yanked her to her feet. He shoved his face up close to hers and narrowed his eyes at her.

"You try turnin' any tricks in my 'hood an' I'm a take a knife to that pretty face," he said. "Got that? Unless you wanna come work for me, that is. My offer still stands." His friends murmured *that's right* and *I heard that*, like a chorus backing him up. He spat to the side and let go of her shirt as passers-by looked and then quickly turned their eyes away. Tess knew that in this neighborhood she couldn't expect anybody to get involved in what might just be a lover's spat — or especially if it was something worse.

Before she could turn away, he grabbed her wrists and began to squeeze. Tipping his head and looking at her almost tenderly, as though he were holding hands with his sweetheart, he whispered, "I know where you stayin' at. I can find you any time I want."

"You don't know nothin'. You seen me on the street, is all. The 'Burgh is a big town, and I go where I please," she hissed, glaring at him. He tightened his grip on her wrists, bearing down until she feared the bones would snap, but she held her face featureless in spite of the pain. The other two goons were watching closely, waiting for her to break down and whimper. She could smell their excitement.

He twisted his hold until her wrists were torqued, and she gritted her teeth to keep from grimacing. She was on the verge of crying out in pain when she heard the sign rattling in the café door and the click of a lock being turned. SloMo released her. Without answering his taunts, she grabbed her bike and put it between the two of them. He smiled and turned slowly, sauntering off down the street with his obedient pack-mates following at his heels. Tess held the café door open with her shoulder and went in, bike and all.

A blonde girl who looked to be college-age came forward.

"Can I help you?" she asked, addressing the question to the bicycle.

"I want to talk to the manager, please," Tess said. "I want to ask about somebody that used to work here."

"I'll see if he's available," she answered, still looking at the bike, and turned toward the kitchen.

Tess moved her bike to the corner of the entrance, trying to avoid blocking the door. She didn't care what the waitress thought of her. She wasn't leaving until she could ask about Antwon, and she wanted her bike to still be there when it was time to go.

After a few minutes, a man in white shirt and slacks but no tie came out of the kitchen. He walked up to Tess and put his hand out, introducing himself as Ted and asking what he could do for her. She shook his hand solemnly and told him she was a friend of Janelle's, and that she wanted to ask about someone who used to work there.

"His first name is Antwon. Tall black guy with a scar over one eye. Can you tell me where he went or what his last name is?"

Ted made a sour face. "I remember him. Antwon Jackson. Walked out of here a little over a year ago in the middle of his shift. And good riddance."

"Did he say where he was going?" she asked.

"He sure didn't. If you're a friend of Janelle's, why don't you ask her about him? Seems like they're friends," he said.

"Used to be, maybe. She doesn't even remember his name right anymore."

Ted's eyes widened a bit as he looked at her. He started to say something, then stopped. The bell on the door tinkled as three people came in and stood by the cash register. Ted glanced over at them, then looked back at Tess.

"Okay, miss, I'm sorry I couldn't be more helpful," he said. "I'm afraid you're going to have to take your bike outside now. The lunch crowd is starting to show up."

Tess decided that was as far as her investigation was likely to get on that particular day. At least she had Antwon's last name. *And Janelle's phone number. Which would be a lot more useful if I had a mobile phone.* She decided that would be her first purchase with the allowance that Irv had promised her.

She got on her bike and rode over to Kennard Park. Plenty of kids were using the playground on this cloudless summer day. She sat on a bench with one eye on her bike, watching mothers push their toddlers on the baby swings. A woman on the far side of the playground caught her eye. *Mama!* She could see her mother's slender figure and smoothed hairdo as she bent over to pick up a dropped sand pail and hand it back to the child standing in front of her.

101

But of course, it wasn't Mama. Tess had been superimposing Rose's likeness on strangers for months. It seemed to Tess as though every time she went anywhere, she saw her mother on the other side of the street, at the far end of the grocery aisle, in the line of cars waiting to pick up kids after school (when Tess happened to be attending school.) Each time it happened, her pulse quickened, her breath became shallow, and her adrenaline started getting ready to set her feet flying toward the woman. Then the stranger would turn her head at another angle or light a cigarette, and the illusion would dissolve.

Now, rubbing her sore wrists, which had already started to turn purple, she thought about her recent encounter with SloMo and her growing certainty that nothing a person did could ever be undone, or probably even ignored for long.

Chapter 12

Irv paid the driver after being escorted to his front door. He generally didn't like to tip, but he figured that as a repeat customer, he'd be wise to stay on the OPT's good side, so he added a bare ten per cent. He went inside hoping to find Tess there, but the house was silent. Making his way to the kitchen, he saw that the back-door key was missing from its cup hook. He resigned himself to making his own lunch of tea, toast and cottage cheese.

He ate in silence, as usual, only this time it felt a bit strange. He began to wonder where the girl was and what she could be doing. After he cleared up his dishes, he moved to his customary spot in the front room and began to leaf through the personal ads in the Post-Gazette. Nothing there held his interest. He laid it aside and closed his eyes, thinking he would nap for a while. Sleep eluded him, though, as he thought more about the situation.

What did he really know about Tess? Precious little, was the answer. He knew that her mother was missing and that she had no father or other family. She had shocked him with a brief account of her first two foster homes and the abuse she suffered there. She didn't seem to want to say much about the third home. Where had she gone after that? She told him that she'd been on the streets for about a month before showing up in his back yard, so that left a lot of time unaccounted for.

Irv had read articles in the newspaper of teenage crime. He thought about the latest case, wherein a fourteen-year-old girl and her boyfriend had stolen a car at knifepoint from a middle-aged woman in a Walmart parking lot. What if Tess was that kind of girl? He may have invited a criminal into his home. His nerves started to jangle in the quiet of the house, where the only sound he heard was the out-of-rhythm ticking of the clocks that surrounded him. Even the cats were quiet, sleeping or grooming themselves or just staying out of sight.

As his unease grew, he remembered the notebook that she was always scribbling in. He had seen her push it under her pillow when he came to the door of her room the other day. He started to wonder whether there might be some information in there that could either set his mind at rest or give him some reason to get rid of her. He knew full well that he had agreed to stay out of her room, but damn it, his safety might be at stake. Furthermore, he was an adult and a homeowner, whereas she was just an underage girl.

Hoisting himself out of the chair with his cane, he made his way to her room. He sat down on the bed and lifted the pillow. There lay the notebook, with PRIVATE – KEEP OUT printed neatly across the cover with a Sharpie. His conscience pricked him, and he laid the pillow down again. Still, he told himself he would only be acting responsibly to learn more about her. It was probably in her best interest, after all. He simply needed more information about this stranger who had taken up residence in his home. It was only common sense. He reached back under the pillow.

Opening the notebook and seeing that each entry was dated, he paged back to the previous September and an entry marked *September 15th, my birthday.*

"Today I am 13 and a full-on teenager. It is my first birthday without Mama. My social worker is taking me to my new foster home tomorrow, since it will be Saturday and I'll be out of school. I sure hope this place is better than the last one."

Irv felt sympathy for the girl, but he was on a quest for background information.

"So it's Saturday and here I am. Soon as we got to the house, I saw how beautiful everything was – the rugs, the furniture, and all the fancy glass things everywhere, like nothing I'd ever seen before. I sat on the sofa while Lorraine and Dolores (that's the foster mom) talked and signed papers. I got a peek at the other girls spying on me. They were all kinds of brown, so I figured I'd fit in. I smelled roasted chicken and right then I planned to stay.

"Only as soon as Lorraine left, things changed fast. Dolores gave all of us girls a list of chores to do. We cleaned and dusted all afternoon, then at dinner time we come to find out the roasted chicken was only for Dolores and her daughter. The rest of us got rice and beans with a few peas on the side."

He flipped the pages, reading each entry with a mix of skepticism and unease. Some of it was just the daily life of an adolescent girl, sometimes major milestones - like her first period - were entered, but her accounts grew darker as time passed in that house. The truancy and drug use both shocked and saddened him. Her reports of Dolores's abuse were alarming, if he could believe them. Perhaps she was exaggerating, the way children do when they feel aggrieved. She was certainly an inventive girl.

Was this account really a description of the foster system that was chartered with shepherding vulnerable children to safety? If only Helen were there to offer her maternal guidance regarding the girl. Irv could not, and would not,

105

believe that very many foster mothers were as unpleasant as Dolores seemed to be. He had just about decided that Tess was using her notebook as a creative writing exercise – witness her account of Christmas on an alien planet, for goodness sake – when he reached the entry describing her afternoon encounter with Carl.

What he read froze his bones. Never had he imagined, in his sheltered academic life, that a child might be immobilized by drugs and subjected to rape within a house that purported to care for her. His horror turned to outrage. If he were to believe this account, then the orderly world that he had known until now was turned upside down. He wished mightily for Helen's calming wisdom. How would she have handled this situation? Sickened, he flipped the notebook's cover shut and pushed it back under the pillow.

He heard a key turning in the kitchen door lock. Rising to his feet with the help of his cane, he smoothed the bed covers and then moved as fast as was prudent next door to his own room. He had no need to pretend that he needed to lie down; his legs were shaking beneath him as he lowered himself onto his own bed.

"Irv? I'm home. Where are you?" she called. He didn't answer, couldn't answer with the shame of what he'd done and the shock of what he'd read burning inside him. He lay still, pretending to be napping. Tess came to his door and looked in on him, then turned back and moved to the kitchen to fix herself a late lunch.

+++

When Irv later asked Tess about her bruised wrists, she told him she'd fallen off the bike and braced her fall with her hands. He let it go, but it worried him to have her running

106

around on the streets alone. He decided to keep her busy over the next couple of days with laundry, grocery shopping, meal preparation, and numerous trips to the garage to search for one thing or another. Having her around soothed his nerves. Also, he was glad to have some help with the chores that forced him to bend over and possibly lose his balance.

Tess was still trying to figure out how she could track Antwon down, and her latest run-in with SloMo had left her reluctant to set off for Lawrenceville again until she had a definite plan. She didn't fully trust the "memory" of Antwon with a gun that had brought her to her knees, but it had been a pretty scary vision. Maybe she could find out where he was without actually having to face him, and that would give her some clues about her mother's whereabouts.

In the end, Irv gave her an excuse to formulate her plans.

Appearing at her open bedroom door later that afternoon, he said, "Tess, I want you to stay close to home for a few days."

"What?" She looked up from her journal. "Why? Did I do something wrong? Am I grounded?"

"No, not exactly. It's just that there are a lot of household chores that need tending. Things have fallen behind around here, and I need you to help out." When she started to protest, he said that he'd put a little something extra in her allowance the next Saturday.

So she settled comfortably, for the time being, into the household role that she had agreed to take on. She spent a few quiet days at home. Although it seemed like Irv had another task for her every couple of hours, she still had plenty of time to write, think, or nose through the books on his shelf.

And what a collection of books he had. Her grandmother had started taking her to the public library on Centre Avenue long before she could read, where she would sit contentedly paging through picture books and making up stories to go along with the illustrations. As she grew older and more independent, that library became a safe place to go while her mother was still at work. Once her homework was finished, she would happily pluck books from the shelves and read until it was time to go home. Now she had plenty to read without even leaving the house. Of course, a lot of Irv's books had to do with history, since that was his profession. Tess wished there were a few more mysteries, thrillers, romances and such, but she found herself drawn into the real-life accounts that she found among his books.

She especially liked reading about the two World Wars. She had skipped a lot of school over the last year or more, and her historical knowledge was lacking, to say the least. The books she found on Irv's shelves covered events she had barely heard of. The personal stories she encountered in diaries and anthologies were the most riveting of all, because these were real people talking about real things they'd experienced. Although the stories were mostly sad, they made her feel less alone somehow.

"Irv," she asked him on the second day, "Who are these 'collaborators' they're talking about in this book? Which side were they on?"

He looked up from his desk to see the title of the book she held. *The Resistance, 1940* was written across the cover.

"Do you know about the Nazis invading France?" he asked her, and she nodded. "The French people were very weary of battle after losing so many young men during the

Great War. Some of them decided this second war would go better for France if they went along with Germany's occupation. Others were vehemently opposed to that idea, and they labeled the ones who wanted to accept the situation as 'collaborators'."

She asked him more questions about World War II, and his answers painted vivid images of both the suffering and the bravery in what she was reading. She wondered whether some day she could write stories that were equally fascinating.

On the third day of this routine, Tess came into the front room to find Irv settled in his chair as usual, with two cats on his lap and a third sprawled on the floor next to him.

"When's the last time you got up outta that chair, Irv?" she asked.

He glanced up at her from under his bushy brows and then returned his attention to the cats that he was petting. "I suppose it was the last time I had to pee, which must have been all of a half hour ago," he said.

"What I'm sayin' is, I am doing all the things you can't bend over for anymore, and now you're just sittin'. That is not good for you."

"Says who?"

"C'mon, let's go for a little walk." She heard grumblings. "Just up and down in front of the house a few times. It's a fine afternoon. If you don't ever move a little, you'll get so stiff you'll be stuck in that chair forever."

"For God's sake, girl. I'll go just to get you to quit nagging." He pushed himself up and grabbed his cane. "I'd better take my key and lock the door after us."

Tess rolled her eyes. "We'll be right out front, Irv. What do you think is gonna happen?" She stood there with her arms crossed while he fumbled in the drawer for his key.

Once they were out the door, she took his arm going down the front steps. He shook her off at the bottom and leaned on his cane instead. They walked slowly past the house on the left, then turned and went just past the house on the right. As they were coming back, the young man who had come to the door the night Tess appeared was exiting his front door with a dog on a leash.

"Hello, there, neighbors," he called out with a smile.

"Good afternoon, sir," said Irv, fixing his gaze on a point just above the man's head.

"I don't believe I introduced myself the other evening. I'm Jake Bernstein. My husband Frank and I just moved in a few weeks ago."

"I beg your pardon? Your what?"

"Yes, my husband. We're both high school teachers, so we're off for the summer. This is our dog, Tubs." Jake walked closer, and the dog – a fat Boston terrier – began to sniff at Tess's feet. She reached down to pet it, and Irv caught her arm.

"It's okay, he's very friendly."

"We are cat fanciers," said Irv, moving as if to continue walking. Jake took a step closer.

"I don't believe I caught your name," he said, extending his hand.

Irv did not respond, so Tess stuck out her own hand.

"I'm La'Teesha, but I go by Tess. This here is Dr. Irving Gladstone. He's a retired history professor," she said with a hint of pride in her voice. Irving scowled at her.

"History, eh? That's my field as well, although I never went on far enough to earn a Ph.D. And where do you live, Tess?"

The question caused her to glance at Irv out of the corner of her eye. After a pause, they both started to talk at once. Tess shut up right away, hoping Irv would think up a good answer. He looked down at her and began again.

"Yes, well, you see...Tess is the daughter of my monthly house cleaner, who lives over in Lawrenceville, not far from here. While the young lass is out of school for the summer, I am paying her a modest allowance to come over from time to time in order to take care of some of my chores. I believe it is important to set a work ethic early in a young person's life."

"Well, that's just splendid, Irving. I hope I may call you Irving? And you must call me Jake. We'd love to have you both over for tea sometime soon." Tubs was by this time pulling on his leash, and they all parted ways.

Irv headed straight for his porch steps without speaking a word. Once they were inside with the door locked and chained, he turned to Tess.

"Do you see what going outside leads to?" he asked. "Nothing but nosy neighbors and problematic questions. We will not be repeating that exercise. Tea, indeed. I should no sooner sit down to tea with that fairy than I would feed one of my cats to his horrid little dog."

He moved to his recliner and plopped down. A cat jumped immediately onto his lap, and he stroked it as he leaned his head back and took a deep breath.

"Isn't that right, Dickens?" he asked the cat with a singsong tone.

"Why's his name Dickens?" Tess asked in a quiet voice. She was seated on the couch with her legs tucked under her and her hands folded. She was a little rattled herself, being on the lam and all, but she was trying not to show it.

"Two reasons. First, Charles Dickens is my favorite novelist. Second, when this fellow was a kitten, he was constantly getting into the trash and dragging bits across the kitchen floor. So I told him he was a little dickens."

Tess looked at him, waiting for an explanation.

"It means he's a little trouble-maker."

"So is that what I am?" she asked. "A trouble-maker?"

Irv looked at her for a long moment before he answered.

"You are a challenge and a puzzle to me," he said. "I think, however, that so far we are each providing something that the other needs. You need a temporary place to live. I need to demonstrate to my son that I am not a helpless old man who must be carted off from his home and made to be a permanent, unwelcome houseguest." He shuddered and returned his attention to Dickens.

"Okay," she said after a silence. "But I'm just sayin' right now that I'm not scared of fairies, and I would love to go to Jake's house for tea." With that, she got up and returned to her room and her journal.

Chapter 13

After a few more days of keeping Tess around the house, Irv began to tire of her constant presence. He ran out of little tasks to assign to her and sank himself deeper into the esoteric subjects that could keep him absorbed for hours at a time. He had almost entirely stopped paying attention to her, until she reminded him one morning that it was Saturday and he had promised her an allowance.

"Yes, so I did," he said, lifting a cat off his lap to retrieve his wallet from his bedroom. He returned in a couple of minutes with his wallet. He peeled off thirty dollars in cash and handed it to her.

"Wait a minute," she said. "Didn't you say you'd pay me something extra for the chores I did this week?"

"Hm. I did say that, didn't I? Alright, here's another twenty. What do you plan to do with this money?" he asked, remembering the accounts of drugs in her diary.

"First off, I'm going to the hardware store to get a bike lock. Then I'm going to get myself one of them – one of *those* – cheap cell phones. That way you can always get a hold of me." She smiled and cast him a wide-eyed, innocent look. He released her hand.

"Well, that all sounds like a responsible idea," he said, moving to his desk and shuffling through a pile of papers. "I have some work to attend to. Shall we convene at dinner?"

"You bet, Irv. I haven't forgot that I'm the cook," she said as she headed to the kitchen door.

Pulling the bike out of the garage, she did some fast calculating and figured she had just about enough money for a bike lock and a phone with a cheap talk-and-text plan. She would then be broke. She was elated and relieved to remind herself that she only had to wait another week to be flush again, and in the meantime, she could eat. She wouldn't have to sign on to any nasty blow jobs on the teenagers in the park in order to survive.

She was feeling optimistic as she pedaled off to the True Value over on Liberty. Once she could keep her bike safe, she figured she could go anywhere. The bike made her feel safer, too. If she spotted SloMo again, she'd be able to outdistance him easily. She had a plan to use the computers at a library to help her track down Antwon Jackson.

+++

A knock on the door startled Irv awake from his afternoon nap.

"Dad, it's me. Are you there?" Joseph was shouting as though his father were deaf, which annoyed Irv every time.

"Coming, coming," he said, as he pushed out of his chair and made his way to the door. He turned the lock and drew off the chain. Joseph stood on the porch next to a boy who looked to be around eight years old, wearing a mud-spattered soccer uniform and knee socks, holding his cleats in one hand. Irv stretched the door wider, and the two visitors came in.

"Sorry, Dad, we're a bit muddy. The fields were wet after last night's showers. Maybe we should sit in the kitchen?"

Irv waved in response and led them through. When they were seated around the small table, he looked at his son and waited.

114

"Dad, this is Dylan," said Joseph. "Marian's son," he added unnecessarily. "He was playing at a park just a few miles from here, so I thought we'd stop in to see how you're doing."

"I'm doing fine, thank you. Would you care to inspect my larder for expired foodstuffs?"

"Um, no, Dad, I don't need to do that. But do you mind if I get Dylan something cold to drink? He was playing pretty hard out there."

"Help yourself."

Joseph opened the refrigerator and let out a low whistle. He drew out a bottle of apple juice, grabbed a cup from a hook, and sat back down. Dylan wasted no time in pouring himself a drink.

"Where'd you get all that food? And what are you doing with it? From what I remember, you can just about make breakfast."

"I told you when you were last here that I have made arrangements to provide for myself," Irv said. "I am perfectly capable of taking care of matters in my own home."

"Okay, Dad." He drummed his fingers on the table. "I guess you don't want to tell me what all kind of a deal you've set up. I'm glad it's working for you. So what else is new? What'd the doc have to say at your last appointment?"

"He said that I am doing as well as can be expected, considering my age, and that no changes in medication are recommended at this time. For which sage advice, I thanked him and left his office minus my co-pay."

Joseph snorted, saying, "Give 'em hell, Dad. The whole medical-pharma industry is a scam." Irving smiled at his son for the first time in a while.

"That's my boy," he said under his breath.

The kitchen door opened suddenly, and Tess burst in at full volume.

"I got me the best deal ever on a flip-phone with unlimited calls and texts," she said with a note of triumph in her voice. Shutting the door, she turned to look at the three figures grouped around the table and fell silent.

"Who are you?" asked Joseph. He turned to look at his father. "Dad, who is this? What's going on here?"

"Joseph and Dylan, this is La'Teesha," said Irv. Three pairs of eyes looked at him, expecting more, but none was forthcoming.

"How do you do, La'Teesha," Joseph said in a measured voice. "I am Joseph Gladstone, Irving's son."

"You can go ahead and call me Tess," she said, looking at Irv for further assistance.

"Tess, can you explain to me what you are doing here?" asked Joseph.

"Son, I don't believe she is required to explain anything to you," said Irv. "The last time I checked, I was the registered homeowner at this address. As such, I am entitled to invite whomever I wish to visit me here. And that is precisely what Tess is doing – visiting."

"Alright, Dad, no need to get testy. I'm just watching out for you, is all. You've got to admit that it's kind of a change for you to be entertaining guests. Guests whom I have never heard of before, by the way."

"Tess has been helping me with some small household chores while she's out of school for the summer. She has been quite reliable in showing up when she is scheduled," he said with a hint of amusement.

Joseph glanced sideways at Dylan and shifted in his seat. Dylan asked if he could have a snack, and Tess reached into the fridge for a couple of cheese sticks.

"See, that's what I mean! How does she know what's in your refrigerator?" Joseph glared at Tess, and she backed up a few steps.

"I repeat, you do not need to be concerned. Now I must excuse myself briefly," said Irv, and he headed down the hall with his cane.

When he figured that his father was out of earshot, Joseph turned on Tess.

"If this is some kind of a set-up, you'd better watch out," he said. "Don't try to take advantage of my elderly father, because I will make sure that you are prosecuted under the full extent of the law. You and whoever you're working with."

"Hey, take it easy, I'm not doin' nothing with nobody," she said. "Me and your dad, we're just friends, that's all. He's givin' me a part-time job while school's out. What he said."

"I like her," said Dylan. "Can we go now?" He had finished his juice and cheese sticks, and he was obviously ready to go home.

Irv reappeared and stood in the doorway.

"So how did the two of you meet?" asked Joseph, looking from one to the other of them. The confusion and distrust were evident on his face.

"She is the daughter of a friend, and she needed a summer job."

"What friend is that, Dad? I thought I knew all of your friends, and none of them are –,"

"Son," said Irv in a firm tone, "I think it's time you took this youngster home for a bath. We'll talk another time," said

117

Irv. Dylan jumped up at once and headed for the front door. Joseph looked at his father with narrowed eyes.

"Are you okay, Dad? Really?"

"If you are asking whether I have fallen prey to some sort of scam upon the elderly, I can assure you that I have not. I am aware of the dangers that lurk for older persons like myself, and I can take my own precautions. Tess is what she says she is – a young girl doing odd jobs for me over her summer vacation." Irv stared boldly at his son, daring him to object.

"Alright, Dad, I get the message," he said as he rose and headed toward the door. Irv followed and locked up after them. He turned back to his recliner, sitting down with a thump and blowing his breathe out.

+++

Tess made a meatloaf for dinner, along with potatoes and collard greens. She knew she was stepping out there with the greens, but she figured she'd eat them if Irv didn't. She was happier than she'd been in a while, and she wanted some comfort food to celebrate. She squeezed a lemon over the greens. The smell of the meat roasting in the oven set her stomach growling. She was pretty settled here, all in all. Chopping up the parsley to go into the potatoes, she made a firm resolve not to live anywhere else until and unless she found her mother.

She hadn't known what to do or say when she came face to face with Joseph this afternoon. Thankfully, Irv had jumped right in there. She only hoped that Joseph would accept Irv's story and let things be. The experience showed her, though, that she wasn't being careful enough with her comings and goings. After all, it wasn't like she was entitled to

118

live in Irv's house. Joseph could cause real problems for Tess if he found out that she had moved in and taken over his old bedroom. She didn't think he'd like that in the least.

Also, the possibility of running into SloMo again was a constant worry. The first time it had happened since she ran off was right here in Bloomfield. The second time, over in her old neighborhood, he'd walked right up to her when she wasn't paying attention. She was going to have to watch her surroundings more carefully.

She wondered whether Social Services was looking for her. She guessed probably not, since Dolores would keep getting paid her support money if they thought Tess still lived with her. So why report her missing? Dolores would have to play it smart when the social worker came by, but Tess could bear witness as to how well Dolores lied, so that wasn't much of a worry. Tess thought of Carl hanging around the house all the time and shuddered. She swore to herself that if the police ever hauled her back there, she'd be out the bedroom window before the cop car had even pulled away from the curb.

All of the clocks began to chime six, and the cats came running into the kitchen. Now that Tess was keeping their litter boxes cleaned up, the place smelled a lot better. She still thought Irv had entirely too many cats, but she had grown fond of a big orange tabby who was lately sleeping on her bed at night. Irv had told her the cat's name was George, after a fellow professor in the history department whose hair had flamed almost as brightly.

"Hey, George," she said softly, bending down to scratch his head. The other cats crowded around, pushing him away and winding around her feet until she picked up the bowl to fill it with kibbles. "You all are a bunch of greedy rascals." She laid down the bowl and turned back to the stove.

"I'm glad you're getting along better with my beauties," said Irv from the doorway. He moved to the table and sat. "Our little confrontation this afternoon was unpleasant. I apologize for my son's behavior. He feels quite protective of me, as you have seen."

"Well, that's not all a bad thing, Irv. At least you got someone lookin' out for you."

Irv was silent, remembering what he'd read the day before in the girl's diary. He pulled out a handkerchief to clean his glasses before he spoke.

"I realize our arrangement is temporary," he said, "but while you are staying here, I feel a responsibility for your well-being. Encounters such as we had today put you at risk for being returned to your last foster home. I gather you would prefer that didn't happen."

"You got that right," she said, mashing the potatoes with a sudden burst of energy.

"Therefore, we shall have to be more careful that you stay out of the way of visitors, neighbors and so forth. I've considered the matter, and I think you need to stay in the house when you have no errands to run for me."

"What?" She turned to him with her hands on her hips. "I can't do that. I got things I want to do, now that I got a way to get around."

"I don't feel comfortable with you running around the city on your own. How do I know if you're safe? Also, the fewer people who know you are here, the better off we both will be. I am well aware of the lack of legality in our arrangement." He had the same 'that's final' look on his face as he'd had when he told Joseph to go home.

Tess was boiling inside, but she decided to let the situation go for now. She would have to plan her attack on Irv's position carefully. She knew already that he was about as stubborn as they come. Arguing with him, especially before he'd been fed, was not likely to end well for her.

She filled two plates at the stove and plopped them down onto the table. Grabbing forks and knives, she sat down across from him and began to eat. He looked at his plate.

"What's that green stuff?" he asked.

"It's a surprise," she said. He raised his eyebrows. "This here is a fair trade, Irv. If I got to give a little, then so do you. Plus, my Gram always said not to insult the cook or you might be cookin' your next meal yourself."

He started in on the meatloaf just as a clap of thunder tore the air, followed quickly by a flash of lightning. The rain began to pelt down on the roof.

"Just as the weather forecast predicted," said Irv between bites. "Severe weather is expected for the next two days — thunderstorms, hail, flood warnings, the whole nine yards. Good thing you're not going anywhere."

Chapter 14

The next couple of days were wet and wild, with rain, hail, lightning and thunder. Wind rattled the windows and slapped the sides of the house with loose pieces of cardboard, garbage can lids, paper coffee cups and soggy newspapers. Tess laid low, mostly reading books from Irv's shelves when she wasn't doing laundry or cooking. Once in a while, she took out her flip-phone and thought about calling Janelle. She didn't know what she would say, but Janelle's was the only outside phone number that she had. She had entered the number in her contacts, as well as Irv's land line number. For emergencies, she told herself. It just seemed safest to keep Janelle in her back pocket. Literally.

By the second afternoon of foul weather, Tess was plenty bored and lonely. What could it hurt to give Janelle a call? She could just say hi. Dialing the number felt a little weird – calling a grown-up like she was a girlfriend or something. But Janelle felt like the only family that Tess had left. The phone rang several times, and then a voicemail message answered: *Hey, Janelle here. Leave a message and I'll get back to you.* The phone beeped.

Feeling sort of sheepish, Tess spoke into the phone. "Hi, this is Tess. I just wanted to make sure this cheapo cell phone worked. You don't need to call me back or nothing." She paused. "Unless you want to. Okay, bye." She hung up.

On the third day, the skies finally cleared. Tess told Irv that she was going for a little bike ride around the neighborhood and that she'd be back in half an hour. He didn't look too pleased, but he could hardly keep her locked up on such a fine day.

Tess headed straight for the Shell station seven blocks away. She locked her bike to a rack and went into the mini-mart. Walking up to the counter, she asked the turbaned clerk for a street map of Pittsburgh. He pulled three off the rack behind him and asked her which she wanted.

"Are any of them free?" she asked.

"Oh, yes, Miss," he said, smiling and tilting his head. "The tourist map from the Chamber of Commerce costs nothing, Miss. It shows all of the major museums, libraries, art galleries, parks, schools, transit stops and tourist areas."

"I'll take that one, please." He handed it to her, and she was out the door.

Once she got home, she disappeared into her room to pour over the map. First she found the Lawrenceville neighborhood where she'd lived with her mother. She drew circles around their apartment house, her grade school, the Kennard playground, and the Shine Café. She had no idea where the first foster mother lived – she'd been too bewildered by the drastic changes in her life to do anything other than try to survive. Then she tried to find the location of the second foster home, but almost all she could remember about the entire experience was the horrid basement. She didn't even know which burg to search.

Next she looked for the fancier neighborhood where Dolores's house sat. She located it by first finding the park where she and the other girls had hung out instead of going to school. Moving radially out from the park, she was able to recognize some of the street names that she'd seen from the bus window when she did go to school. After searching for a

123

while, she found the block where Dolores's house was located and drew a circle around it as well.

She was pretty familiar with Bloomfield by now, having initially reached it on a city bus from her old Lawrenceville neighborhood and explored it on her bike since then. Still, she drew a circle around Irv's block. She wanted to be able to trace all of the places she'd been since her mother had disappeared. Somewhere there would be a clue. She just needed to know where to look.

The map showed a lot of city landmarks. She studied the legend at the bottom and saw a symbol for Library, then looked around for the one on Centre Street where she'd spent so many hours after school. Moving south on the map, she saw another icon labeled Main Library and was elated to see that it was in Oakland, an easy bike ride away. She remembered her mother taking her to Schenley Park, near the Main Library, on the bus one Saturday. They didn't have the money that day to go inside Phipps Conservatory, but the little girl had been overwhelmed by the glass structure that looked like a fairy castle. She and Rose had walked all around the park, enjoying the gardens, and Rose had pointed out the beautiful library building. Tess determined right then that the Carnegie Main Library was tomorrow's destination.

The next morning Tess was awake before George had even stirred on her bed. The early morning sun poured in through her window, setting her mood so that she was convinced of great possibilities for the day. Dressing hurriedly, she met up with Irv in the kitchen.

"Good morning," he said. "You're up bright and early. And what are your plans for the day?"

"I'm off to the main library. I figure I can do some good research there," she said.

"What if you run into that hooligan again?" he asked.

"Oh, Irv," she said. "I can't live my life being afraid all the time. I can deal with SloMo."

After feeding the cats and eating a hasty breakfast, she hurried out the back door to retrieve the bike from the garage.

She didn't figure the library would open before 10:00 or so. Still, she had to see it. She rode her bike over to Forbes Avenue, and what she saw took her breath away. It bore no comparison to the modest branch library on Centre Avenue where she had spent so many peaceful hours. It looked to her more like a palace than a library. The building's cornerstone showed that it had been built in 1895. It was huge and grand, with granite steps, Greek columns and porticos, statues on the well-watered green lawn, and the general air of a place where Tess instinctively felt she did not belong. Yet over the massive iron doors were carved the words *Free to the People*. Reassured, she locked her bike to a rack and sat on the grass, waiting for the doors to open.

While she sat eating the last of a PB&J sandwich she'd brought along, an elderly woman approached and perched on a nearby bench. The woman reminded Tess of her Gram, except that she was older and a bit darker, with her gray hair pinned up neatly on top of her head. The woman smiled at Tess and asked her if she was also waiting for the library to open.

"Yes, Ma'am," Tess said. "I can use a computer for free there. It's real handy."

The woman nodded. "I'm not any good on a computer," she said, "but my book group meets here every Wednesday morning, so here I am." She glanced at her watch and stood.

Tess stood also and shifted from one foot to the other.

"Ma'am, would you mind me coming in with you? I've never been here before. Maybe you could show me where to go."

"I would be delighted, my dear. And you can help me up all of those steps. My name is Mrs. Robinson, by the way."

"I'm pleased to meet you. I'm Tess."

They climbed the imposing stairway together, and Tess held one massive door open for the older woman. Inside, she looked up at the tall ceilings and hanging light fixtures. She felt even more intimidated than she had when gazing on the huge building from the lawn. She followed alongside her companion, who guided her to the Information desk and then moved on.

"May I help you?" The youngish woman behind the desk looked up at Tess.

"Yes, Ma'am, I want to use a computer."

"Do you have a library card?"

Tess's hopes sank. She shook her head.

"Well, that's all right. Here's an application for you to fill out. There's no charge, we just need your contact information so that we can keep track of anything you might borrow."

Tess took the form over to a table that had pens standing in a cup. She filled in her name and the number of her new flip-phone. What should she write as her address? She hadn't paid any attention to the number on Irv's house, she simply knew it by sight. She decided to use the address of the apartment that she and her mother had shared – an address that Mama had taught her to recite when she was barely three years old. Putting it down on the form felt strange, as though she could just go back there and everything would be the same. Tears pricked her eyes, and she blinked to clear them before she handed in the form.

"Thank you," said the librarian. She tore off the copy and handed it back to Tess. "You can use this as your temporary card. We'll mail the permanent card to you in a few days."

Uh-oh.

"Could I maybe just pick it up the next time I come in?" she asked. The woman looked at her with a slight frown.

"Is there a problem? We need to have your permanent address before we can allow you to check books out."

"Well, see, our mailbox got took down while they're painting our building. I just think it's safer if I pick up the card myself." Tess felt like she was getting pretty good at making stuff up on the fly, but it was becoming tiresome.

"I see. Then of course, we'll hold it here for you until you come in for it."

Tess smiled at her and moved off to find the computers.

+++

Irv was sleeping later these days – dozing, really - now that Tess was taking care of the cats in the morning. It felt good to let his bones rest and his mind float a bit, time-traveling between the past and the present in the early morning light. Once he did open his eyes, he had to look around the room for a few minutes to bring himself back to the reality that he was now an old man and Helen was gone. Still, rather than being unsettled by it, the time that he'd spent roaming around the years usually left him with a warm feeling. He reflected that he'd rather talk to Helen in his dreams that not at all.

He rose and hitched off to the kitchen to heat the tea kettle. Glancing at the cup hook near the door, he noticed that the key was gone and felt both annoyed and worried that the girl was going off without even asking. Then he remembered that he wasn't actually responsible for her. At least not that anyone else knew. He fixed his tea and moved to the recliner, where a cat jumped into his lap the instant he sat down.

He stroked the cat while he sipped at the tea, the sweet creamy liquid sliding down his throat and warming his arthritic joints. As he sat and thought about the young girl who was temporarily sharing his home, he again had a sharp desire to know more about what had happened to her. Where was her mother? How could she have been left to drift on the streets, knowing too much for her still-tender age? He didn't expect her to tell him, and he wondered how he would ever find out.

With a sharp feeling of guilt, he remembered the diary in her bedroom. Irv had always thought himself to be a man of his word, and he still felt shame that he had gone into her room after promising to stay out of it. Not only that, he had read her most private records. And yet, she was a minor, and he wanted to protect her. Somehow that fact made him feel that he had a right to look after her best interests, as well as his own.

Once, when Joseph was a teenager, Irv had caught Helen going through their son's dresser drawers while he was at school. Shocked, he had asked her what she was doing. She replied self-righteously that she was protecting their son by staying aware of the threats that confronted him. Irv hadn't felt at the time that he had a convincing rebuttal to that statement, and perhaps she'd been right. Now he thought he was facing a similar situation.

He struggled with his conscience through the rest of his cup of tea. Then he pushed the cat off his lap and made his way to Tess's room. Sitting on the edge of her bed, he pulled out the diary from under the pillow. He found the place where he'd left off when Tess had come home the other day, and he resumed reading.

May 5 – I got out of the house with just what I could grab. I forgot my jacket, but I got my duffle with most of what I need. It's kind of cold. I'm gonna sleep in the park with all my clothes on me. I took a granola bar and an apple off the kitchen counter, that's all I could find. Then I ran. I didn't want Carl coming after me.

May 6 – Don't know what I'll do today. At least it's sunny. I'm hungry, though. I found a six-pack of Gatorade on the sidewalk outside the 7-Eleven, so I took it. I hate Gatorade. Mama says it's sugary piss water, and I think she's right. But I get thirsty.

May 7 - Today I snuck onto the back of a bus headed up Penn Avenue. I stayed on all across town til I got to my old neighborhood. I got off at 40th and walked to Arsenal Park. Guess I can sleep here as good as anywhere. Least I know where I am.

May 8 – Still cold at night. Still hungry. I found some food in the trash can behind the McDonald's, so that was good. Some slick dude name of SloMo came up to me last night while I was hunkered down in the park. Said he could help me earn some money for food and stuff. He didn't look too straight, and I told him to piss off.

May 9 – Sometimes I wish I was back at Dolores's. At least I had a warm bed. Except Carl would be there too.

May 11 – Didn't write yesterday, I lost my pen. Took one today from a hair salon counter when nobody was looking. SloMo keeps coming around to the park where I'm hangin. He says I only got to do blow jobs, not the "real number" on account of I'm young, and he'll give me a cut.

Seems to me like if I want to do that kind of stuff, I can do it on my own. But he's kind of scary.

Irv cringed at the thought of poor Tess in such grim circumstances. He wondered whether her abuse in the foster homes had hardened her enough to deal with these new horrors. This SloMo fellow sounded plenty dangerous, and Irv hoped never to lay eyes on him.

May 12 – Okay, I got to eat, right? Otherwise I die. It's not so hard to put some kid's pecker in my mouth if it means I can buy some food after. But I got to say it's disgusting. I'm sorry, Mama. I think you'd like me to stay alive so I can find you, and this is how I'm doing it for now.

May 13 - SloMo took a share of my money like he owned it. Man, that pissed me off. I got to stay away from this dude. Out of sight. Run when I see him.

May 14 – He showed up again, said he'd cut me if I didn't deal him in. Said he doesn't allow 'free operators' in his hood. I got to stay clear of him somehow.

May 15 – Did a teenager and got me $20. I'm heading straight to McDonald's.

May 16 – I walked as far as I could and then took a bus a ways. I think I'm out of SloMo's hood, but how would I know? I never been a gangsta and I don't know the rules.

Irv winced, then skipped ahead a few pages. It was all too graphic and painful for him. The next few entries found Tess hiding in backyards, raiding kitchen trash bins for leftovers. She stayed out of the way of people, but she was chased by dogs a few times. Irv's heart was hurting for the girl. Finally he found the page that she'd written the night he let her in the back door.

June 2 — I got me a real house to sleep in for tonight. I even took a bath. I got to see if I can work a deal, make this last a while. The old man that lives here seems okay so far except for being grumpy and kinda stuck up. I'm gonna watch him real close so's he can't pull nothing on me. Meantime, I got to come up with a plan for how to stay here.

Irv shut the notebook and slid it back under the pillow. Grumpy? Stuck up? He started to feel insulted until he remembered the adjectives were those of a thirteen-year-old street waif. Oddly, though, her opinion of him did seem to matter to him, more than he would have thought.

Chapter 15

When Tess found the room with the computers, she was disappointed to see that all of them were in use. She sat at one end of a polished oak table bearing only two computers but with four chairs lined up in front of it, enjoying the air-conditioned coolness and watching for an open spot. The room was very quiet, except for clicking keys and the occasional cough. After about half an hour, she noticed that the young woman sitting next to her had started coughing quite a bit. Finally, after a sneezing fit, the woman got up and left. Tess quickly slid into the empty seat and laid claim to the keyboard in front of her.

Tess was pretty good on a computer, but she'd never tried very hard to find someone before. She stared at the Google icon and wondered what she should type in. She started with just *Antwon Jackson* and got 621,000 results. She'd have to pare them down, so she added *Pittsburgh PA,* which gave her 43,200 results. But not all of them were about Antwon spelled like she'd seen on a note her mom once left for him on the kitchen table. Some were Antoine or Antwann or Ant'wan. And some had different last names, or they were articles with an Antwon and a Jackson who were two different people.

She thought back to the social studies classes she'd had in the computer lab at Arsenal Middle School. The teacher had told the class that if they wanted more exact results, they should put single quotes around the words they were looking for. She tried that and came up with only 29 people listed in something called the White Pages whose names were Antwon

Jackson and who supposedly lived in Pittsburgh. She opened the site and looked at the list. It turned out some of those people only used to live in Pittsburgh. Then she wondered whether *her* Antwon would even have an address. Seems like he'd been pretty good at freeloading off of other folks.

Her hands drifted off the keyboard as she tried to plan what to do next. She'd been so eager to log on and start the hunt that she'd barely noticed the room in which she sat. Now, for the first time, she took a real look around her. As she raised her eyes to the ceiling, the full glory of her surroundings hit her.

A domed ceiling made up of patterned and recessed white squares stretched high over her head, lit softly from underneath along the tops of the walls. A row of tall arches lined the walls on each side of the room, and two long rows of oak tables lit with green-glass lamps led down the center. The soft gold-hued lighting, the huge yet hushed room, the beautiful ceiling all combined to both dwarf her and comfort her. She remembered a time when Gram had taken her to Sunday school and the teacher had talked about the Great Hall of Heaven. What she was seeing reminded her of the pictures she'd had in her head while she listened to that lesson.

Suddenly a crackly voice blared over a loudspeaker like a truck horn, cutting the silence in two. *'Attention, all library patrons. We have been advised by the police that this library has received a bomb threat. We must ask you all to gather your belongings as quickly as possible and exit the library. Do not use the elevators. Police are on hand to assist with an orderly and safe evacuation. Again, please exit the building immediately.'*

As soon as the voice stopped speaking, an alarm began to sound in a continuous series of deafening electronic beeps.

Tess covered her ears and looked around. People with worried faces scrambled to gather up books, papers, eyeglasses, pens, stuffing them into backpacks and tote bags or just carrying them in their arms. Tess had only her phone and her house key in her pockets, and she moved toward the door. The reading room that she'd been in was on the top floor. She joined the line that was descending the stairs, trying to keep hold of the railing so that she wouldn't be knocked down by all of the people around her. Lots of folks were talking on their cellphones, telling their families, or whoever, what was happening, which added to the noise and confusion.

When the mass of bodies reached the ground floor, Tess was propelled along with them to the exit doors like a fish in a stream. Once they were out of the building, the clump of people broke apart as they scampered down the long flight of cement steps as fast as possible and then started running.

"Tess!" She heard her name and looked around for a familiar face. She saw Mrs. Robinson standing a few feet away, clutching the handrail at the top of the stairway and weaving slightly. Tess joined her.

"Dear, can you help me down the stairs? I'm afraid I'll lose my balance with all of these people rushing around." She kept hold of the railing on one side and grasped Tess's arm with her free hand. Together they descended one step at a time, placing their feet as though they were just learning to walk. Tess would have preferred to go it on her own without being slowed by her companion. She couldn't just leave the elderly woman, though, and she noticed that people were skirting around the pair to avoid bumping into them.

When they reached the bottom, Tess pulled free. "I got to get my bike, Ma'am," she said. Mrs. Robinson nodded and sank down onto a bench, dabbing at her face with a handkerchief. Tess returned with her bike, and the two of them continued across the lawn to the street below.

"Have you called your mother to tell her what's happened?" asked Mrs. Robinson. "She must be plenty worried about you, it's probably on television. I just don't understand about all of these bombs and shootings and all. I'm going to take the bus straight home and watch the news, but I'll bet this was just a false alarm, most of them are, you know. My son is always telling me not to go to public buildings, he says they're targets for extremists, but I do love the library."

She stopped talking to take a breath and looked over at Tess, whose face was streaked with tears.

"Oh! Oh, my dear, you mustn't get upset. You're safe now, you can just ride your bike on home to your parents and not worry about it anymore."

Tess despised herself for her silent weeping, and the angrier she became, the faster the hot tears rolled down her cheeks. She didn't seem to have any control over it. She wanted to scream and swear and kick something, and her rage and anguish must have shown because Mrs. Robinson took a step away from her. Tess swung herself onto the bike then and pushed off, tossing a final bitter comment behind her as she left.

"I don't know where my mother is."

When she got back to Irv's, Tess rode first to the front door where she could see the house number above the mailbox. She pulled the flip-phone out of her pocket and made an entry in her Contacts folder. Then she rode around the corner and pedaled up the alley to the rear of the house.

After putting the bike in the garage, she let herself in through the kitchen door and clomped into the front room with heavy footsteps. She plopped down on the couch with her arms folded across her chest.

Irv peered over his newspaper at her blotchy face and arched his eyebrows. "What's wrong with your face?" he finally asked. "And where have you been all morning?"

"There's' nothin' wrong with my face. You got a TV in here somewheres?" She jumped up and started moving boxes around, peering into them, tossing items out so she could dig deeper.

"Stop that, you're making a mess," said Irv, and Tess rolled her eyes. "The television is serving as a table surface at present, since I never watch it. It's under that blue quilt next to my desk. I don't even know whether it works."

Tess took books and papers off the top, piling them on the desk, and pulled away the quilt to reveal a Sony television that didn't look exactly ancient, even though it wasn't a flat screen like they'd been making for the last several years. She knelt to turn it on, changing channels until she found a local station that was broadcasting a news report. The camera was pointed at the main library, showing all of the front entrances taped off and surrounded by police. A newscaster held a microphone as he talked to the camera. Tess turned the sound up.

". . . *shortly after noon today. Police are trying to trace the person who made the call. As yet, they have uncovered no explosive devices, but the main library will be closed for the remainder of the day. This is Charles Walker with WPGH-TV News.*"

She switched the set off.

Whirling around and glaring at him, she said, "That's where I was all morning. Till they kicked us all out 'cause some damn fool called in a bomb threat."

"What? What's that you say?" Irv took off his glasses and sat up straight, furrowing his heavy brows.

"You heard right. And now I got some things to do in my room." She turned to go, then stopped. "See you later, Irv," she said, softening the edge in her voice a bit.

Irv stroked the cat on his lap, chewing on his bottom lip. Hearing Tess's door click shut, he rose and headed to the door at the bottom of the stairs. He opened the door and climbed carefully, following the hallway to Helen's sewing room. The light was fine in there, the indirect afternoon sunshine making the room glow with a soft warmth. This was the time of day when Helen loved to work on her crafts. He closed the door after himself and sat down on the small day bed.

"Ah, Helen, I do miss you," he said to the empty room. "What am I going to do? We never had a girl, you and I. How am I supposed to keep her safe? And why is she even here?"

He picked up one of Helen's samplers from a basket next to the bed and turned it over in his knobby hands, tracing with his finger the quilting lines that she had stitched so carefully while she still had control of her hands. What had upset the girl so when she ventured into this room?

"Well, Helen, she is here, and I'm not going to turn her out until I have a good solution for her. No more sleeping in parks, no more being attacked where she should be safe. I think I'm going to have to look into the situation with her mother, though I have no clue how to begin."

+++

Tess emerged a few hours later and got busy in the kitchen. Irv had pushed the collard greens around on his plate the night before and taken a few bites, but Tess realized that she'd better set her sights lower and get him to eat frozen peas and beans first. The leftover meatloaf was handy, and it didn't take her long to put dinner together. She fed the cats promptly when the clocks chimed six, and then she told Irv to come and eat.

As they sat down at the small table and shared their food, Irv began to shuffle his feet back and forth underneath him. Never one for sparkling dinner conversation, he seemed tonight to be unusually distracted. Tess kept eating, her thoughts focused on the day's events and the puzzle of how to proceed from here. Suddenly Irv broke the silence.

"You are starting to remember what happened to your mother, aren't you?" he asked.

Tess froze with her fork half-way to her mouth.

"How you figure that, old man?" She was immediately on the defensive, wondering what he knew about her that she hadn't shared. No way was she going back to the foster system. She'd rather run.

"I just think so. But you're being careful. Otherwise you'd tell me what you know. So where do you think she is, and how are you going to find her?"

Tess didn't know how to answer, so she sat silently, wondering the same thing.

"You're thirteen years old," he said. "You can't do much sleuthing on a bicycle. Don't you think you'd better involve the police?"

"I'm almost fourteen." Tess glared at him. "And I already told you, the police are done lookin'. They got my mama

138

pegged for a druggie, which she surely is not. And if I go to the cops, they gonna throw me right back in the house with that creep Carl. You don't know about him, but believe me, he's bad news. I gotta do this on my own."

"Well, how much have you remembered about the night she disappeared?"

"I just see some pictures, is all. Mama was packin' up Antwon's stuff when I got home from school, she was gonna throw his ass out of our apartment. I was dancin' around the bedroom 'cause the radio was playing Stevie Wonder, and I love him. Plus, I was feelin' pretty good to hear that Antwon was gonna be history."

She stopped and closed her eyes. Irv ate slowly, watching her but not pressing. After a moment, she continued, still with her eyes closed.

"That's when the pictures get scary. I see Antwon come in, and he's got a gun in his hand. They start fighting, they're throwing things at each other and yelling. I grab the quilt my Gram made me, I guess I'm trying to hide under it, and then somethin' hard hits me on the head. And that's all."

"You woke up in the hospital?"

"Yeah. I didn't remember even that much of the story when I first woke up."

"What did the police report say about the whole thing?"

"How should I know? I was twelve years old. You think they gonna show a police report to a twelve-year-old? They just said my mother disappeared, and next thing I'm in some damn 'group home' and I got no say about that or anything else." She pushed her plate away and shoved her chair back from the table.

"It looks as though someone needs to see that police report. Since you're not supposed to be living here, and I'm not supposed to be involved, I'll have to put some thought into the matter." Irv folded his hands under his chin with his elbows on the table and looked at her steadily.

"You want to help me?" Her eyes lit up even as her brows arched with skepticism. "Why?"

"That is a fair question, my dear girl. One to which I have no answer at present."

Chapter 16

The cats started yowling at about 6:30 the next morning. Irv was by now accustomed to relying on Tess to get up and feed them, and he turned over to continue sleeping. This time the racket didn't stop, though. He put a pillow over his head and managed to doze off for a while, until their complaining woke him again. Had the girl slipped out without feeding them? Grumbling, he sat up and waited to regain his balance, then shuffled off toward the kitchen.

He managed to feed them without tripping over any of them and straightened to put away the kibbles. It was then that he noticed the key hanging on its cup hook next to the door. A shiver of apprehension ran down his back and settled in his gut. He went straight to her bedroom and knocked on the door.

"Tess? Are you in there?" No response. He knocked again. "Tess? Are you alright?"

He thought he heard a faint sound, but he was too deaf to make it out clearly. He turned the knob and cracked open the door, prepared to slam it shut again if she wasn't properly dressed. She was lying in bed with the covers pulled up to her chin, shivering on this warm June morning.

He went in and stood over her, placing his hand on her forehead. She was burning with fever. Looking up at him, she swallowed painfully and licked her lips.

"Irv." She licked her lips again. "My throat feels like it's got daggers in it." Her voice was a croak that he could just barely hear.

He stood still, wondering what to do. Whenever Joseph had fallen prey to childhood illnesses, Helen had bustled around making tea, bringing aspirin, and if necessary, calling the doctor. Irv had been pretty much useless and well aware of that fact, and so, after offering his sympathy to his son, off he would go to the university to earn the money to pay the doctor bill. He felt that he was doing his proper bit, and he confidently left the rest in Helen's capable hands.

But Helen wasn't here. He went into the bathroom and wetted a cloth in the sink with cool water, wringing it out and bringing it to lay on Tess's forehead. He knew where the aspirin was, but he didn't think she'd be able to swallow it if her throat was that sore. Then he remembered a trick that Helen had used: she would smash the aspirin with a teaspoon of her home-made apple jelly so that all the patient had to do was suck it off the spoon. He went to the kitchen with a couple of pills and found some Smucker's grape jelly in the refrigerator. He figured that would have to do.

He brought the mixture back to her and offered it, but she shook her head, tightening her lips.

"I know your throat hurts. Don't you want it to feel better? Just suck the jelly off the spoon and let it melt down your throat. You hardly have to swallow." He coaxed her like a mother bird pushing a reluctant chick out of the nest. Partly he was nurturing her, and partly he wanted to win this contest of wills. She let him push the tip of the spoon into her mouth, and he relaxed his grip, feeling that he had prevailed.

Suddenly she was hot, pushing the covers off and lying spread-eagle on the sheets in her T-shirt and panties. Irv felt extremely uncomfortable and was ready to flee, until he realized that she was unaware he was even in the room. He looked at her and hoped the fever would die down on its own, as so many childhood illnesses do. Mothering a sick child was not in his wheelhouse, and he didn't know what else he could do for her. Leaving as quietly as he could, he kept the door ajar in case she should call for something.

After fixing himself a cup of tea, he sat in his recliner and thought. She was really just an adolescent, in spite of the harsh situations she'd faced, and wasn't he starting to feel grandfatherly toward her? He wanted to protect her, keep her safe, and maybe help her find her mother – assuming that her mother wanted to be found. He wondered what he would tell Tess if he learned that her mother was dead, or perhaps worse, really had abandoned her. All these feelings had arisen in a relatively short time period. He hadn't known her all that long. Maybe he should slow it down a bit, pull back some.

"Irv."

He sat up when he heard her faint call. What now? He tried to ignore her small voice, reasoning that he had already used the only nursing skills he'd learned from Helen. After all, she wasn't dying. But that thought raised more concern, knowing that he was all she had right now. It was no use. Against all reason, he was worried about this waif who had connived her way into his home.

Through the weekend he tended to her, but the fever continued off and on. She still couldn't swallow more than a little juice through a straw and the jelly-aspirin spoons with which he dosed her at proper intervals. It was time to get her to a doctor.

That realization, of course, presented new difficulties.

+++

143

"It's definitely a strep infection," the doctor said as he washed his hands. "I'll write her a prescription for an antibiotic. You can get it filled at the Walgreen's next door. She's to take the pills until they're gone. And try to minimize the number of visitors you allow in your home, as strep is quite contagious."

"Thank you, Doctor. As I've told you, she's my housekeeper's daughter. I simply volunteered to accompany her, as her mother was unable to come. I'll pass along your message." The doctor left the room, giving no indication that he had heard. These 'doc-in-a-box' drop-in clinics didn't seem to want personal details if one was prepared to pay in cash. Irv put a sweatshirt around Tess's shoulders and took her back to the nurse's desk to pick up the prescription and pay for the visit at the Urgent Care clinic.

After a quick trip to Walgreen's, Irv caught another cab to take them home. Tess dozed against Irv's shoulder all the way, but when the cab pulled up at their address, she rallied enough to help him out of the car and up the steps to the front door. Once inside, she crawled back in bed while Irv lit a burner under the tea kettle and mashed up a prescription pill in some jelly. While he was working on the mixture, someone knocked on the front door. When he went to the door and peeked out the spy hole, he was surprised and alarmed to see the cab driver, a small, dark Pakistani-looking man.

"What do you want?" he shouted through the door. "I've already paid you."

"Yes, sir," came the reply, "but you dropped some money getting out of the cab." The man was holding up a fifty-dollar bill.

144

Astonished, he slid back the deadbolt and opened the door just a crack with the chain still in place. Looking the man over for a gun or a knife, he was prepared to slam the door and yell, "Help! Police!" Instead, the man carefully proffered the bill through the gap, bowing his head slightly. With trembling fingers, Irv accepted the cash.

"Thank you," he said in a voice that was barely audible. He ducked his own head in acknowledgment and shut the door.

+++

Tess was in bed a lot over the next ten days or so. When he wasn't taking care of her, Irv busied himself with his research, combing through old newspapers, cutting out articles and taping them into notebooks, consulting historical volumes residing on his shelves. He typed away at a PC that had seen better days and not unfrequently froze up on him. Being suspicious of the internet, he used it only sparingly, preferring primary sources and reputable journals for his work.

One day, however, while researching some government regulations regarding his potential access to formerly classified documents, he took a detour. He'd been wondering in the back of his mind how he might get a look at the police incident report of Tess's situation. Exploring that idea, he clicked on first one government link, then another, and soon he was down a rabbit hole of nested sites – a place he'd sworn he would never go.

He ended up at the Allegheny County website for children and families. That was the government arm that had put Tess into foster care. He wondered what the employees there had been told when they committed her to a group home to await placement. Had anyone on their staff seen the police report? Even if they had, there was no way that he would be allowed to look at it.

The situation would require subterfuge, this was obvious. He realized that he was starting to enjoy the role-playing that had been involved in sheltering this girl. He had never before imagined himself as a super-hero, but he had to admit to himself that taking on the part of her rescuer was exciting in a way. And he wanted to see that police report. He thought for a few moments and then picked up the phone.

+++

After two weeks and a full round of antibiotics, Tess was ready to roll. She'd had no success chasing down Antwon on the internet. It was time to talk to Janelle again – the only person she knew, besides the manager at the Shine Café, who might have some information. She thought about calling first, but in the end she decided to just drop by. She remembered how welcoming and warm Janelle had been the last time they met, so like family, such a dear friend. Why be formal with someone who was like an auntie to her?

She knew she had to demonstrate to Irv that she was fit enough to get out of the house, so she threw herself into her chores. She cleaned the cat boxes, swept the kitchen, grocery shopped, and took particular care to cook dinners that Irv would be sure to enjoy – meatloaf, frozen peas, tater tots.

She did whatever was needed to get him to stop following her around like a nervous hen, and then she announced to him that she was going back to the library to do more research.

"I don't like that idea at all," he said in response. "You're barely over your strep infection, and by the way, you probably contracted it at the library, using their filthy public equipment."

"Irv, I got to make some progress here. If you won't let me go, I'll just climb out a window."

He could see that he wasn't going to be able to stop her. "Alright, but call me as soon as you get there. And wash your hands after you touch anything!"

She smiled and ran off to get the bike out of the garage.

The library was, in fact, the first stop on her route. She wanted to pick up that card that was waiting for her before the library staff tossed it out, on account of her never showing up to get it. That would be just her luck. It turned out the card was still on hold at the information desk, and she gratefully pocketed it.

Her next destination was her old apartment house, where she hoped to find Janelle still at home. She confidently maneuvered her way back to the neighborhood, keeping to side streets to avoid the heavy traffic. She loved being able to cruise her old haunts on a bike – it was something she'd never had when she was younger. She felt so powerful being able to get across town without buying bus fare or relying on someone else. She sped up and down the streets, often passing cars stuck in traffic, and wondered why anyone would want to travel any other way.

As Tess was pedaling up the street toward the house where she'd been raised, Janelle's front door opened and a figure emerged. The sight shocked the girl so badly that it seemed as though all of the strength was drained from her legs. Wobbling from one side to the other and narrowly avoiding a fall off the bike, she made a quick turn up a side street to a spot where she could still see the front of the house.

The man on the porch looked for all the world like Antwon. What was he doing at Janelle's apartment? The realization that Janelle had been lying to her caused her to doubt every assumption she had made. Horrible suspicions rose in her mind. What had really happened to her mother?

The man (she was sure it was Antwon) tossed a cigarette onto the front walk and ground it out with his toe. Turning back, he shouted something at Janelle where she stood in the doorway. He walked to the curb, got into a car, and started it up. Tess strained to see the license number, then texted it into her flip-phone. She tried to add a description of the car, but car ownership not being part of her upbringing, she was pretty much clueless as to make and model. She got down that it was blue and that the name of the car started with an H.

After her nerves settled a bit, she pushed off on her bike, circling the neighborhood as she struggled with conflicting emotions. Part of her wanted to confront Janelle straightaway. She was furious with the betrayal that she was certain she'd seen. Her mother had considered Janelle to be her best friend. Were Janelle and Antwon hooking up? If they were, what did Janelle know that she hadn't told Tess the last time they met? Did Janelle know what had happened to Rose? The anger in her welled up as she pumped harder and harder, until her bike was screaming around corners and shooting through stop signs.

Shit! Who's left that I can trust? She remembered Janelle telling her that she couldn't invite Tess in because she had a visitor. Janelle had also claimed not to remember Antwon's last name. That had to have been a lie. Tess felt confused, angry, double-crossed. She was also frightened. If Janelle was part of the reason her mother was missing, what would she do once she knew that Tess was on to her? What would Antwon do? Tess had not erased from her mind's eye the recently recalled vision of Antwon bursting into her mother's bedroom holding a gun.

As all of these thoughts tumbled around in her head, she wondered what was real and what wasn't. She began to see herself as ridiculous, powerless, delusional for thinking that she could do anything on her own to find her mother. Suddenly she was utterly drained of energy. Her feelings of defeat brought tears and hot shame flooding through her, along with an aching sense of loss.

She turned her bike toward the Bloomfield neighborhood and pedaled slowly, unable to put any muscle into the ride. Her mother was missing, a trusted friend had betrayed her, Antwon was on the loose, and Tess felt as weak and blind as a newborn kitten. She longed only to hide away for a while in the quiet of Irving's packrat burrow, pulling the covers over her head until she could think what to do next.

Chapter 17

Phones were ringing on several desks as Irv opened the door and walked in. Having never been inside a police station before, he wasn't sure where to start. He took a seat in one of the wooden chairs lined up under the windows. All of the officers that he could see had receivers to their ears, muttering intermittently as they took down notes. As one officer hung up her phone, she glanced his way.

"Can I help you, sir?" She smiled. "Please, step on over."

Irv approached her desk with what he hoped was a stern expression on his face.

"I'd like to make an inquiry about someone's whereabouts," he said. "Her name is Rose Baxter, and she owes me a fair amount of money. She stopped answering her phone almost a year and a half ago, and the letters I send her are returned to me by the post office."

"I'm afraid the police can't assist with bill collections, sir. You might want to engage a collection agency."

"Well, that won't do me any good, since I don't have a trail to send them on."

"A collection agency can try to trace her from her last known address."

"Yes, I've already tried that route. She seems to have disappeared off the face of the earth."

"Sir, I wish I could help you, but the police have other, more urgent matters to attend to."

Irv raised his voice. "Look, I pay taxes in this city, and the way I see it, you work for me. Can't you at least look to see whether someone by that name was involved in anything criminal here in Pittsburgh in the last several months?" He scowled and slammed his fists on her desk. "I never should have trusted her."

"What would you like me to do, sir?" the officer asked in a less friendly tone.

"Just tell me whether or not you have some kind of police report concerning her. I obviously can't get money from a woman who's dead or in jail, and I don't wish to waste a lot more of my time if it's fruitless."

"I can search for her name in our incident report archive, sir," she said. "Was that B-a-x-t-e-r?" He nodded, and she typed a few keystrokes into her computer.

"I have one report here that shows a call concerning a disturbance on Fenway Avenue in March of last year, in an apartment rented to a Ms. Rose Baxter. Officers responded to the call within one hour."

"That's her," said Irv, trying to hide his excitement. "Did they arrest her, or did they find her dead, or what?"

"The report states that the officers found only a minor female who was injured. They transported the minor to a hospital, and she was later remanded into the custody of the Allegheny County foster care system."

"Well, they must have investigated the scene, since an injured child was left there. What about a forensics report? Did they look for blood? Maybe Rose was murdered and hauled away."

The officer looked at him with a face that expressed some distaste for the man's grisly interest in the details. She turned back to the report and scrolled down the screen.

"The only blood samples found in the apartment matched those of the minor individual. The notes state that the minor could not provide any information, having been found unconscious and, when questioned later, remembering nothing about the incident. The case was subsequently classified as that of a Missing Person and was eventually archived, since no adult family members stepped forward to pursue it, and in fact, none could be located. A warrant for the arrest of Rose Baxter was issued on charges of child abandonment."

"Well, might I request the re-opening of the case, on the basis of my financial interest?"

"No, sir. But if you do find her, please follow up with the police, as the warrant is still in effect."

"I'll be sure to do that," he said, and he walked out the door to hail a cab.

+++

Tess walked in the kitchen door a little while after Irv's cab had dropped him off out front. He looked up to greet her as she passed through the front room, but she went straight to her bedroom and shut the door.

"Damn," he muttered to the cat on his lap. "Here I thought I was done with teenage moodiness once Joseph finally grew up and moved out."

Sitting cross-legged on her single bed, she wrote furiously in her journal. Every so often, she threw down the pen and sobbed, then picked up the pen and started scribbling anew. This catharsis went on for at least an hour until, exhausted, she leaned back on the pillow scrunched behind her and fell asleep. Mockingbirds sang on the power lines that stretched over the house, infiltrating her dreams, sounding like a radio that played while she screamed for her mother.

152

The afternoon light had moved to the west when she awoke and wandered out of her room, tangled hair hanging in her face and an oversized T-shirt almost covering her shorts. She went to the kitchen and lit a burner under the tea kettle. She saw no sign of Irv, which was normal – he napped almost as often as the cats did, frequently surrounded by several of their sleeping forms.

After pouring the water for her tea to steep, she thought vaguely about running a load of wash. It had been a while since she'd done so, due to her illness, and she was in need of clean clothing. It was hard to rouse herself from her current nap-induced stupor, but she shook herself firmly and went back to her room to gather up a bag of her laundry.

She was halfway to the garage when Slo-Mo stepped out from behind a bush and stood in front of her.

"Whatcha doin' girl? How come you ain't checked in wit' me?" he demanded, staring her straight in the face.

Setting the laundry down, she met his look. "I got me a new gig now, Slo-Mo. You ain't my pimp, and you never was. So step aside."

"Tell you what, girl. I own you and the corner you stand on, and I'll kill you if you flag on your own."

"No, you don't own me. Cause I'm in a different hood, and I got me a new deal. You don't claim around here. What you doin' here, anyways? How'd you find me?"

He stepped closer and grabbed her T-shirt just under her chin, tightening it so that she found it difficult to catch air. His breath, reeking of tobacco and booze and something else, sickened her as he spoke close to her face.

"I been watchin' you. I followed you home from Fenway today, hung around the block till you showed your face. You turned a coupla good dimes with me, and I ain't lettin' you go all that easy. You're young and you still got some miles to go. I want you to fix a situation for me, girl."

They stood glaring at each other, nose to nose. Tess was struggling to breath, wondering if this was a nightmare, he seemed so out of place. She'd felt safe in this neighborhood filled with the sounds of kids skateboarding, car stereos thumping, and mothers calling from porches. Was her world falling apart again?

"I got a job for you," he said in a low voice. He loosened his grip on her shirt enough so she could answer him.

"I told you, I don't do that kind of stuff no more. I got me a real job that feeds me, and I'm off the streets.

"Not that kind of job," he said with a grin.

Just then a shotgun fired over their heads. SloMo instantly let go of her shirt and disappeared into the alley. Tess stood still, waiting for her heart to slow down. After a minute, without looking back toward the house, she walked into the garage to start her laundry load.

Irv followed after her, still holding onto the shotgun.

She loaded the washing machine, not looking up to where he stood gripping the gun's barrel, and then she spoke.

"We got to get that garage door fixed so's we can lock it," she said. "Until we do, I'm gonna park that bike in my bedroom."

+++

Tess called Irv to dinner after she'd wrangled the cats. She plopped the filled plates down onto the table and sat waiting for him.

She wasn't much interested in eating. She was very interested in keeping a roof over her head and a lock between her and SloMo. On that account she had prepared yet another meal. That was the deal, after all, that she and Irv had struck. It was a deal set to expire at the start of the new school year – just a few weeks away - and what she would do then, she did not know. It was now mid-July. She figured she'd better start thinking about it.

Irv made his way to the table and sat.

"Looks good," he said as he stared at the macaroni and cheese with a side of some kind of vegetable. Tess didn't answer.

"I went down to the police station today." He loaded a fork with mac and cheese and shoveled it in. After chewing and swallowing, he continued. "Guess what I found out?"

Tess looked at him with a glimmer of interest on her face.

"The only blood the police found in that apartment was yours, apparently from your head wound." He laid down his fork. "Which means that your mother was probably alive when she left the apartment."

"Probably?"

"Very likely." Irv was unwilling to bring strangulation, or other means of death without bleeding, into the conversation. He didn't want to introduce more horrible possibilities to her, and he did want to give her some hope. He also wanted to be careful that neither of them should jump to conclusions from what he had learned.

"Now," he said, patting his mouth with his paper napkin. "What are we going to do about this fellow who accosted you in the back yard today?"

"I don't know, Irv. I'll take care of it. It's really not your problem. But the bike stays in my room until that garage door is fixed."

"I don't object to you keeping the bike in your bedroom. I didn't like the look of that fellow, though, and if I find him bothering you again, next time I won't shoot over his head."

"Just so your shots don't hit me," was all she said.

+++

Saturday finally arrived. Tess had been looking forward to getting her allowance. She was wearing Joseph's outgrown T shirts and running shorts almost all the time now, since her own much-worn clothes had just about disintegrated after being washed a few times. She'd been saving her money so she could replace a few things.

She spent the morning changing cat box loads, sweeping up the kitchen, and washing Irv's clothes. After a quick lunch, she reminded him of her allowance.

"Is it Saturday already?" he asked. He went to his room and returned with the promised allowance and a good amount extra. "I noticed you have been wearing Joseph's old clothes lately. I thought you might get yourself something more suitable for your age and gender."

Tess was surprised and touched. She thanked him as she stuffed the bills into her pocket, and a few minutes later she was out the door with the bike.

Her mood lifted considerably once she was pedaling her way across town to get to the Target over on Penn Avenue. She reflected that mobility was a fine thing to awaken some perspective in a person. She was no longer stuck in one place, feeling abandoned and powerless. It wasn't like she had a master plan to solve her troubles or anything. The world just seemed to have a lot more possibilities when she could move through it freely and expand her view. She could also keep a lookout for danger and take *evasive action*, as Irv would call it.

156

Having studied her street map and chosen her route, she decided to bike across the University of Pittsburgh campus. Green lawns, beautiful old brick buildings, and the occasional statue gave her a pleasant break from the road traffic. A few people were walking between buildings, and she passed a group of parents and teenagers standing around listening to an orientation spiel, but the campus was pretty quiet overall. She imagined what it would look like in the fall, when the term would begin and throngs of students would again crowd the walkways. For just a minute, she pictured herself in that crowd of future students.

Like hell, she thought. *I'll be lucky to finish high school, the way I'm going. I don't even know where I'm gonna live when school starts up next month.*

She left the campus and was back on the street with traffic flowing around her. Time to pay attention again. The truth was, Tess always paid attention these days. She was vigilant about her surroundings at all times. She'd been sort of a dreamy little girl, picturing stories in her mind and likely to bump into things when she was out walking with her mother. Gram used to say she had her head in the clouds. The last few years of her life - really, ever since Gram died and Antwon moved in - had changed all that. She wasn't telling herself stories any more.

When she got to the Target store, she locked her bike to a rack and went inside. Pushing a cart to the teen department, she looked around at the other girls who were shopping. She hadn't been in school all that much the last year, and she wasn't too sure what girls were wearing right now. Plus, she'd be starting high school next month (if she made it that far), and that alone was intimidating. She wished she had a girlfriend to shop with. Or to talk to. Or to get a frothy coffee drink with.

A couple of girls nearby were holding up dresses and laughing with each other. "Omigod, do you believe this?" Tess made a mental note to stay away from the dresses. Not that she was very tempted. It was hard to look tough wearing a dress, and while Tess didn't mind feeling attractive, above all she wanted to look tough.

Moving on, she found some suitably skimpy shirts that would barely cover her midriff, like those the girls around her were wearing, and tossed a few in the cart. She'd need a new hoodie by fall, so she grabbed one of those as well. Underwear came in three-packs at just the right price for her budget. The jeans presented a problem, because Tess despised trying things on at the store. She couldn't go too far wrong with shirts, but jeans were another story. Choosing four pairs, she sighed and took the cart to the dressing room area. She very quickly emerged again, keeping two of the pairs of jeans and tossing the others to the attendant.

Tess was a speed shopper. Her mother had loved to shop when she had any money, but Tess had no patience for it, and she was in and out as fast as possible. Maybe if she'd had a friend along, they could saunter between the racks, squealing and laughing at private fashion jokes. Since that was not the case, the entire ordeal was boring, and the smell of the cheap fabric dye was giving her a headache. She could hardly wait to get back outside on her bike and feel the wind in her hair.

As she guided her cart toward the check-out lines, she realized that a man had been following her throughout her shopping expedition. Every time she noticed him, he got busy looking over the merchandise on a shelf. Then when she changed locations, there he was again, looking at her while pretending not to. It started to give her the willies. Finally, she whirled on him.

"Why you followin' me around, you creepy old man? You better stay away or I'll scream. My mama taught me to watch out for perverts like you," she said, loudly enough for the elderly lady next to her to turn down the next aisle with a worried glance over her shoulder.

The man's face reddened. He reached into his shirt pocket, producing what might have been some kind of badge, if Tess had bothered to look at it. "Store Security, miss. I'm just doing my job." She stared at him until he looked away.

"Well, do it somewhere else 'cause you are scaring me, mister, and I'm gonna call for help if you don't back off." She turned her cart and proceeded to the nearest checkout counter, head held high, where a gangly young clerk had been watching the proceedings with his mouth hanging open.

After paying for her purchases, Tess went outside, slung the shopping bags over the handlebars, and headed home. She smiled to herself as she thought about her improvised put-down to being profiled. Mama would be proud.

Chapter 18

At precisely 2 p.m. the doorbell rang. "Hello, Dr. Gladstone, it's Mrs. Hollander here for your monthly cleaning," she shouted.

Irv unfolded his frame from his recliner and slowly made his way to the front door. After making sure that it was really her, he loosened the chain on the door and let her in. They exchanged greetings, and then Irv returned to his recliner to stay out of her way as she got to work.

He had never really thought about Mrs. Hollander one way or the other. She came once a month to clean. Joseph paid her from Irv's account, on which Joseph was a signatory. Irv would raise his feet when Mrs. Hollander told him to, so that she could vacuum underneath his footrest. Normally, they barely exchanged two words during her monthly visits. If he had been pressed, he probably wouldn't have been able to recall a single conversation they'd shared.

So today, as ever, he returned to his newspaper and paid no more attention to her. The vacuum cleaner buzzed from room to room, and then suddenly it stopped. The next thing Irv knew, Mrs. Hollander was standing in front of him with her hands on her hips. He looked up from his newspaper and raised an eyebrow.

"Dr. Gladstone. There's a bunch of girl stuff in your son's bedroom."

"That is correct."

"Well, are him and his girlfriend living here now? Because if they are, I've got to raise my rates. The more the people, the more the mess. I'm sure you can see how that would be fair."

"No, Mrs. Hollander, my son still has his own residence. My niece is visiting from out of town for the next six weeks or so. I'm happy to pay you an additional $20 per month while she is here."

"Your niece! Well, that's a surprise. I've been cleaning for you for some years now, and I never heard of a niece."

"Actually, she's a great-niece. From my late wife's family. She's adopted," he added lamely.

"Pfft. That doesn't matter. Adopted or home-made, it's all the same to me. Family is family, and I'm just as glad to hear you've got some." She returned to her work, and Irv picked up his paper.

Mrs. Hollander was just finishing up in the kitchen when Tess came in the back door. The girl was startled by the sight of yet another stranger, and she froze, not sure what to do. She looked around for Irv, afraid to speak for fear she would accidentally untangle a knot in their ever-growing web of lies. The older woman looked up and smiled.

"You must be Dr. Gladstone's great-niece," she said as she stuck out her hand. "I'm his once-a-month cleaning lady, Mrs. Hollander."

"Yeah, okay, pleased to meet you," said Tess as she took the woman's hand in her own, feeling how rough and dry the palm was compared to her mother's own smooth hands. "I'm La'Teesha, but they call me Tess. Do you know where my, um, Great-uncle Irving is?"

A cane thumped into the room, followed by Irv's slightly bowed figure.

"Aha! I see the two of you have met. Tess, dear, Mrs. Hollander has been helping me with the cleaning for quite a number of years now. I'm afraid she has her hands full, as I am no use at all between her visits."

"I got to say things look a bit better around here, Dr. Gladstone. Your Miss Tess here must be pitching in some," said Mrs. Hollander. She looked at Tess. "How long you stayin' for, honey?"

"Oh, just until school starts later in August," said Tess. She glanced at Irv, but he had nothing to offer. After an awkward pause, she continued. "I've been helping out with Great-uncle Irv and, uh, doing some research for a school report."

"Well, isn't that fine?" said Mrs. Hollander.

"Can you excuse me? I've got to put some things away," said Tess. She took the Target bags and went to her room, shutting the door behind her. *I got to lay low until she leaves. Me and Irv have got to keep our stories straight. It's no good if I mess up his version of things.*

She spent the next hour happily cutting off tags and folding away her purchases. The shirts, jeans, and underwear were the first brand-new clothing she'd owned since the Days Before. Imagining herself at home with her mother once more, she pictured herself as a confident high-schooler wearing just the right outfits. She didn't come out of her room until she heard the distinctive sounds of the deadbolt turning and the chain slipping into place on the front door.

Irv was in the kitchen heating the tea kettle when Tess came and sat down at the table.

"Okay, who am I now?" she asked with a mischievous grin. "I'm kinda hoping I'm named in your will, me bein' a dear relative and all."

He gave her a sidelong glance and turned back to the stove without a word.

"C'mon, Irv, I'm just kidding. But seriously, we got to keep track of what we tell people about me, and which people we tell, or one of us is gonna slip up and blow our cover."

At his usual deliberate pace, he silently took a cup down off a hook and placed a teabag in it, then poured boiling water over the top. While it steeped, he went for the cream and sugar. At just the right point, he stirred everything together. When his cup was finally ready, he sat down across from her. Throughout the process, Tess was barely managing to hold it together and not explode with impatience.

"Well, let me see now," he said, stirring his tea. "We told the next door neighbor, whom I hope never to see again, that you are the daughter of my cleaning lady and that I have employed you for some menial tasks during your summer vacation."

"Yeah, that made me feel real proud," she said with a smirk.

"And I have just told my cleaning lady, Mrs. Hollander, that you are my adopted great-niece on my late wife's side."

"I like that story better."

"And I told the police that your mother owed me a good sum of money and that I was trying to locate her, which was how I learned that only your blood was left in the apartment when your mother disappeared."

"And the police didn't even want to know about me, right?"

"Their records show that you were remanded to the foster system, and that's where they think you are right now."

"Well, that's cool. I mean, I wouldn't want them thinking nothin' else, given the situation. But it's kind of harsh that they just lost track of me, like I don't count for anything."

"Tess," said Irv. "You count. You've got more guts than most of the people I've met in my miserably long life. And I'm confident that you will find out what happened to your mother."

After a silence, Tess spoke. "Would you tell me about my 'Great-aunt Helen'? I never met her, you know."

Irv looked hard at her to be sure she wasn't playing a joke. When he decided that she was serious, he settled in with his teacup and began to speak.

"Helen was very intelligent, but she was raised by parents who taught her that a woman was supposed to look for a husband to provide for her. We met in college, where she was majoring in psychology. She thought she'd like to work in the schools with children."

"So did she ever do that?" asked Tess.

"Nope. She married me instead. And when I finally earned my PhD and managed to grab an associate professorship, she immersed herself in the social life of academia. Oh, she hosted many a dinner party for cohorts at the university, teas for graduate students, brunches for the wives, all of that. She was very good at it."

"Did she like doing that?"

He looked at his teacup. "I don't know, really. She did the hostess bit very well, and then, finally, Joseph came along. He was her shining star. She thrived with taking care of him, and she became even more domestic. She started baking bread and

164

making quilts. She was even writing children's stories that she hoped to publish." He stopped talking.

"Then what happened?" asked Tess.

"Well, Joseph grew into his teens, and I suppose he required less nurturing. So Helen thought again about pursuing her master's degree in psychology and really doing something with it. But then she got sick."

"What was she sick with?" Tess thought about her Gram, and the sudden way she had died. She had no personal experience with other ways of giving up one's mortality.

Irv sat in silence, pondering what to say, considering how much he was willing to share.

"Cancer," he said finally. "She fought it hard. Chemo, radiation, the whole program. It went into remission for a while, and she was able to attend Joseph's high school graduation. Over the following summer, she spent some good times with him before sending him off to college. Then it seemed like the minute he was gone, she just let the air out of all the tires. I hadn't realized how much she was struggling to stay upright for his sake, but when it was just the two of us, she faded fast."

Tess listened quietly. She couldn't picture her own mother being ill, because Mama had always been strong, never even had a serious cold that Tess could remember. When she tried to visualize her mother now, she just saw a big gaping hole where once had been someone whose presence she had assumed as much as the air she breathed.

"That sucks," she said finally.

"It does, indeed."

"So, like, what did you do then? Did you pray or something?"

"I prayed harder than I ever thought I would, given that I have never believed in God. I begged. It was pitiful."

"My Mama used to tell me that prayer is just asking somebody else to take care of the shit that you got yourself into. She used to say it was only wishful thinking."

"My dear, Walt Disney taught us to believe in wishes from early childhood. How are we to blame?"

"Yeah, I guess. I really liked 'Aladdin', though. Wish I had me a genie."

"I wish you did, too."

Tess said nothing. The many clocks ticked, and a few of the cats showed up to dig in their sandboxes. She felt the silence like a blanket around her, and the feeling was comforting rather than suffocating. She realized that she liked this old man, even with his quirks and his formal way of speaking, like he was Moses come down from the mountain. The ultimate authority. Except she knew that he knew that he wasn't.

Chapter 19

Monday came around, and Tess decided that this was the day she would confront Janelle.

The Shine Café would be closed. Janelle would be sleeping off whatever partying she'd partaken of the night before. Tess was familiar enough with the lives of restaurant employees to know the routine. She dreaded facing Janelle, but she could see no other way to uncover the truth about her mother.

Irv was occupied with his research and barely acknowledged her when she told him she was going for a bike ride. Setting out in the late morning, she pedaled off toward the old neighborhood, taking Fifth Avenue straight across town. She passed pho eateries, bail bonds offices, nail salons and coffee shops, interspersed with apartment buildings and dental offices. It felt so good to be under her own power, zipping between cars waiting in traffic jams, weaving in and out of queues. Her bike gave her wings.

When she reached the house on Fenway Avenue, her buoyant mood sank like a stone. She was fearful about the possibility that Antwon would be there also, and she wished she'd told Irv where she was going. Suddenly shaky and sweating, she locked the bike onto a porch stave and sat down on the front steps. What would she say, knowing what she now presumed? If Janelle and Antwon were hooking up, did that mean that Janelle knew what had happened to her mother? And if she didn't know, how could being here help her? She was saved from thinking about it further when the door opened.

Antwon stepped out, knee-length robe wrapped around him, looking for the newspaper, and almost tripped over the girl who sat on the top step of the porch with her knees hugged into her chest.

"Whoa! I 'most stepped on you!" He froze in place when he got a look at her.

"Hey, Antwon." She had nothing else to say. She still wasn't sure whether her memory flashes were real or whether they were stories that she told herself. But she definitely wanted to find out which it was. The thing she felt pretty certain of was that other than herself, he was the last person who had seen her mother.

"Li'l Stuff! Well, I be damned just lookin' at you. Where you come from? Where you been?" He smiled broadly and came toward her with his arms open, but she scooted away. He was acting way friendlier than he'd been for almost the last year they were living together on the first floor of this house. It had seemed as though after he and Rose started to argue more frequently, he had changed his manner. He no longer teased and joked with Tess; instead he took to staring and brooding whenever she was around. When she complained to her mother, Rose just shrugged it off, telling her they needed his share of the rent money. Now Tess looked up at him warily, wondering where to take this conversation next.

Hearing footsteps descending the stairway, she watched his face as Janelle opened the door and sucked in her teeth at the sight of the girl. Antwon's eyes darted toward Janelle and back to Tess.

"Janelle, we need to invite this young lady upstairs for a proper visit," he said, his voice oozing with politeness.

"We can talk out here, far as I'm concerned," said Tess. "I like the air."

"But as you can see, I'm not dressed. I insist you come inside with us," he said, taking her arm and pulling her to her feet. He marched her up the stairs ahead of himself as she struggled to free the arm that was bent behind her. Janelle brought up the rear, still not speaking a word. Once inside the apartment, Antwon lowered Tess into a chair and sat opposite her, staring. Janelle stood against the wall smoking, her left arm tightly folded across her stomach and holding her right elbow in a protective stance.

"What you doin' here, baby girl? And where are you supposed to be right now?" Antwon crossed his legs and leaned back, the master in command.

"I been here before, to see Janelle. I wanted to see her again," was all that Tess said.

"Yeah, Janelle and me, we're old friends. She introduced me to your mama, you remember."

"So where is my mother?" Her question hung in the air for a moment.

"I wish I knew that. She just took off and left me. Left you, too, looks like."

"Mama wouldn't do that."

"You don't know your mama as good as you think. She stole my money and ran, I don't know where she got to."

Tess jumped to her feet. "That's a lie! My mother would never steal."

Antwon stood as well. Tess said, "She was throwing you out – ," when a blow hit her face. She fell to the floor, and a foot kicked her in the gut. She crumpled, trying to draw air into her lungs and failing, when a new punch threw her face to the side. She felt herself being picked up and tossed, landing hard on the floor. Her ears rang, the room turned upside down, and she was kicked again, sending her far away into a landscape of pain and confusion. Through the fog, she heard Janelle scream, "That's enough, God damn you." She heard no more.

After a while, she came around enough to crawl to her knees before vomiting. Sitting back on her heels, she tried to stop the room from spinning. The silence helped to calm her ringing ears, and she realized that she was alone. She could feel a mucky mass in her underpants. Kneeling in a puddle of piss, she was too hurt to even be disgusted.

Janelle came into the room, still smoking.

"He's gone. Don't ask me nothin'. Just get yourself on home, wherever that is. I can't help you none. And don't come back here again, neither. I'm just sorry, is all."

+++

Tess managed to push the bike to a bus stop, and then she sat down on the sidewalk, peering through the eye that wasn't swollen shut, waiting until she saw a bus with an unoccupied bike carrier across its nose. The driver looked like he'd rather do anything than to get involved in her troubles, but he silently hoisted the bike onto the rack and allowed her reeking self to board his bus, once she pulled out the correct amount of cash.

When she finally pushed her bike up the alley and opened the back door, the first thing she saw was Irv standing in the kitchen, reading the back of a box of noodles. He looked up sharply when the door opened and the stench of Tess's persona invaded the room. Her bloody mouth and bruised eyes set alarm bells clanging in his head.

"What on earth! What happened to you? Are you alright?" He caught her just as she sank to the floor, not so much holding her up as cushioning her fall. "Did that thug who accosted you in the backyard do this to you?"

"I hurt. I'm so tired. Just throw away my clothes and put me in the tub," she whispered. Irv somehow found strength he didn't know he had and managed to half-drag her to the bathroom, where he stripped off her clothes as the water ran in the tub.

He ducked into his room and returned with two pills in his hand. He filled a cup that was standing at the edge of the sink and held it out to her along with the pills. "This should help," he said. "It's OxyContin, left over from when I broke my arm last year. Try to swallow it."

She found herself reclined up to her chin in a warm bath, with Irv hovering worriedly just outside the door. He spoke to her from the hallway, asking who had done this to her, telling her they should call the police, wondering whether she should go to a hospital and whether she thought any bones were broken. Tess didn't answer other than to tell Irv that it would be okay. Then she stuck her washcloth back in her mouth and bit down to stanch the bleeding from her loosened teeth.

His voice was a soothing drone of grandparent-ish mutterings in her ears. She wanted only to stop hurting, and Irv's stash of OxyContin was doing the job. She was very relieved not to stink anymore. She was reassured to know that she had somewhere to sleep that night. Beyond that, she just couldn't think right now.

Irv tried to respect her privacy, but he had to help her out of the tub eventually. He quickly wrapped an oversized towel

171

around her to absorb as much damp as possible. She clung to his back as he knelt to hold her pajama pants so she could step into them. Once she had a shirt on, he tucked her into bed, then gently felt her limbs and ribs but felt no broken bones. She fell into a deep drug-induced sleep almost immediately, her arm encircling George's furry orange body.

Irv was exhausted as well, both from the shock and from the physical effort he had expended to get her cleaned up. He was too agitated to sleep, though, so he and Dickens settled into the worn recliner. He sat up late into the night pondering who had done this and why, what he should do next, worrying about their situation being found out and whether that meant the authorities would take Tess away from him. He wondered what he'd gotten himself involved in, for someone to beat up a young girl like that. The old Irv would have been scared for his own safety, but this Irv was angry. Angry for Tess's sake.

+++

The inhabitants of the house awoke later than usual the next morning. Wonder of wonders, even the seven cats slept in. After tossing kibble into the cats' bowls from a standing position (he missed the target on a few), Irv went to check on Tess. He helped her to the toilet, then steadied her back to bed. Time for another pain pill, duly administered.

Irv made a habit of reading the newspapers regularly and thoroughly, and he was well aware of the dangers of the pills he was giving her. He meant them only for temporary use, and he hid them well between doses. But sweet Jesus, she was a mess, and if they weren't going to take her in for treatment, what he had in store would have to do.

He had decided during his night ruminations that he needed some feminine help here. He thought first of Mrs.

Hollander. She was convinced that Tess was his great-niece, and she had seemed quite welcoming on their first encounter. But how would he explain the bruises to her? He certainly didn't want anyone to get the idea that he was abusing Tess. Far from it.

Tess woke a couple of hours after she'd taken that morning's pill with the aid of a straw. Irv had been peeking into her room every so often, and now that she was awake, he went in and sat on her bed.

"Are you going to tell me what happened?" he asked as he gently took her hand.

She shook her head very slightly. Her face was badly swollen, one eye was mostly shut, and her lower lip was split.

"Can you tell me if it was a fight?"

"Cah't talk," she muttered. "Lemme sleeh." She closed her eyes, signaling that the interview was over.

Irv went back to his recliner and thought about possible stories that he could tell Mrs. Hollander. He came up with a story of a bicycle accident, a hit-and-run encounter. Tess had been tossed from the bike and limped her way home, pushing the bike in front of her. That was it. That would be his story.

He called Mrs. Hollander later that morning and got a recording, so he left a message asking her simply to call him back. He knew that she cleaned houses three days a week, and she had told him that she also took in some bookkeeping. No doubt she was busy earning a living, but he was hoping she could at least stop by and see the girl. In the meantime, he sat down at his computer, determined to make peace with Google.

Irv was an academic – a historian. He retired well into the internet age, but he had always maintained a deep distrust of information that did not come from primary sources, or at least thoroughly vetted secondary sources. He placed his confidence in books, newspapers and manuscripts. He used the on-line libraries, medical and scientific sites, and occasional government sources available on the internet. He held Google in contempt, however, on account of the amateurish, misleading or downright lying drivel that he had to wade through in order to find a source worth consulting.

He now found himself in the middle of a situation that he didn't know how to classify, and he knew very well that classifying the problem was the first step toward finding solutions. One had to know where to start looking, after all. And he didn't have a clue. Helen would have been intuitive in her approach, but along with cooking skills, intuition was something that Irv fell far short of in comparison with his late wife. Diving in, he bumbled along with the search engine, keying in various thoughts that came to him. *Runaway foster youths. Applying to be a foster parent. Emancipation of foster youths. Missing persons. Missing persons in Pittsburgh, Pennsylvania. Child abandonment penalty.*

His wanderings were leading him nowhere other than down rabbit holes, deeper than he ever wanted to go and still with no answers. He had to admit to himself that he didn't even know where to start. Along the way, though, he picked up additional information about the underside of the foster system that deepened his understanding of Tess's struggles. He started to grasp her feeling that law enforcement wouldn't help her at this point, although he still had his doubts about that.

The phone rang, and he picked it up to hear Mrs. Hollander's voice. He described to her the bike accident and explained that he felt Tess would be comforted by some female companionship, being so far away from her mother and all. He wondered if she could stop by and spend some time with the girl, see if there was anything she needed that Irv, clueless male that he was, had not provided. He assured her that she would be paid the hourly rate for her time. He argued against her protestations about pay, saying that Tess needed a woman's touch and an old widower could not provide that. They finally settled that he would pay for a taxi to bring her around the next morning at ten.

Without Tess to fix dinner, Irv resorted to home delivery. First he went into her room and asked her what she'd like.

"I duh no. I cah't chew." The last word was pronounced with some difficulty.

"How about some soup, then?" he asked.

"Sure. Do I ge' a pill now?"

"Not until you have some soup." He moved off to the kitchen to search through the possibilities.

Thumbing through his many coupons, he found a place that he hadn't tried before, so he ordered Chinese. He didn't always eat the strange-looking vegetables, but he loved the crunchy noodles, the water chestnuts, and all of the meat. He included in his order some broth that he could feed to Tess with a spoon or a straw. When the food arrived, he was taken by a rare fit of generosity and tipped the delivery person (he couldn't actually tell if it was a male or a female.) He went to bed that night wondering about himself but feeling pretty good all in all.

+++

Mrs. Hollander arrived at ten, as she had said she would. Irv greeted her and took her back to Tess's room. Tess was sitting up, with an ice pack on her eye, pretty groggy but not yet drugged. Her last dose had been at four that morning, so she was about due, but Irv could see that she was holding it together pretty well. He was proud of her.

Grace, as she insisted they call her, took a look at Tess and tsk'ed mightily. "You poor child, who could do such a thing and then just drive away?" she asked. "I brought you some chicken soup, all pureed, so you can just slurp it through a straw."

"T'ank you, ma'am. I 'preciate you comin' to see me," Tess slurred through her swollen mouth.

"Did you tell your mama about what happened?" asked Grace. "She must be fit to be tied. Where does she live, anyways?"

Here Irv interjected himself. "She doesn't want to worry her mother. Tess is a very independent type, and her mother would find it difficult to travel just now. That's why I called, I was hoping you could just visit with her and be a comforting female presence. But perhaps it was a mistake?" He looked at Tess, who shook her head very slightly.

Grace looked piercingly at Irv. She turned her head to the girl. "No, I think I'll sit with her awhile," she said quietly. Irv took the hint and left the room.

The door shut behind him with a click. Grace leaned in close and spoke softly.

"Child, who did this to you? This was not a bike accident, this was a fight."

Tess did not respond.

"I promise I am not going to hurt you. I'm here to help. Are you going to tell me what happened?"

176

"Jus' fell off my bike." Tess closed her eyes and leaned her head back on the pillow propped behind her.

"Where is your mama? Really?"

Tess kept her eyes closed tight, but the tears leaked through and streaked down her face in silent weeping.

Chapter 20

Irv stayed in the front room during Grace's visit. He could hear low voices and some nose-blowing, but he didn't try to eavesdrop. Didn't want to. He had learned long ago to stay away from female business if at all possible. Still, he was glad that Tess had someone to whom she could pour out her troubles. Poor kid. He doubted that she would be able to find out what had happened to her mother without a lot of help, but he'd come to understand why she had no faith in the police.

Not that he knew what to do about it. He assumed her mother was either dead or on the run, and he didn't expect Tess to ever learn anything more about it. He was occupied with trying to figure out what he would do when school started in late August and he was still harboring her. He couldn't picture throwing her back into the foster system after what she'd been through, but what other solution was there?

Grace emerged from Tess's room around noon. She came over and sat on the couch, smoothing her blouse over her slacks and tucking her legs under her. Irv watched her silently, noting the smudged mascara and the tight lines around her mouth.

"What's she told you about what happened?" Grace asked him.

"Pretty much nothing," he said. "I didn't press her. I was too concerned about her injuries. She's been sleeping a lot, and I thought that would help her to heal."

Grace fixed her gaze on him, and he grew uncomfortable. "She's not your great-niece."

"No." He looked down at his hands. "No, she isn't. But she might as well be."

Grace sighed heavily. "I can see that you care about her. And you're helping her the best way you know how. But she's going to need more help than you can give her from inside these four walls. And if you dig into this, you may be endangering yourself."

"I know that. It's partly why I called you."

"Dr. Gladstone," she began.

"Irv, if you please."

"Well, then, Irv it is. I'm gonna tell you some hard truths, Irv. When a female is black and poor, 'specially when there's no man around, nobody with any power listens. Nobody listened to that child in there. So she just got scooped up and plopped into the foster system. I think she told you some of what-all went on there for her."

Irv grimaced.

"And now she found herself a place to hide for a bit, hoping to track down her mama. You are both living under the radar, that's clear to me, and I got no mind to interfere with a situation that's workin' for both of you. I just don't know how to help her."

"Who did this to her, Grace?" Irv looked straight at her, gripping the arms of the recliner.

She shifted uncomfortably, weighing whether or not to confide before she spoke. "It was Antwon, her mother's boyfriend," she finally said. "She really doesn't understand why he beat her up. Maybe when she's healed a while, she can think of something. She insists that Antwon doesn't know where she is. For now, I say we should let her rest."

Irv heard the word "we" and took some heart in it. He hadn't got so far as to think how Grace might help, other than she already had with her visit, but his spirit grasped like a drowning man at the possibility that he wasn't facing this situation alone. He chose to ignore the fact that by getting involved, Grace might be legally putting herself at risk as well.

He admitted to himself with some shame that he had never really viewed Grace as an individual before. Joseph had found her through the want ads, and he paid her for her monthly cleaning. Irv barely noticed her as she worked around him to clear the dust. Now he saw for the first time that she was a handsome woman, perhaps in her early fifties, with an air of no–nonsense about her that reminded him strongly of Helen.

"Do you have a family, Grace?" he asked.

"I have a son." She raised her head proudly. "He was killed in Afghanistan five years ago. I am still his mother, and I'll be his mother until I die. His father and I haven't been together for a long time."

"I am truly sorry. Grief spares no one, it seems." He heard the inadequacy of the cliché as it fell from his lips, but had nothing better to offer. It struck him that he could have been less of a stranger to her for all of these years that she'd been cleaning his house.

Grace stood. "I'm planning on taking the bus home, and I won't hear another word about it. I'm glad you called me," and here she hesitated, "Irv."

"Mrs. Hollander," he said, holding out his hand. "Grace. Thank you so much for coming."

She took his hand. "Call me in a few days, let me know how that child is comin' along. Meantime, I'll be thinking about how we might help her find out about her mother."

+++

Irv must have dozed off after Grace left, because he awoke with a start to hear thumping noises coming from Tess's room. When he shuffled over and opened her door, he found her knocking her fist weakly against the headboard. He wondered whether she was manifesting her sorrow and frustration somehow, and what he should do about it, when she looked at him and lisped out one word. "Pill!"

She was overdue for a dose of Oxycontin, and she was cranky. He turned to fetch the bottle from its hiding place and returned with a half-tablet and a glass of water with a straw poked into it.

"Wha' dis?" she asked, scowling at what he held out. "Where da rest ob it?"

"I've already explained to you that this is a narcotic. It has been two full days since your 'accident,' and I am weaning you slowly off of the drug."

"Bullshit! I s'ill hurt," she said.

"I understand, but we need to gradually reduce your dose until you can get along with ibuprofen or something milder. I am following the procedure that my doctor led me through when he prescribed it for me.

"Fuck da docto'! He not da one got da pain."

Irv thought it over. She was a spitfire, and he wasn't going to win an argument easily.

"Alright, Tess," he said calmly. "Take this half now, and I'll go get the other half. I'll be right back." He held out the half-tablet and then helped her with the water glass until she

181

got it down. Setting the glass on the bedside table, he turned and left the room. A couple of minutes later, he came back and peeked in at her. She was sound asleep. He closed the door gently and went to the kitchen to fix himself some canned soup.

+++

Grace returned on Saturday, having telephoned first to see if it was okay with Irv. She knocked on the door and called out his name. Irv opened up to find her holding a small cooler in one hand and a few flowers in the other.

"How's our girl today?" she asked as she entered.

"Well, she's coming along. I've got her on ibuprofen starting today, and the swelling's going down. She doesn't eat much, though."

"I brought her some ice cream, maybe that'll get her interested," said Grace. "May I see her?"

"You can see me 'cause here I am," said Tess as she came into the room wearing an oversized t-shirt and shorts, her bare legs marked with yellowing bruises. The purple around her eyes had turned green, and her cheeks were almost their normal size. She stretched her mouth into a tight-lipped smile.

Grace held out the flowers. "These're just somethin' from my garden," she said. "I wanted to brighten your room a bit."

"Thank you," Tess said with almost no lisp. She gave them to Irv, who went off to find a glass to put them in, and sat down on the couch. Grace sat opposite her in the armchair, clearing her throat and folding her hands in her lap.

"Have you told him what really happened?" asked Grace while Irv was in the kitchen.

"I'm not sure," Tess said. "I been kinda hazy the last few days, but my head is clearing now. Do you think I should tell him?"

"I think," said Grace carefully, "that he's the only person you can trust right now. Besides me, I hope."

Irv came back with the flowers and set them on the side table, then sat in his recliner. A cat immediately jumped up to join him, and he stroked it absently in a silence broken only by the ticking clocks.

"Grace," he said after a bit, "are you fond of cats?"

"Well, yes and no, Mr. – Irv. Some I like and some I don't, but all in measured doses. I got to say your brood is on the upper limit of what I can tolerate, but Tess here seems to be keeping the mess down. Or she was."

"That's just what I was thinking. I wonder whether my 'brood', as you say, is a bit too much for Tess and myself these days."

"There's rescue places you can call if you want to relocate some of them. They don't have to go to the pound, you know."

"I couldn't send them to the pound where they'd likely be killed. I couldn't stand that. But maybe I can find another way."

Grace stood up suddenly. "I forgot about the ice cream!" she said, and she took the little cooler to the kitchen. While she was making a clatter with bowls and spoons in the other room, Tess spoke up.

"Irv. It was a fight. It was Antwon did it."

"I know, Tess. Grace told me about it. But I'm glad you're telling me yourself."

"Okay, then."

"Yes. Okay, then. Do you know why he did it?"

"I figure it's because he knows what happened to my mother, and he don't ... he doesn't want me snooping around."

"That seems logical. What do you think should be done about it? Have you put any thought into that question?"

"I have put me a *lot* of thought into it," she said. "And so far, I come up with nothin'."

"What about involving the police?" he asked. "Isn't it about time for that?"

A guarded look came across Tess's face. "I told you, I don't figure the police will do anything except throw me back in the system. No way. I want to stay here with you"

Grace came back with bowls of ice cream on a tray and handed them around. Tess tucked into her dish, wincing at first as the cold hit her sore teeth, then just letting the treat melt in her throat. The heat of the day and the aches in her ribs faded away as the frozen concoction slid down her insides. She had a kind of a family feeling for the first time in over a year while the three of them silently sucked on their spoons.

+++

Monday found Tess sitting on the front porch with a glass of iced tea in her hand. It felt great to be outside again after mostly lying in bed for a week. Her sunglasses hid the remaining discoloration around her eyes, and she felt pretty normal. She hadn't dared to sit out front like this for the first part of the summer, but now she just didn't care. She had decided that no one from CPS was looking for her, and she missed the comings and goings of a neighborhood. No more hiding in the shadows for her. It was clear that she wasn't any safer that way.

As she sat watching people and traffic passing by, Irv was inside on the telephone. He had located a cat rescue organization that promised a no-kill policy. In a shaky voice, he arranged for their employee, someone named Pat, to come by and pick up most of the cats the next day. As soon as he hung up the phone, he had a strong urge to call back and cancel. He held tightly to Dickens, who had curled up in his lap.

"Never you, my rascal. Not you, and not George. The girl loves George," he said as he stroked the cat, eliciting strong purrs.

He continued talking to the cat. "I don't know how we came to be so many. I just couldn't turn any of them away when they showed up at the kitchen door. But we can't take care of them all any more, that's clear. You understand that, don't you?"

"Understand what?" asked Tess as she came in through the front door.

"Just…we can only any of us be expected to do so much. That's all."

"I got you, Irv. But sometimes it all seems too hard, you know? And then it turns out, our best just isn't enough."

He looked at her, and his heart broke just a little bit.

The phone rang as she plopped down on the couch. Irv picked it up and listened for a long minute before speaking.

"I understand your concern, Joseph, but really, everything is fine here….Yes, I am eating regularly…The last doctor report was just more of the same, I am in fine health…Is that so? No more soccer for now? …Well, I'll be happy to see you

185

on Sunday, but I am really not in need of provisions…Then I'll see you around ten. Goodbye."

"Joseph worries about you, Irv," said Tess. "Why don't you want to move in with him?"

He was silent for a moment, looking down at Dickens.

"Helen and I shared this house throughout our marriage. I feel very much as though she's still here. Sometimes I even talk to her. I don't want to leave, I just want to stay here until I die. Is that so difficult to understand?"

"No, I don't guess so," she said. "But it's hard to be alone sometimes."

He looked at her and then shifted his gaze out the front window.

"You and I are not alone, Tess," he said.

Chapter 21

A knock on the front door Tuesday morning sent Tess back to her bedroom as Irv went to answer it. "Feline Friends Rescue Service," a voice called out.

Irv cracked the door open and saw a middle-aged blonde woman in jeans and a flannel shirt holding a pole with a net on the end. "I changed my mind," he said as he shut the door.

"Irv. You promised," Tess called softly from her room. "You know they'll be better off, and so will we."

Sighing, he opened the door again and waved the woman toward a chair. "I'd like to get the details on your organization first," he said. "I want some guarantees."

"That's fine, sir," she said as she sat. "My name is Pat, and I'm here to set all of your worries to rest."

"I'm afraid that would indeed be a great undertaking," he said. "My cats are the present issue, however, and I want your assurance that they will not be euthanized before I let you take them."

"No, sir, absolutely not. We have a strict no-kill policy at Feline Friends. If we can't place a cat after three months, we send him or her to a local farm to work as a mouser. Your kitties will be safe and happy," she said with enthusiasm. Irv looked grim in the face of her jollity, but he realized that it was too much to ask of Tess to care for so many animals.

"Very well, then," he said. "The two cats who are sequestered in the front bedroom are not to be disturbed. The other five are hiding somewhere around the place. If you can find them, you can take them."

Pat retrieved a couple of carrier cages from the front porch. Then she pulled on some leather gloves, took her net in one hand and a flashlight in the other, and set about peering underneath furniture and inside boxes, pulling blankets off piles of detritus and generally poking around everywhere Irv didn't want her to be. She thoroughly searched his bedroom as he stood in the doorway supervising her every move. Within ten minutes she had netted one cat after another, loading two cats each into carrier boxes, until only one cat remained.

"I'll have to go back to my truck for another cage," she said as she walked out the door carrying the two filled boxes, each emitting yowls of protest. Irv sank into his recliner with a defeated grunt. He spied the remaining cat hiding underneath the television where it was parked in the corner, covered by a tablecloth. The cat's yellow eyes stared at him as it growled menacingly, daring him to betray its hiding place.

"Give'er hell, Casper," he whispered.

+++

Tess was looking pretty good by Wednesday, at least in her opinion. She figured she could make a trip to the Aldi in a pair of sunglasses and not attract too much attention. After lunch, she pulled on some jeans to hide the bruises on her legs and went out to the garage to fetch the wagon and a chain lock.

Irv handed her the grocery list along with some cash. He looked at her with concern.

"Are you certain you're up to this?" he asked. "I could go with you, just to make sure you're all right."

"Irv. You would slow me way down. I'm gonna go crazy if I don't get out of this house for a while. 'Sides, we're out of food. So, yeah." She turned and headed off to the alley, making a left and towing the wagon down to the sidewalk. It felt great to get out in the neighborhood again. The day was fine. Half a dozen kids were playing kickball in the street. A dog barked as she walked by. She was starting to lose the feeling of insecurity that had plagued her since the shock of the beating.

When she got to the supermarket, she locked the wagon to a bike rack. Giving the combination dial a twist to set it and standing up, she found herself looking straight into SloMo's smirking face. Her heart slammed against her chest as she stared back at him. A few seconds went by before either spoke.

"What are you doin' here?" she finally said. "Why can't you leave me alone 'stead of creepin' up on me everywhere?"

"Relax, girlfriend. I just need to talk to you without that old man blowin' my head off." He was clearly enjoying the effect he had on her, and he blocked her path to keep her there. "I got something to discuss with you."

"I already told you, I'm not doin' that stuff anymore. I got me a place to live and food to eat, so why ever would I wanna do the dirty?"

"I know you ain't in the business no more. That's not what I wanna talk about. Here's the deal - we got us a mutual problem, and his name is Antwon."

"How you know Antwon? What's he done to you? And how do you know he's a problem for me?"

"Girl, I already told you, I been keepin' track of you. When you went back over to the house on Fenway last week, some of my boys let me know. I was down the street when you come stumblin' outta there all bloody with your clothes torn. I don't know what his beef is with you, but I thought you might wanna know where he lives so's you can maybe do somethin' about it."

"What's your thing with him?" Tess looked at him warily, wondering what his angle was.

"The man sold me some bad shit. I passed it along to one of my customers, and the guy turned up dead. That is not good for business, which I'm sure even you can dig. So he owes me. Either that, or he's tryin' to crowd me out of his market. Whichever, I got his number."

"Why don't you go after him yourself, then? Why talk to me?"

"Here's why: I got a record. I got a parole officer breathing down my neck. I ain't gonna call the cops and complain about a deal gone wrong. And I ain't sending my boys after him 'cause he got some, how you wanna say it, 'associates' in high places. This deal ain't worth a shitstorm to me, but if I can get him called up on something else…well, that would be sweet. Now you get it?"

"I guess I get it, but I don't like it. Besides, I already know he lives on Fenway with Janelle now."

"No, he don't, he only stays there sometimes. He got his own place over in Garfield. I can show you."

"Look, I got no reason to trust you. Right now I got to get me some groceries and be home before I'm missed. But I'll think about what you're sayin', and I'll let you know. Gimme your cell number."

"Tell me what yours is, and I'll call you."

"Nope." She held out the grocery list and a pen. He smiled and wrote the number down. She grabbed the pen and paper and turned to go into the store.

"You be careful, girlfriend," he said to her back. "Think about your answer. I be waitin' on your call." He sauntered away, and a couple of his homies joined up with him at the corner.

When Tess came out of the Aldi later with her cart, she looked around carefully. SloMo was nowhere to be seen. Rasheed, however, was standing near the bike rack smoking a cigarette. He smiled when he saw her.

"I thought I recognized that wagon," he said. "Where you been lately? I kinda missed you comin' around."

"I been busy. And I told you, I don't like cigarettes."

"I'm tryin' to quit," he said as he ground out his smoke with the toe of his shoe. "Can I walk you home? I'm off work as of ten minutes ago."

Tess lifted her chin in an I-don't-care pose and tossed her head. *This boy is fine, and his smile is blinding. But do I want him to know where I live?*

"You can walk me part way, but that's all." After transferring her bags of groceries, she unlocked the wagon and started towing it, but Rasheed took the handle from her. She accepted the gesture, and they walked slowly down the street.

"Do you go to Allerdice High?" she asked.

"Yup. I'll be a junior this year."

"I'll be a freshman. Maybe we'll see each other around." Tess had no solid reason to think she'd be placed in the high school in that district, but she could always imagine. She adjusted her sunglasses, trying to hide the bruises around her eyes.

"I hope so. I play basketball, I made the varsity team for this year. What do you like to do?"

No one had asked Tess that question in a very long time. Her mother, naturally, had always wanted to hear about everything that Tess was doing at school. Rose heaped constant and indiscriminate praise on Tess's artwork, her spelling quizzes, her book reports and her math results. Tess was confident that she was the shining star in her mother's galaxy. But what did she herself like the most?

"I guess I like lots of stuff," she said. "I don't know what I like the best. But I got lots of time to figure that out." She walked on, lost in thoughts about the journal she'd been keeping and all of the events recorded there. A vision of the reading room at the central library flashed into her mind. The quiet in that room was like nothing she'd ever experienced in her noisy life.

"So, I like to write things down. Real things. Not made-up stories."

"Oh, journalism," said Rasheed. "Like the school paper."

"Yeah, maybe. Whatever."

They reached the corner of her street, and she took the wagon handle from him.

"Thanks, Rasheed. I'll go on from here."

"What's your name? You know mine 'cause of my nametag, but I don't know yours."

"I'm Tess. I'll see you around, maybe." She turned the corner, looking back once or twice to make sure he wasn't following. Then a shy smile spread across her face and she forgot, for once, about her bruises.

+++

Irv was waiting when she pulled the wagon up to the kitchen door. He insisted on helping her to unload, and they got everything put away faster than usual. He seemed agitated, and Tess wondered how she could calm him down. She put the kettle on for tea and poured out two cups when the water was ready, adding milk and sugar after it steeped. Bringing the mugs into the front room, she called Irv to sit down.

"What's up, Irv?" she asked. "What did you do while I was gone?"

"Oh, I don't know. I looked through some of my papers, then I started to sort my coupons."

Tess sipped her tea in silence.

"I miss those cats," he said after a moment.

"I know, Irv, but they were just too much for the two of us. You can see that, can't you? And we still got Dickens and George, they're the ones that love us the most."

"I suppose so. It's hard letting go, though."

They sat with their tea while the clocks ticked out of rhythm and the refrigerator hummed in the kitchen. The two of them had grown comfortable with silences in the couple of months they'd lived together. Finally Irv spoke.

"Can you help me to sort out this mess I've created?" he asked her.

She was uncertain of his meaning. "What mess is that, Irv?"

"You know. All of the recycling, the old magazines – the things I have such a hard time getting rid of. I want to impose some order onto all of it."

Tess continued to drink her tea. She twirled her foot, reached down to scratch George's neck, then looked off into space. Finally, she cleared her throat.

"Irv," she said. "I don't know. You're pretty attached to your stuff, and I just see us fussin' and fightin' over things.

I'm not sure I'm up for it. Right now I got other things on my mind."

"I need your help, Tess. Joseph won't let up until he's satisfied that I can keep order in my life according to his terms."

"Why'd you let stuff pile up in the first place? Has it always looked like this around here?"

Irv was silent for a moment before he spoke.

"No, Helen would never have allowed it. As I told you, she died while Joseph was away at college. The boy came home for a few weeks, but he was already fully out of the nest by that time, and he soon returned to school. Somehow, I never could bring myself to empty Helen's craft room, and then I started to let things pile up in the living room as well. It got harder to throw anything away. I just wanted time to stop. I thought if everything remained static, maybe it would seem like she was still here as well."

"Well, I'm sorry about that, Irv. But look, I got me a good deal goin' here. If we get on opposite sides about the clutter, where does that leave me?"

"Tess," he said. "This is your home, too, at least for now. I think that maybe with your help, I can let go of some things that have me kind of stuck. Just please think about it."

What she thought about was her surprise to discover that she had become useful – maybe to Irv, maybe to SloMo. It was a new experience for her, and although it left her feeling somewhat empowered, she wasn't sure she liked it. She mostly preferred to operate in solo mode, where the only person she had to trust was herself. And after her recent run-in with Antwon, she feared that her search for her mother was about to get more dangerous. Going at it alone meant that the only

194

person whose safety she risked was her own. Those were terms that she could live with.

Chapter 22

"Why the heck don't you throw out these pizza boxes soon as you're done eating the pizza?" Tess was filling her arms with a second load of cardboard from the fireplace. When the pile reached her chin, she edged her way toward the kitchen door. "Wouldn't that be easier?"

"Those boxes are for the recycling bin, which is more than twice the size of my wet garbage can. I'm supposed to move both bins out into the alley on pick-up day, and the big one just got to be too much for me. I never use the fireplace anyway."

Tess came back in the kitchen door with empty arms. She was making some progress with the cardboard, but Irv had stopped sorting the bulk mail pile that sat next to his chair. He seemed genuinely troubled.

"What if I suddenly need a window screen replaced, and I've tossed the advertisement for Windows-R-Us? I can't know for sure that my dentist won't retire, leaving me in need of a new provider such as this Smile, Inc. that sent me an offer for a discount on my first visit. How am I supposed to find services when I need them?"

"You get on your computer and do a search, read the reviews. Or you ask a neighbor for a referral - or your son."

"You see, that's just what I don't want to do," he insisted. "I prefer to be self-reliant."

Tess sighed. A thick pile of catalogs on the bookshelf caught her eye, and she leafed through a few.

"Bicycling catalogs? Really, Irv? When's the last time you rode a bike?"

"Those were Joseph's catalogs. He rode distances in his younger days."

"Yeah, he must'a been way younger. These are all at least twenty years old. Out they go, before they disintegrate into piles of dust."

"No, no, those are keepsakes! They don't even belong to me, strictly speaking."

"And *strictly speaking*, this is the kinda stuff your son is buggin' you about. Man up, Irv. You got to show Joseph that you can deal with living on your own."

+++

At the end of two full days of wrangling, the front room was cleared of a large amount of flammable material, with the exception of the stacks of newsprint remaining along the wall under the front windows. Tess was exhausted, both physically and spiritually, from hauling, sorting and convincing Irv to let go of stuff. The place still wasn't 'Home Makeover' material, but she really didn't think she could do any more without permanently damaging her relationship with Irv. They'd been working together peacefully for a couple of days, and a feeling of companionship had made the work feel lighter.

She did enjoy the fact that the house smelled better without the usual abundance of used cat litter and old pizza crumbs. After opening a few windows to let the breeze in and air the place out, she took a bath and went to bed with George curled up at her side.

A scraping sound awakened her, and she opened her eyes without moving. A half-moon dimly lit the room, casting shadows. George stretched in his sleep and rolled to the side of the bed. Tess very slowly turned her head to see a male figure climbing in through her window. Instantly, she rolled off the bed, landing soundlessly in a crouch. She slid her hand under the mattress and grabbed hold of the hunting knife. Pulling it out, she leapt to her feet and held the knife under the man's throat.

He grabbed her wrist and twisted it, causing her to drop the knife. At the same time, he clapped his other hand over her mouth, stifling all but her desperate squeaks. He lowered her onto the bed, her eyes rolling in terror.

"Shut up," he whispered. "It's me, SloMo. I ain't gonna hurt you unless you make me. You and me gonna go pay a visit to Antwon."

Keeping one hand over her mouth, he twisted her arm behind her and shoved her out of the room, pulling the door shut behind them. Irv's snores continued unabated while she struggled to get away as he pushed her toward the kitchen. He grabbed the key off its cup hook and unlocked the door. Tossing the key onto the counter, he forced her out the back door and closed it. Once outside, he kept her moving all the way to the alley, where he allowed her to shake herself free.

"What the fuck are you doing?" she demanded, rubbing her arm. "I could'a stuck you with that knife." She glared at him.

"Yeah, girlfriend, you almost had me," he said with a smirk. Then, turning serious, he said, "You never called me."

"So what? I was still thinkin' about your 'offer'."

"It's gotta be tonight," he said. "I seen Antwon gettin' wasted over at the Night Owl, then his girlfriend, she hauled him outta there to her place. Now's the time for me to show you where he lives."

"What if I don't wanna go? What if he comes home and beats me up again?"

"Just get in." He pulled her over to a dark blue sedan, opened the door, and bowed dramatically to her as he thrust her into the passenger seat. The stars were just beginning to pale as they set off toward Garfield.

SloMo drove down streets lined with low-income apartment buildings, then past empty weed lots interspersed with run-down mid-century houses. He pulled up to one of them and said, "This is it. You gotta know where he lives if you gonna report him for beating you up. That way, the cops can find him quicker. Plus, you gonna do some scouting for me. Have a good look around. See what you can see, then come back and tell me. I be waitin' for you in the car."

Tess got out, shutting the car door as quietly as she could, and walked up alongside the driveway, keeping on the far side of a row of bushes. She peered at the back of the house, noting blank unshaded windows with a dim light shining in one of them. Creeping up to that window and standing on her toes, she saw a kitchen lit only by the bulb under the stove hood. The table was covered with various items: measuring cups, glass beakers, spoons and syringes, a kitchen scale, pipes, zip lock baggies, a couple of cardboard shipping boxes, a small covered kettle. She'd never seen a druggie's prep station before, but she figured that was more or less what she was looking at. Dropping back down, she turned to look behind her.

A one-car garage sat at the end of the driveway, its shingle siding peeling with age, weeds growing next to it on both sides. She walked up to it, then circled it carefully. The windows had been boarded up with plywood, and the side door had no window at all. Coming back around to the front, she noticed that the roll-up door was bolted to the driveway with large iron hooks imbedded in the cement. Unlike the rest of the place, the hooks looked fairly new and shiny.

Wondering what was the use of a garage with a door that couldn't be opened, she glanced up and noticed a skylight. The only way she was going to see what was in the garage was through that rooftop opening. An old apple tree was growing right next to the garage, and she climbed up till she could step onto the roof. The sky was getting lighter now, so she flattened onto her belly and started snake-crawling toward the dome of the skylight. Her bare toe caught on a small apple lying on the shingles, and when she dislodged it, the sound of it rolling down the slope and hitting the rain gutter felt to her like a fire alarm going off.

She lay still until she was sure that no one and nothing had reacted to the noise. Then, continuing her crawl, she reached the edge of the skylight. Peering over the rim, she froze with shock. A woman wearing a flimsy night dress was lying sprawled out on a bed. She was rail-thin, with a snarl of matted black hair tumbling over her head. She lay with her face in the pillow and stick-like arms spread wide to either side. Tess couldn't see the woman's face. She didn't recognize anything that she could make out in the glancing rays of the early morning sun that lighted only a part of the room. Once her eyes became accustomed to the dimness, she searched more carefully, her heart racing. When she spotted her own quilt bunched on the floor in a corner, her breath stopped.

Oh, my God! Who are you?

Her heartbeat was almost deafening, her blood slushing in and out of her ears like the surf. She tried to get a better look around the room, but her vision was blurred by the adrenaline pumping through her body. Panic seized her as she ran her fingers around the edge of the skylight. It was sealed tight. She started tapping her fingers on the glass, trying to rouse the woman without alerting the neighbors. The woman didn't stir. Tess looked around and found another hard green apple within reach. She grabbed it and used it as a heavier knocker.

The woman turned onto her back, matted hair still covering her face, arms flung out next to her. Now Tess could see her more clearly, and what she saw was needle tracks up and down those thin brown arms. Was this emaciated woman with the knotted hair and ripped nightgown her mother? Tess could not – would not - believe that. Her mother had never used drugs. Her mother was very particular about her hair and her appearance. This vision lying below Tess was a nightmare.

Antwon must have taken her quilt from the apartment, she reasoned. She remembered looking for it when she went back with the police for some clothing and toiletries, but it wasn't there. She'd been hiding under it when she was hit in the head, so it must have had some of her blood on it. Was that why Antwon had taken it? Or did her mother grab it first? Irv had told Tess that the police found her blood on the scene, but it could have soaked into the carpet.

If that woman in the garage was her mother, how was she going to get her out of there? And if it wasn't her mother, what should she do about it? For all Tess knew, the woman was just some druggie squatting in Antwon's garage. Or maybe one of his customers, trading sex for heroin. The sun was rising quickly, and trying to break into the garage struck Tess as a very bad idea until she had made a plan. She backed her way off the roof to the apple tree and climbed down.

Retracing her furtive path alongside the bushes, she opened the passenger door of SloMo's sedan and hopped in.

"Wassup? What'd'you find?" He was sitting low in the driver's seat, a cap pulled over his eyes, obviously watching for passing cars and pedestrians as the neighborhood awakened. Once she had climbed in, he turned the key in the ignition and moved off at a low speed with the engine purring softly until they cleared the block and turned onto a side street. Tess kept her mouth shut until they had rounded the corner. Then she sat up straight and looked directly at SloMo.

"You know what I found," said Tess. "He's sellin' you drugs, so you know what's there. Why even axe me?" She was disgusted with the whole situation, but she was also thinking about how she might use SloMo's new offer of an alliance to her advantage. He had a loyal gang that followed him around, keeping him safe. Maybe they could keep her safe, too, at least for a while. For sure, she was not going to tell SloMo what she had seen in the garage. Not yet.

"What'd you see in the house?" he asked.

"I saw plenty, and it was right out there in the open, spread out all over the kitchen. You know all about it. So why'd you bring me here? What do you want from me?"

"I want you to bring that mothafucker down for me, and I ain't gonna leave you alone until you deliver. I wanted you to know where he lives, so's you can report him beatin' you up. All's I need is for the cops to have an excuse to search his house, and you're gonna serve it up." He twisted his hat around backwards and stared out the windshield, his hands gripping the wheel tightly.

"Why you need me to do this? Why don't you do it yourself?"

"Girl," he said in a voice that was almost a growl. "I already told you why I don't go after him. I can't call the cops, even anonymously. They'd find me, and then Antwon's friends would find out right away, and so would my parole officer. But you could explain to the cops that he beat you up, you bein' a minor an' everything, and that would turn up the heat on him."

"There's a problem with that," she said calmly. "I am personally missing from the foster system. And I do not want CPS to know where I am, 'cause they'll throw me into the soup and I be right back where I escaped from when your bad black ass found me the first time."

SloMo never stopped the car as he rolled slowly and quietly down the alley behind Irv's house. Tess had to jump out and trot beside it long enough to press the door shut with a click. She cut through the neighbor's side yard and slipped back in through the open window of her bedroom, noting with relief that the door to her room was still closed. The clock on the side table showed that it was 6:38, and she wasn't surprised to hear Irv rattling around in the kitchen. After brushing some leaves and dirt off the T-shirt and running shorts that she'd gone to bed in and still wore, she opened the door and wandered off to join him, with George trailing after her.

"Morning, Irv," she said as she yawned and stretched her arms over her head. "Sorry I haven't fed the cats yet. I must've overslept after all that cleaning and sorting yesterday."   She rustled the bag of kibbles, which brought Dickens running from wherever he'd been curled up.

"That's fine," said Irv. "The two of them must have been tired as well. I do want to thank you for your efforts to clear

203

the place out some, in spite of my cranky objections. It needed doing, especially since there will be an inspection tomorrow."

Tess looked at him curiously, then smiled when she understood that he was talking about his son's visit the next day.

"Oh, yeah. Joseph oughta be pleased with how orderly things are getting around here," she said. "You can tell him what a great job I'm doing. Maybe that'll keep him off your back for a while." She turned to put the cat food back and noticed the Schlitz keyring lying on the counter, right where SloMo had tossed it after opening the door to shove her out in the early hours. Irv was fussing at the stove, adjusting the flame under the tea kettle with his back to the counter. She quietly edged over behind him, picked up the keyring, and hung it back on its cup hook. Then she pulled a mug down from a different hook and busied herself with finding a teabag.

"By the way," he said, still with his back turned. "I noticed this morning that you failed to lock the back door when you went to bed last night. That is a serious breach of security which could leave us vulnerable to criminal activity. I hope that you will not repeat the lapse."

Tess tucked her chin and sighed with relief. If that was the only thing that Irv had noticed was amiss this morning, she was lucky indeed. She shivered at the thought of what she'd seen in the early hours and wondered what, if anything, she was going to do about it.

"Yes, sir," she replied.

Chapter 23

The next morning her ringing phone woke Tess from a dream so deep that she had to fight her way out of it. She'd been trying to swim upstream with her legs bound tightly together while a crowd of people, supposedly family members, cheered her on from the banks. She opened her eyes and tried to get her bearings in a room that at first looked as unfamiliar as Oz must have looked to Dorothy. She was sure she didn't know anyone from her dream. Then she wondered who could be calling her, since the only person she'd ever called from her cheap cell phone was Janelle, and just the one time. She decided not to answer it.

Pushing herself out of bed, she made her way to the bathroom to wash up. It was probably just a junk call. One thing she knew from hanging with the street kids who had phones was that robocalls were a daily annoyance. She was actually less annoyed by the experience than she was happy to be able to share in it. It made her feel normal somehow.

In the hall she heard the phone ding for a voice message, and she stopped. She wanted to hear the message from her first ever real phone call, to make sure. Janelle was the only person she'd ever called, but what could Janelle possibly have to say after what had happened? She went back to her room and put the phone to her ear. When she listened to the message, she heard a familiar low, slurred voice. She sank down on the edge of the bed.

"Hey girlfriend, you figured out yet how you gonna get back at that dude?" SloMo demanded. "You better come up with a plan or I be comin' up with my own plan, and it won't be no easy ride for you. Don't forget I know where you live. Call me." Click. Silence.

Tess sat staring at the opposite wall, thinking. She picked up her hairbrush off the little table and brushed the snags out, lost in thought as she started to work her long, wiry black curls into a braid. Irv was still snoring as she quietly pulled on her clothes. She wandered off to the kitchen to start a flame under the tea kettle and feed the two cats, thankful for the quiet house and a chance to consider her options.

Joseph would be there by 10:00. It was now 7:15, too early to pay Janelle a visit, but Tess definitely wanted to be gone before Irv's son arrived. She needed to confront her mother's old friend, to cut through the lies and find out what Janelle knew - or at least, what Janelle believed. And they needed to talk when Antwon wasn't around. She no longer trusted Janelle to protect her, but she didn't fear that the woman would try to hurt her. Tess could see that Janelle was the kind who needed a man around in order to feel okay about herself. She'd never confront Antwon openly, but Tess might be able to scare her into being a little more honest, as long as he wasn't around to hear her.

Irv came in while Tess was eating some scrambled eggs. He was still in his pajamas and robe. His skin was pallid, even for an old white guy. Tess noticed that he hadn't shaved for a couple of days, which was unlike him. He chose a mug, poured some hot water over a tea bag, added sugar, and sat at the little table across from her. Staring absently into space, he stirred and stirred, continuing long after the sugar had dissolved, the spoon clicking steadily against the sides of the mug.

"You okay, Irv?" she asked, as much to get him to stop stirring as anything else.

"What's that? Yes, I'm fine. Fine." He continued to stir.

"You remember your son is coming over this morning, right?" She prompted him gently, watching for his reaction. At that, he looked up and seemed to focus on her for the first time.

"Oh, yes. Did he say 10:00? I wonder what he wants this time."

"I think he prob'ly just wants to see you, Irv. And don't worry, I won't be here. I got to see a friend today. I'm gonna be gone before he ever gets here."

Irv looked startled. "Why ever should you go away? You *live* here. *He* doesn't live here."

Tess wondered whether Irv was fully awake. She looked more carefully at him. The remaining wisps of his white hair were stuck to his scalp with sweat. His whiskers gave him a grubby look. His eyeglasses were covered with smudges, and his bathrobe hadn't been washed in quite a while. If Joseph saw his father like this, he'd drag Irv off to assisted living or whatever, and that would kill him. She decided Irv would need some assistance with his grooming before Joseph arrived. Much as she hated to admit it, the groomer would have to be her.

"Okeydokey. Why don't you just drink your tea for now? Lemme fix you a bowl of oatmeal, maybe put some raisins and honey and almond bits in it. Just the way you like it."

That last part was a lie that she hoped he would ignore. Irv was a corn flakes kind of guy, definitely not a granola fan. Tess hadn't forgotten his seizure on the kitchen floor, though, and she snuck some nutrition into him every chance she got. She hoped never to have to drag him up off the floor again.

After he'd eaten most of the oatmeal in his bowl, he laid down his spoon.

"I'm tired," he said. He grabbed his cane and stood, moving off to his chair in the front room. Tess glanced at the clock on the stove and saw that it was 8:30. She followed after him as he sat, and she pressed the button to recline the chair. Dickens jumped into his lap.

"I'm gonna run you a warm bath, Irv," she said as she hovered over him. He had already closed his eyes and didn't respond, but his hand moved gently over the cat's back, eliciting loud purrs. "I'll come get you when it's ready."

Tess had never shaved anyone or anything before, except for one time when she was eleven. She and her friend Delia had decided to shave their legs out on the back porch. Delia had taken her father's razor and shave cream, and they used a garden hose to rinse themselves off. Tess had nicked herself a few times, but not badly, so she decided she knew the basics. At least she was confident that she wouldn't fatally cut Irv.

She set out a razor and some shave cream in the bathroom while hot water filled the tub, then she darted into Irv's room and pulled open drawers until she found his clean underwear. She grabbed a pair of boxers and a t-shirt, then a shirt and pants from the closet, clean socks and some moccasins. She laid it all out on the bed and went back to turn the water off. It was time to collect Irv.

He had fallen asleep again, but his color looked a little better than it had when he first got up. She put her hand on his shoulder and squeezed gently. He opened his eyes.

"Time for a bath," she said. "C'mon, I'll help you outta this chair." She pressed the button to lower the footrest and set him upright. Dickens jumped off. Grabbing his cane, he leaned slightly on her shoulder as they walked to the bathroom. This time he didn't protest, he just meekly allowed her to undress him and help him into the bath. She was unfazed, tending to him as she would to a grandfather who had lost some mobility. She was not surprised to realize that such was how she felt.

That's what really worried her, she realized. From the formerly stiff and proud Professor Gladstone to docile Irv was a big change. Instead of brooding on it, she got busy shaving and cleaning him until he was presentable. Helping him out of the tub, she wrapped him in a towel and retreated to the hallway.

"You get dry, Irv, and then you'll find your clothes all laid out in your room."

When he finally emerged from his bedroom fully dressed, he looked almost like his old self. Tess was relieved that his son would not see him in such a feeble state. Still, she wondered what had happened to change his demeanor so. She realized that she had been busy with her own affairs for the past few days, not really paying much attention to him. In fact, she kind of resented having to fuss about him at all.

Her grandmother had been an important part of Tess's life until she was eleven. Gram was a handsome woman without a line on her face; a slight silvering in her hair was the only clue that she was "of a certain age." But then Gram was gone, seemingly overnight. Tess had never seen anyone grow old before, not really. It was not a pretty sight. And she didn't feel equipped to deal with it. Aging was uncharted territory for

Tess - it was beyond her experience and her skill set. Yet here it was, smacking her in the face.

"I'm about ready to take off now. You gonna be okay without me till Joseph gets here?" she asked him.

"Yes, of course," he said as he settled himself into his recliner again.

"I'll leave this piece of paper here by the phone, it has my cell number on it. Call me if you need anything."

He grunted his assent and picked up the newspaper. Tess inspected him one last time and then took herself out the back door, locking it afterwards with her spare key. Irv didn't seem like his usual overly careful self this morning. She figured she'd better try to keep the house - and Irv - safe.

As she rolled the bike into the alley, she thought again about the horror she'd seen in the early hours of the previous day. The woman in the garage could not have been her mother. Tess refused to believe it. Still, she had to cut through this web of lies and find out what, if anything, Janelle really knew. Was she aware of the locked garage? Did she know what was in there? How deeply was Janelle – her 'auntie,' her mother's friend – involved? Tess was determined to find out what she could.

+++

Irv was sitting in his recliner, unable to answer the front door, his body not responding to his order to stand. He could hear Joseph calling to him and knocking with increasing strength. The noise ceased after a bit, then he heard the sound of the kitchen door being unlocked. When Joseph walked into the room and stood in front of him, he looked up vacantly. His eyes were not tracking together, they seemed almost to be looking in different directions. He forced a lop-sided smile and mumbled something unintelligible.

"What, Dad? What did you say?"

Irv uttered another set of meaningless sounds. The cat sitting on his lap pushed its head against the hand that lay next to it, but nothing happened. Irv's other hand, his right, reached out slowly and settled on the cat's head.

Joseph grabbed the telephone and dialed 911, telling the dispatcher that his father seemed to be having a stroke. He waited on the phone for what seemed like ages, answering questions and then being asked to hold again. He paced back and forth, the receiver to his ear.

"Hello? Hello?" he said when he next heard a voice. He listened for about ten seconds and then yelled into the phone to for god's sake send an ambulance, what was taking them so freaking long, he should just drive his father to the hospital himself. The voice on the other end spoke in a rising volume as Joseph interrupted repeatedly, until a knock on the front door caused Joseph to drop the phone. In two strides, he managed to throw off the chain, turn back the deadbolt, and fling the door open. Two EMTs in uniform stood on the porch.

One of them knelt by his father and started taking his blood pressure, measuring his blood oxygen level, asking him questions the entire time. Joseph couldn't see that the man was getting any understandable responses from his father, but he seemed to have an agenda to work through. The other man was bringing in a stretcher and laying it out. When they were ready, they hoisted Irv onto the stretcher and began to ease him out the door. As they carried him, his eyes went wide and his agitation increased noticeably. "Tsh, tsh," he was mumbling.

"Dad, I'm coming with you. It'll be okay. I'll be with you the entire time." Joseph locked the door and went out through the kitchen with his key, then followed the stretcher to the back of the ambulance and climbed in after it.

+++

The old neighborhood was just as quiet on this Sunday morning as it had always been. Half the folks had gone to church, the other half were still sleeping off their Saturday night activities, and all of the businesses were closed except for the gas stations, a few convenience stores, and the Aldi. A few people were walking their dogs or putting coins into newsstands, but the foot traffic was light. Lower Lawrenceville was peaceful. Tess's heart was not.

When she got to Fenway, she carefully cased the street. She knew what Antwon's car looked like, and she had to make sure it was nowhere near Janelle's place. After riding around the block, looking up and down the side streets, she figured she was safe. She locked her bike to a porch railing, then walked up to Janelle's door and leaned on the bell. When there was no response, she started pounding as hard as she could.

"Janelle! Hey Janelle! I wanna talk to you. You come on down here or I'll keep yelling till you do." Tess didn't care if she disturbed the neighbors – the more witnesses who knew she was here, the better, was what she figured.

Finally, and probably just to shut her up, Janelle appeared in the doorway in her bathrobe, the usual cigarette dangling from her hand.

"Well, come on in here 'fore you get me throwed outta this here apartment," she said, her voice low and gravelly.

"Nuh-uh. We talk out here. I'm not gettin' beat up again or locked in some damn closet till Antwon comes around, or whatever you thinkin'." Tess was already sitting on the top step.

"Suit yourself." Janelle sat down next to her, with a comfortable space between them. No more hugs. No more Auntie Janelle.

"Where's my mother?" Tess asked her immediately.

"Girl, I got no idea. It's like I said, she – the both of you – y'all just disappeared. Then I run into Antwon, and he says your mama robbed him and took off with his money. Well, that don't sound like Rose, but then she never did say goodbye to me, so what do I know about where she went? Maybe I didn't know her so good after all. I have had me some so-called 'friends' disappear before, and it don't feel good. I really cared about your mama, and she left me with not a word."

"And you hooked up with Antwon, just like that? You believed him over what you knew about my mother?" Tess's voice was full of scorn.

"I didn't have a reason not to believe him. The police, they didn't find nothin'. I went down to the police station to ask for myself. They only told me they couldn't find your mama. They wouldn't tell me nothin' about you since you was a minor. I about fainted when you showed up on my porch, but you couldn't tell me where your mama was neither. So why not go with Antwon's story?"

"Why'd you let him beat me up?"

Janelle took a deep drag on her cigarette and blew the smoke out slowly. "I stood by to see he didn't kill you or maim you. I called him off you finally. But he had to get the anger

213

out of him, or else he'd of just had to come after me. He's been mad at me before. And I didn't want that, no way."

Tess looked at Janelle and realized that she herself really didn't have any answers about what had happened. She also understood a few things about survival that she hadn't previously known. Both she and Janelle had simply had to maintain, make choices, survive, and do the best they could. She decided that judging other people's decisions, at least for now, was not her most important job.

She was getting ready to leave when the question that had been hiding in the back of her mind suddenly popped out.

"How do you know SloMo? You must'a given him my cell number. Why'd you do that?"

Janelle got a sly look about her, shifting her eyes to the bottom porch step.

"Antwon got his own business now," she said. "He does okay, and SloMo once in a while comes over to, uh, talk business with him. Seems like they had a falling-out, you might say. I don't know nothin' about it."

"Yeah, SloMo got a lot of 'commerce' going on. But what's your deal?"

"Well, he comes over here yesterday morning when Antwon's not around. He starts askin' about you. At first I tell him to piss off, then he pulls a knife, says he wants your cell number and he figures I got it, seein' as how you and me is old friends and all. So then I give it to him. He can't hurt you none over the phone, is what I'm thinking."

Tess stared at her. She looked a mess right then, but she could still clean up pretty nice. Tess thought it was a shame she didn't seem to think much of herself.

"Janelle," she said, looking at her with a mixture of pity and disgust. "You can do better for yourself than Antwon." Standing up, she unlocked her bike and pedaled off.

Chapter 24

Irv lay in a hospital bed, feeling somewhat disembodied after the procedure that they told him was a CT scan. He'd been wheeled down a hallway on a gurney afterwards and settled in this room. He wasn't in pain, he just felt light-headed and weak. A nurse, or someone, had hooked him up to a variety of tubes dangling from bags that hung from a pole above his head. People in green uniforms came and went, arranging things around him without asking his permission. The funny thing was, for about the first time in his life he felt okay about not being in control.

After a while (how long?), he heard a little commotion on the other side of the curtain that divided his part of the room from the remaining space. It sounded like another patient was being settled into the next bed. He wondered idly what was wrong with the new roommate. He mostly hoped that whoever it was would be quiet, as noises and lights seemed to bother him quite a bit right now.

Some time passed. How much? He didn't know. A man in a white coat sat down beside him and introduced himself as Dr. Ashwan. He asked Irv a few questions that Irv had some trouble answering, as he was getting very sleepy. He must have dozed off, because the doctor was gone when he awoke. Nurses came and fussed over him once in a while, but otherwise he was alone.

He came half-awake once to realize that Joseph was sitting next to him, talking into his phone.

"Hi…I'm at the hospital…No, not me, it's my dad…He seems to have had a stroke…Yeah, I used my back door key when he didn't answer, and there he was, just sitting in his recliner…Because he wasn't making any sense…Well, I called 911 and got an ambulance…No, don't come into town, just take care of Dylan…I'll let you know when I know…Okay, yeah, 'bye."

Irv kept his eyes closed. He didn't want to try to talk. Finally, Joseph must have gone away for a while, because when Irv peeked, the chair next to the bed was empty. Another period of time passed pleasantly enough, with Irv feeling like he was floating. Then the doctor returned, and this time Joseph was with him. They both sat by the bed. Irv listened carefully but did not stir. He pretended to be sleeping.

"Mr. Gladstone, your father has suffered a mild ischemic stroke. This is good news, as a hemorrhagic stroke would be far more serious and require immediate surgery. We can treat this type of stroke with clot-clearing drugs, and indeed, we have already begun to do so. Physical therapy and speech therapy will also be prescribed as needed as soon as he is ambulatory." The doctor paused.

"Well, uh, that's good, I guess," said Joseph. "How long will he be hospitalized?"

"He may be able to leave tomorrow, as it was a relatively minor stroke. But we'll be monitoring his vitals – blood pressure, blood sugar, oxygen levels, and etcetera – before we release him. Were you aware that your father is hypoglycemic? That means that he has low blood sugar."

"Um. I'm not sure. My mother always took care of those things."

"Yes. Of course. The implication with hypoglycemia is that he needs to be careful of his diet. Does your father live alone?"

"He does. I've been trying to get him to move in with us — with me — but he's determined to stay in the old house on his own."

"These are often difficult conversations to have with an aging parent. I am afraid for the immediate future, his choices are to live with you or to have a home caregiver on a drop-in basis. That option can be somewhat expensive, depending on the type of insurance that he holds."

"My father is very indisposed to spending money. He's going to have to stay with me. How long do you expect his recovery to take? He'll want to know."

"That depends on many factors. It's good that you found him when you did. Test results indicate that he had already had a TIA — a transient ischemic attack — earlier in the day or perhaps during the night. The sooner treatment is begun with a stroke patient, the better is the prognosis for a full recovery."

When the conversation paused, Irv's eyes fluttered open.

"Hey, Dad. It's me, Joseph. How are you? Are you comfortable?"

Irving turned just his eyes toward his son. He said, "Mmm-hmm," and squeezed Joseph's hand softly.

"That's good, Dad. Hey, I talked to Dr. Ashwan here. They say you'll only have to be here for a day or two, and then you can come home and rest. Home to my house, where I can take care of you."

Irv started to shake his head back and forth, and his right leg made slight kicking motions. "Wanh go home." His speech was still slurred, but it was plain enough that he disagreed with Joseph's plan. What would happen to Tess if he did not go home? He continued to struggle, mumbling, "Tsh. Go home."

Dr. Ashwan spoke up. "Your father is still somewhat disoriented. This may not be the best time to discuss post-treatment alternatives."

Joseph looked alarmed by his father's agitation. He pressed the call button for a nurse.

"Yes, sir, can I help you?" said the nurse when she appeared.

"My father seems to be quite upset. Can you do anything to quiet him?"

"I can take care of that. I'll give him a mild sedative so that he can rest." Then she said, "You'll need to go down to Admissions next and check your father in. There are papers to fill out concerning insurance and what-all."

Joseph and the doctor both left the room, and Irv started to panic. He didn't fully understand what had happened to him nor why he couldn't speak clearly, and that alone was terrifying. The worst thing, though, was that no one knew about Tess. He couldn't go home with his son. What would happen to Tess if he didn't go back to his house? He fretted while the sedative the nurse had given him took effect.

After that his thoughts came in fragments, and sometimes it seemed as though he was just drifting, with no feelings of immediacy about what should or shouldn't be done. That was the best feeling of all. It was kind of like what he had always imagined surfing or skiing to be like. He had never experienced either one, but he knew instinctively what it would feel like to fly. He had dreamed of it often enough.

Floating felt just fine, and he would have been content to check out right then and there, except for Tess. Why the hell should he be concerned about her, when instead he could have peacefully sailed away?

He loved her like a grandfather. That was the scary truth. Scary because it left him so damned vulnerable. She didn't belong to him. She had her own community — or did she? — and her own concerns. The sudden realization that she would come home to an empty house jolted him into full consciousness.

He pressed the call button and an attendant appeared. What did he want? He insisted that he wanted to leave. The attendant nodded reassuringly, as though she understood every word of his garbled speech. Then she took his vitals, emptied his bed pan, fed him some more pills, and left him alone to fall asleep once more.

Sometime later, he came around enough to hear Joseph sitting nearby, talking on his cell phone again. He kept his eyes closed and drifted pleasantly for a while. Joseph started out speaking softly, but his voice became more animated, and Irv paid closer attention.

"I know it's been hours . . . We'll just have to do that next Sunday. You can explain it to Dylan . . . Look, this is my father we're talking about . . . Yes, I *understand* that your parents seem to do very well with your once-a-year visit to Florida. That is not my situation . . . Well, maybe I *do* care more about him . . . Fine. Think about it yourself, Marian." He ended the call and sat back with a huff. Irv breathed evenly behind closed eyes as he listened.

Joseph left after a while, and a nurse came in to take his vitals and switch out his drip bag with another one. He had to pee, and he was elated to find that he could make himself understood enough to be given a bed pan.

When he had concluded his business, she removed the pan and raised his bed so that he could sit upright.

"Your dinner will be coming shortly, Dr. Gladstone. The attendant will stay while you eat so that you can have help if you need it."

Irv waved his right hand weakly, trying to indicate that he would not require assistance with his dinner, thank you very much. He was frustrated and irritable, angry with his disobedient left side, and wishing he could let loose a volley of complaints to anyone within earshot.

Presently an attendant came into the room and set down a tray bearing little covered dishes.

"Here you go, Dr. Gladstone," the young man said cheerfully. "I'll stay in case you need any assistance."

Irv growled softly as he used his right hand to uncover a cup of red Jello. He picked up the spoon and tried to use it, but the cup slid away from him. The attendant was leaning forward, intending to hold the cup still for him, until he noticed Irv glaring at him with a furrowed brow. Wisely, the young man retreated.

Picking up his unresponsive left forearm, Irv placed it on the tray and used it to block the cup in place. He managed to extract a small spoonful of Jello and transfer it to his mouth. He swallowed deliberately. Then he laid the spoon down and leaned back on the pillows that were propped behind his back.

"Good job, Dr. G," said the attendant, whose name tag identified him as Mehir. "Use it or lose it, that's the best way to get back into gear. The more you try to do for yourself, the faster you'll recover."

221

Irv closed his eyes with a sigh. He was worried about Tess, wishing he could speak clearly enough to call the house and tell her where he was. He desperately wanted to go home. What would she do when he failed to show up? He realized that she didn't have anyone else to call. At that thought, sadness clogged his throat and a stray tear rolled down his cheek. He was too old and infirm to be responsible for such a young girl, he thought, and he never should have allowed her to stay. But he had allowed it, and he missed her now.

+++

With all of Sunday still in front of her, Tess decided to stop off at a park and rest for a bit. She found a bench under a shade tree and sat down, watching the activity on the playground, watching the parents chatting with each other as they kept track of their kids. Part of her wanted to be in there with the other children, running and climbing, feeling safe under the observant eye of a parent. Things were a lot simpler when she was a kid, or at least it felt that way. It seemed to her as though more than those two or three years had passed since she was playing on the swings. She didn't feel ready to face adolescence without her mother. She knew she couldn't go back and erase what had happened, but she yearned to fill the hole in her soul that her mother's absence had left. She just didn't know what to fill it with.

So far, Irv had been treating her fairly, and she was grateful for that. He could be stubborn and difficult sometimes. He certainly had some views of the world that her mother and grandmother had taught her to shun. Plus he was a stuck-up old white guy, the sort of person she had never imagined she would have to rely on for anything other than trouble.

On the other hand, he had given her a roof over her head, food, a way to be useful, and plenty of freedom. She couldn't complain, especially when she compared it with the treatment she'd faced in her foster placements since her mother had disappeared.

She started to wonder how Irv was doing. He hadn't looked so great this morning, but he had come back from less than perfect situations before. She was confident that he could do it again. She told herself that she didn't need to worry about him. But she worried anyway. Because he was both her meal ticket and the safest person she'd found so far.

Lost in her thoughts, she had stopped paying any attention to what was going on around her.

"Can you please give me back my ball?" The question came from a very small boy who was standing in front of Tess. She looked down and discovered that a large blue ball had become lodged beneath her bench. She dug it out and returned it to the boy, who promptly ran off with it to rejoin his game. Deciding it was time to head out, she stood and stretched.

Traffic was light on this Sunday afternoon. Tess was in no hurry to get home. She was struggling with the vision of the woman in the garage. It couldn't be her mother – but what if it was? The thought of Antwon catching her on his property was terrifying. She pedaled slowly, trying to think up a plan, turning up the bike path that followed the river. Other cyclists were out, along with skateboarders and people walking dogs. Young couples pushed strollers and children followed after their parents, awakening the same yearning in Tess that had been burning in her for a year and a half. She had only a slim hope that her mother was still alive, but she had to know either way.

Her quilt, the one her Gram had sewn for her, was in Antwon's garage. Tess's head injury had left the only blood the police found in the apartment, but she had seen enough crime shows to know that there were many ways to kill people. Kill. People. Her imagination created terrible images. What had Antwon done with her mother?

Janelle's story didn't convince Tess. Rose would not have stolen from Antwon, she was trying to break up with him. Tess was determined to get inside Antwon's garage. She thought about breaking in, about how she would do it and the tools she would need. She wondered whether she dared try to use SloMo's gang as a security force, or at least as a look-out team. Maybe she could make it sound like she wanted to get Antwon arrested for something. That was what SloMo wanted, for sure. And Tess had learned very well by now that you don't get something for nothing.

Tess was afraid of Antwon. She was afraid of SloMo too, or maybe just wary of him, but at least she knew what he wanted from her. She didn't know what Antwon wanted, and that made it very hard to imagine making any kind of deal with him. Which left her feeling powerless.

Antwon had become the monster in the dark. The enemy that you don't see coming. When had that happened? She thought back on the days when he first moved in with her and Rose. He'd seemed pretty normal - smitten with Rose, likely to come home late and drunk after his shifts, but nice enough on his days off. His behavior changed, though, when Rose started to complain about his drinking and partying.

After the first year or so, Antwon began treating Tess differently, and she noticed. He would stare at her when Rose wasn't in the room, which made her feel creepy. Her mother seemed less flirty with him, more business-like. On many nights, from her curtained corner in the front room, Tess heard angry whispering coming from the bedroom, muttering, words hissed out and then hushed. Once she heard a loud thump followed by the slam of the bathroom door. And then the Day came when her world changed forever.

She had to break into Antwon's garage. The thought of that undertaking gave her chills, despite the warm August air. She had always disliked this sticky, humid time of year. The damp made it almost impossible for her to brush her hair, which was always a challenge anyways. Braids were the answer, said her Gram. Mama used to tell her to be proud of her hair, and to let her curls fly free. She'd never been sure which voice to listen to, since she loved them both. Now, though, she knew what she heard. It was her own voice that spoke the loudest to her, telling her what she must do.

Chapter 25

Tess let herself in through the back door and headed straight for her room. Passing the recliner along the way, she noted that it was empty and assumed that Irv was napping. She pulled her journal from under her pillow and curled up in the corner of her bed to write down her latest thoughts on life, the nature of folks, and the disappearance of her mother.

She didn't have a lot of new information about her mother, but she was now fully aware of the lies that Antwon had been telling and Janelle's need to believe him. Did Janelle know about the woman in Antwon's garage? Tess hadn't dared to bring it up and reveal to Janelle that she'd been snooping around Antwon's place. There had been a time in her life when she had thought of Janelle as a safety net. No more.

What was she going to do about it all? SloMo was threatening her with some kind of deadline - she wasn't sure what that meant. She knew she couldn't rely on the police, they had closed the book on the whole situation. Janelle was no help. Irv, bless his heart, was too old. It was up to her, and her alone.

After writing for a while, she wandered into the kitchen and made herself a sandwich. Still no sign of Irv. Maybe his son had taken him out for a ride, she mused. That would be nice. He hadn't looked like himself this morning, and she was glad to pass his care onto someone else for a change.

She finished her lunch and cleared her plate. As she was washing up, she took note for the first time of an ancient-looking radio that was almost buried beneath a pile of old junk mail. She flipped it on and turned the dial, trying to find a station that wasn't baseball, Bible sermons, or call-ins. Near the end of the dial she found a Spanish station playing a slow love song. Grabbing the dish towel as though it were a scarf, she danced around the room, moving her hips with the beat. When the song ended, she tossed the towel on the counter and turned off the radio.

Sinking down onto a kitchen chair, she realized that she needed help from SloMo. The plan would take some thought. She had to make it worth his while to help her, but she didn't want to tell him too much. She had learned by now that the more information someone had about you, the more ammunition they had to use against you. No way was she going to confide to him her fears about her mother.

For the next half hour or so, various plans ran through her mind, most of them terrible. She was also starting to worry that Irv would suddenly return with Joseph and she'd have a lot of explaining to do.

Back in her room, her phone started to ring. It took her a while to get to it, she wasn't yet attached to it as a life source the way the kids on the street were. SloMo's name showed on her screen, since she had saved him into her contacts. She made an instant decision about what she would say to him.

"Yo, girl," was all he said when she connected.

"I heard your message," she answered. "And I been thinkin' about it. You and me both want Antwon busted. You want me to report that he beat me up so's the cops will search his house and find the drugs, right? Only I didn't report the fight when it happened, and I'm pretty well healed up by now."

"Yeah. Right." Silence while the wheels in SloMo's head turned slowly. "So now what?"

"So. When I was over there yesterday, I poked around some, and looks to me like he's got somethin' fishy goin' on in his garage."

"Fishy like how?"

"Like maybe he's hiding someone or something in there. It's all boarded up and locked down tight, but I saw a skylight I could look through if I can climb up on the roof. If we can get him on pimping or trafficking, that's way better than a drug bust."

"Hm. You got a point. He could go away for a long time on somethin' like that."

"So I want to go back and find out what's going on. But I need your help."

"I hear you. What do you need?"

"First, I got to know that he's not gonna be there. Second, I need a ride. That's it."

"I'll send my boys to scope it out. Pick you up in the alley at ten if it's go. If not, I call you."

Tess remembered the windows that were covered over on Antwon's garage. She thought it might be easier to pry the boards off of one of them than to try to force the doorknob. There was always a chance that the woman inside would come and open the door, but Tess didn't want to count on it. She seemed pretty drugged out when Tess had seen her from the skylight.

She went out back to Irv's garage and started rummaging around, looking for tools. She found a hammer with a claw, two kinds of screwdrivers, a box knife and some pliers. She also came upon a musty old canvas sack that she could use to

228

carry the tools. After locking up the garage, she went back in the house to wait and plan. She added to her toolset a working flashlight that Irv kept in a kitchen drawer. It was three o'clock, and Irv still wasn't back from wherever. She felt uneasy about him being gone so long, but since he didn't have a cell phone, there was nothing she could do about it.

She didn't want him to know about her planned nighttime activity, since he'd certainly try to stop her. He was usually in bed by nine-thirty, and she could then sneak out, closing her bedroom door as though she was asleep in there. She'd leave the Schlitz keyring hanging on its hook and lock up with one of her spare keys, confident that she would be home before midnight. All she had to do now was wait for darkness.

She was waiting for Irv, too. This just wasn't normal. Could Joseph have hauled him off and stuck him in a nursing home? But that didn't make sense. Joseph had been plain about wanting his father to move in with him. If he finally succeeded in convincing Irv, they would have at least spent some time packing his clothes, as well as the papers and books spread across Irv's desk. Irv would never leave his work behind.

Would he have left her behind? She turned her mind away from the thought; it hurt too much to bear.

+++

Around six o'clock, the two remaining cats started yammering for their dinner. Tess had been immersed in a book of diary excerpts from the First World War, and she was surprised to see how late in the day it was. She laid the book aside and went off to feed them, wondering where Irv had gotten himself to. If he was spending the night at his son's house, he could have told her so. She was more than a little irritated to find herself feeling concerned about him.

Having only herself to feed at dinnertime was unusual. She'd only been living there for a couple of months, but she had fallen into a routine of shopping, cooking and laundry that had become as familiar to her as if she'd been doing it for years. She took the opportunity of dining alone to make herself a big salad with lots of veggies, tuna, and a hard-boiled egg - something that definitely would not satisfy Irv. *If he's just gonna take off and not tell me a thing about it, I'll please myself.*

With dinner out of the way, the time seemed to drag slowly. It was hard to keep her mind focused enough to read. She checked the contents of the canvas bag, picturing how she could use the tools to get into the garage. She still didn't know what she was going to say to the druggie who was squatting in there. Chances seemed slim that the woman would know anything about what had happened to Rose, but slim was better than none. She was the only lead Tess had at the moment.

SloMo still hadn't called to stop the plan. At a few minutes before ten, Tess closed her bedroom door, put her phone in her pocket, and went out the kitchen door. She had the canvas sack slung over her shoulder, and she took care to lock up with one of her spare keys.

Standing in the darkness near the alley, she stepped out when SloMo's car drove up. She hopped in as he slowly rolled by, pulling the door shut quietly after herself.

"Yo. What's the plan?" he asked her.

"I'm gonna try to climb up on the garage roof and see what's in there. Then if I can break in, I'll get a better look around. It'll take maybe an hour. You gonna wait while I'm in there?"

"Naw, girl, that don't look so good. I'll come back in an hour. You be waitin' out front or I'll keep on driving. I don' wanna get pulled over for bein' DWB."

"DWB?"

"Driving While Black."

Tess hadn't figured SloMo was going to wait around, and she was reassured by his answer. She stayed silent for the rest of the drive. He let her off in front of the house and took off.

The house was dark. Antwon's car did not appear to be parked anywhere nearby. Tess could see a faint glow coming from the skylight on top of the garage, and she headed up the driveway. As she reached the side door, a dog started barking, and she froze. A man's voice yelled sharply, and the barking stopped. She knocked softly at the door.

"Anybody there?" she called. Silence answered back. She knocked again, then tried the doorknob. It didn't budge. Moving over to the window a couple of feet away, she shined the flashlight on it. The boards looked as though they'd been there for a while, and they had shrunk a bit as the wood had dried out. Tiny gaps appeared between a couple of them – enough, she thought, for her to jam the claw of a hammer between them. But the window was positioned so high that it was out of her reach. She set the canvas bag on the ground and took out the hammer. Still no sounds came from within the garage.

Maybe she's gone. Or maybe she's just riding a needle. Either way, my quilt is in there, and I want to have a look around. Climbing the apple tree just far enough to reach one of the gaps, Tess jammed the claw between two boards and pried until one of them loosened. Encouraged, she went at the boards harder and managed to widen the gap enough to see a narrow slice of light.

She listened carefully and heard what sounded like something being scraped across the floor. What if the woman was getting ready to attack her? Dropping the hammer, she climbed further up the apple tree and belly-crawled to the skylight for a look. When she peeked over the edge, she saw that the woman had pulled a low table up to the window and was standing on it. Tess peered down at the top of her head and those skinny, needle-tracked arms holding the edge of the window. The woman was trying to look out. Tess couldn't spot any knives or guns lying around. She decided that even if that emaciated scarecrow went after her, there was no reason to fear harm. She felt only pity for the woman.

She backed carefully off the roof and climbed down the tree, just far enough until she could reach out and grab one of the loosened boards. It was splintery, and she wished that she had found some gloves to bring along. Ignoring the slivers that bit into her hands, she wedged her foot in the crotch of the tree for leverage and pulled with all of her strength. The board came loose with a groan, hanging by a few half-pulled nails, and Tess stared directly into the gaunt, barely recognizable face of her mother.

The girl's throat went dry. Her entire body started shaking as she sank, half-fell, dropped out of the tree like a falling apple. Her knees buckled so that she was crouched there on the ground, eyes shut tight and hands clamped over her mouth to keep herself from screaming. Or vomiting. Or any other noise that would betray her. She stayed like that for several heartbeats – long enough to calm her trembling limbs and stand.

Taking the hammer and the canvas sack with her, she climbed back to where she could reach the window. Her mother's frightened face mouthed her name: Tess! Tess! The girl held a finger to her mouth, signaling that they needed to be as silent as possible. She had heard a car's motor shut off at the street. She was hoping it was SloMo, although she had no idea how much time had passed. Had it been an hour since he'd dropped her off?

Tess waved to her mother to get out of the way, then she pried another board off. Now what? If she smashed the glass with the hammer, it would make a lot of noise and there would be shards everywhere. The window was too small for either of them to climb in or out, especially with broken glass around the edges. She decided to use one of the screwdrivers to puncture a smaller hole in the glass, then chip away at it until she could widen it enough to pass the tool to her mother. Maybe her mother could then use it to get the door open.

She tapped the handle of the pointy screwdriver with the hammer until it went through the glass. So far, so good. Drilling around in circles with the screwdriver, she managed to widen the hole until it was about the diameter of a quarter, then a half-dollar. She reached into the bag and retrieved the other screwdriver, the one with the flat tip. Pressing her lips to the hole, she whispered to her mother.

"Take both of these screwdrivers. Try to use them to get the door open. If you can't do it, come back and I'll think of something else."

She shoved the two tools through the hole and then waited while her mother passed from her view. Pressing her ear to the hole, she could hear Rose — it really was Rose! — working at the lock on the door. It sounded like she was poking, prying, shaking the knob with no results. Tess climbed down the tree and stood outside the door, hoping against hope that her mother was clear-headed enough to tackle this challenge. Since neither of them had any experience at picking locks, it was not a sure bet. But it was all they could do.

Suddenly she saw the knob turn, the door swing open, and her mother standing triumphant, screwdriver in hand. A rush of pure adrenaline went through Tess as she clasped her mother in a tight embrace. She ignored the fact that her arms reached all the way around her mother. It was relief beyond words for them to hold each other again.

As they stood there hugging each other, a strong arm suddenly shoved both of them back into the garage. The door slammed shut behind them.

Chapter 26

Antwon stood in front of the door with his hands on his hips.

"Li'l Stuff," he said quietly. He sighed and shook his head. "Wasn't that whuppin' I gave you enough to teach you not to be so nosy? Why, my daddy used to whup me way worse'n that when I messed around somewheres I didn't belong."

Tess looked at her mother. Rose's eyes were downcast, her face expressionless, her hands folded in front of her like a parlor maid. Tess looked back at Antwon, who was smiling now. For some reason, his smile frightened her worse than his scolding. Something seemed off about him, and she didn't dare to speak.

"You came around Janelle's place lookin' to find out about your mama, and all the time she was perfeckly happy here with me. There wasn't no need for you to be worryin' about her. But now that you found her, it's all the better. Yes, sir, I'm just as glad you're here." His words chilled Tess.

"Let her go, Antwon." Rose kept her eyes lowered as she spoke. "Please. You got me, let that be enough."

"Aw, Rose," he said with a wheedling voice. "Don't you see? Now we can be all one happy family again. Just like I always wanted us to be. Wouldn't you like that, too?"

Rose scratched nervously at her arms and shoulders. She raised her red-rimmed eyes to look at him, then quickly glanced away again. "I don't think this is right, Antwon. She's just a girl. Let's you and me keep this between ourselves."

"Hush, Rose. Your gal turned out real pretty. I think I might want to keep her around for a while."

Tess took a step back and bumped into a chair. Suddenly the garage seemed like a very small space. Antwon was still staring at her, and his smile broadened. They stood in silence, Rose scratching at herself and shaking her head. Tess jumped when her cell phone started ringing. Antwon put out his hand, and she reluctantly gave it to him. He lifted it to his ear and listened.

"Well if it ain't SloMo. You know why folks call you that, right? It's 'cause you so stupid, that's why. Your girl ain't available just now."

He listened for another moment, then said, "You show up here, Bro, and you dead. You hear me?"

He ended the call and tossed the phone on the floor. Looking straight at Tess, he stomped on the phone, grinding it into scattered pieces of plastic. She flinched and glanced at Rose, who kept her gaze trained on the floor.

"You don't need a phone here, Li'l Stuff. You got your mama, you got me - you even got room service." He grinned and bowed slightly. "Now settle in for the night. You can sleep with your mama just like in the old days. I got to make some repairs, and then I gotta figure out what I'm gonna do with you."

He pocketed the screwdrivers that were lying near the door and went outside. They could hear him scuffling around. After a bit, hammer blows hit the door as he used the scrap wood and nails to close them in. His footsteps receded, but he soon returned with more tools and materials to repair the door. Last of all, he fastened a new half-sheet of plywood over the damaged window.

After a while, the hammer and drill fell silent, and there was no sound at all. No cars. No barking dogs. Not even crickets. Tess looked around. She saw that the walls were lined with old mattresses. Pulling one of them out until a small gap appeared, she saw a thick layer of fiberglass insulation. She could probably scream her head off without anyone hearing her.

She turned to her mother. "You been living here all this time?"

Rose nodded, tears escaping as she held her face immobile and her chin high.

"How did this happen, Mama? I been tryin' to find out where you were for the last year and a half. Are you gonna tell me what's going on?"

Rose began to cry with great heaving sobs. She pushed Tess away and started to scream at her.

"Why did you come here? Why couldn't you just stay away? Now you got to see me like this, all messed up and strung out. And I don't even wanna think what Antwon's gonna do to you."

Tess stood in shocked silence for a moment before she spoke. "I had to find you, Mama. I didn't have no life, living in nasty foster homes, running off into the streets, picking through the trash for food. You're my mother, you're supposed to take care of me! Why did you go off and leave me?"

"You don't know nothin'. You don't know what you got yourself into here," Rose shouted. "Me and Antwon got a deal goin', and I need what he's got for me. This is real bad."

She started to shake, and the scratching got worse. Finally, she fell onto the mattress, rolling into a ball. Tess tried to calm her, but she flailed her arms and kicked her legs until Tess backed off. She watched her mother having what appeared to be a fit of some kind until it wore itself off and Rose passed out. Tess crawled in next to her, pulling the blanket over both of them, and succumbed to her own emotional weariness.

Sometime in the night, Tess awoke with the need to pee. She crawled around on the floor, trying to explore without the risk of tripping, until she found a small washroom. It was not much more than a closet, but it had a toilet, a sink, and a tiny shower enclosure. She was relieved to know that at least her mother had indoor plumbing. She also heard a low hum that had to be some kind of air conditioning system. Otherwise, how could her mother have lived in this sealed-off tomb for so long?

Crawling back to their shared mattress, she found it hard to fall back to sleep. Unanswered questions crowded her mind, and she was desperate to hear her mother's explanation of this bizarre situation. Antwon had to be crazy to keep her mother prisoner for more than a year. Tess doubted whether he would let her get away alive after what she'd seen here. Her mother didn't look to be in any condition to protect her, either.

She wondered if Irv had missed her yet. He was probably still at his son's house, she realized, since it wasn't even morning yet. Why hadn't he told her about his plans? Didn't he think she might worry? She suddenly faced the fact that she hadn't shared her plans with him, either. That was probably a mistake, one that could cost her and her mother dearly. The anxiety exhausted her, and she drifted off into a restless dreamscape.

Dawn came early through the skylight, suffusing the room with indirect brightness and waking Tess. Glancing at the clock next to the bed, she saw that it was six-fifteen. Her mother was still asleep. She stared at the arm that lay on top of the blanket. Needle tracks marked the skin and left scars that had surely imbedded themselves in the brain as well as the body. Tess knew that her mother was in trouble, and she would be even if they managed to escape. She would never leave her mother again until Rose was well.

Antwon showed up at their door around seven, letting himself in with a key and locking the door again from the inside. He held a tray with a towel laid over it.

"You see this, Li'l Stuff? I told you there'd be room service. Just like the finest hotels."

He set the tray down on the small table and pulled the towel off. Two plates each held a biscuit, an apple, and a boiled egg. Two mugs of tea set off steam. A needle with a filled syringe lay next to one of the plates.

"This here is a special occasion - kinda like a family reunion - so I went to some trouble. I sure do hope you like it." He smiled with his mouth while his eyes remained impassive, almost dead. Tess looked warily at him, and his smile disappeared. "Rose. Wake up, Rose. You got company, look lively there!" He clapped his hands, and Rose opened her eyes.

Seeing that she was awake, he went on. "I brought you some sugar, Rose, but you only get it after you eat your breakfast. Can't have you gettin' too skinny on me. You know, I don't like that. You hear me, Rose?"

Rose sat up with a groan and shoved her hair out of her face.

Antwon sat himself down on the floor with his back against the door, staring at the two of them. He looked like he planned to sit there until breakfast was finished, so Tess slid over and picked up one of the biscuits.

"There you go, girl, help yourself," said Antwon. "No need to go hungry. In fact, I got to insist that you eat the apple and the egg, too, otherwise my feelings might be hurt. Don't want nobody saying I can't take care of my family or see you get all raggedy. That would be a crime."

Tess looked over at her mother, who was just climbing off the mattress. Rose stared at the tray holding the food and the needle.

"I'm not too hungry this morning, Antwon," she said with a whine in her voice. "Can't you just give me my medicine?"

"You say that every morning, Rose dear. If I was to leave you to your own choice, you'd waste away. Look at you. Naw, you got to eat your breakfast first."

Rose sighed and crept over to the little table, reaching out for the tea. She took a few sips from the mug, then set it down and grabbed the apple, biting into it like a wild thing. Tess had to look away. She ate it rapidly, tossing the core onto the tray when she was finished and picking up the biscuit. After choking it down, washed with great swallows of tea, she popped the whole egg into her mouth. Chewing and swallowing, she gloated at Antwon.

"I did what you said. Now you do what you said."

He rose and took the needle from the tray. Wrapping an elastic tie around Rose's arm, he swabbed a spot above it with alcohol and injected her with the contents of the syringe. Her eyes rolled back, her lids fluttered, and she sank onto the mattress behind her.

240

Tess looked on in shock. She had never imagined seeing her mother lying in a drugged stupor. She felt like she didn't even know this woman, with her sunken eyes and knotted hair, who bore no resemblance at all to strong, confident, pretty Rose Baxter.

Antwon stood up. Looking at Tess, he said, "Now let's talk about you, girl." He shoved her into a corner and leaned in close, speaking in a low voice. "You never shoulda come around here. I tried to warn you off. What you thinkin' anyways, I can just let you walk out of here now? Me and Rose, we got a good situation here. She'll stick with me forever, so long as I got dope for her. I can't let you go talking to the cops, now can I?"

Tess watched him closely. "What's your plan? Are you gonna hook me on that stuff, too, so you can keep me quiet?"

"Naw. That would just be wasteful. I gotta get rid of you, that's for sure, but maybe you're worth more to me alive than dead. I know some folks that would offer a good price for a pretty girl like you."

Tess felt sick with fear, imagining where he might send her or what he might do to her.

He pushed her into a chair and stood looking down at her, rubbing his chin. "I got to think about this situation. No sense hurrying things. You and me could have some fun together first."

Tess turned her face to the side in disgust. Antwon snorted.

"Your Mama'll be fine now. Just let her rest some. I'll be back around noon. You wait here for me now." He turned and left, locking the door after himself.

Tess sat still, immobilized by the scene she had just witnessed. It was no wonder that at first, she hadn't thought this woman was her mother. It hurt to see Rose behaving like someone else, almost sub-human, after all her preaching to Tess against drugs. The girl felt disoriented as well as frightened. She watched her mother half-dreaming with a lazy smile on her face, and her feeling of helplessness grew. How was she going to get the two of them out of here and away from Antwon with Rose acting like a zombie?

By the time Antwon appeared with a late lunch, Rose was awake again and sitting with her head in her hands. When Tess heard him unlocking the door, she sprang to her feet, ready to argue, plead, make a deal, whatever she could do to keep him bargaining with her. This time, though, he just set the tray on the table and left without a word. Tess listened to the lock shooting into the bolt and felt her strength slide all the way down her spine and out through her feet, as though someone had pulled a drain plug in her. She realized she was no more to him than a zoo animal at feeding time.

Rose spoke to her at last.

"I'm sorry you came and found me like this, Tess. I wish you'd stayed away and made a life for yourself," she said.

Tess sucked in her breath, and her fists clenched. "Just how was I gonna do that without you, Mama? Huh? I woke up in the hospital one day, and you were gone. Are you planning to tell me what happened that day? 'Cause I have spent a year and a half wondering, and now all I want to hear is your story."

"Looks like we got plenty of time for storytelling," Rose said quietly.

Rose told her daughter that Janelle had come to her finally with the details of that Monday afternoon when Tess had been molested in her mother's bedroom. Outraged and worried, Rose had wanted to call the police and file some sort of charges against Antwon, but Janelle had talked her out of it. She said that nothing had happened in the end, there was no way to prove it, and Rose would be better off just throwing Antwon out. So Rose laid her plans.

On a day when she knew that Antwon had a dinner shift and wouldn't be home until late, she started packing his clothes. That was when Tess had come home from school and wondered what was going on.

"You seemed so happy that it would be just the two of us again, it made me sorry I'd ever let him live with us in the first place. "

"Why'd you do it at all, Mama?"

"After Gram died, I knew I needed some help with the expenses," Rose said. "I thought, since he and I were dating anyway and he seemed to get along with you, that it would be okay. But Antwon got way too serious about the relationship. It wasn't working out, he was coming home drunk all the time, and I just didn't feel like I had anything in common with him except for the rent and the grocery bills. But every time I talked to him about breaking up, he'd start to cry and beg. It was pitiful."

"So, you felt sorry for him?"

"In a way, yes. Until Janelle told me what had happened to you. After that I wanted him out of there as fast as possible. That's when you saw me packing up his stuff."

"I sometimes have a nightmare that he came into the bedroom with a gun."

Rose paused, then said, "It happened like that, baby girl. He told me he couldn't live without me. We started fighting, I threw a vase at him, but I think it hit you instead. I'm sorry. I'm so, so sorry."

For a moment Rose, reliving the moment, fell into silent weeping. Tess stroked her mother's arm, feeling shaken herself as her mind cleared and the events slowly came back to her.

"I was trying to hide under the quilt that Gram made for me," she said. Her mother nodded. "I noticed my quilt the first time I spied on you here."

"Your head was bleeding. I tried to hold onto you, but Antwon started to choke me, and then I passed out. When I woke up, I was in this room with my wrists zip-tied together. And the first thing he did before he even untied me was to shoot that poison into me."

Tess wrapped her arms around her waist, rocking slowly back and forth with her eyes squeezed shut and her jaws clenched. After a few moments, she spoke.

"Mama, do you like the heroin?"

Her mother snorted. "I got to have it, Tess. I get real sick if I don't get my daily dose now. And it was a way to numb the pain."

"What pain, Mama? Did he hurt you badly?"

"Not with his fists, but with words. And—" She stopped talking and squeezed her eyes shut, her lips trembling. "Antwon told me you were dead," she said finally in a quavering voice, "and all the hope just went out of me like snuffing a candle. I wondered if I killed you when I threw that vase, but Antwon wouldn't say any more about it." Her voice caught in a sob. "I wanted to die."

For the rest of the afternoon the two of them talked, filling in the blanks on a year and a half of misery and heartache for both of them. Tess told her about the foster homes, leaving nothing out. Part of her wanted her mother to know that she had suffered as well. Mostly, though, she didn't want there to be any secrets between them.

Finally, she told her mother about Irv and her unlikely alliance with this crusty old man who had been sheltering her from life on the streets.

"This Irv guy, do you think he'd come looking for you? Would he try to find you?" asked Rose, her voice rising with hope.

"He doesn't even know I was coming to look for you. And I think he's gone to visit his son, anyways."

"Well. . . Wouldn't he worry when he finds out you're gone?"

"Mama, me and Irv are more, kind of like, transactional, you might say. He gives me room and board, and I take care of his shopping and cooking so his son doesn't haul him off to live somewhere else. The deal works for both of us. I was thinking he sort of cared about me, but just lately I don't even know where he is, so maybe not."

Rose fell silent. She plucked at her clothing and scratched her shoulders. Tess watched her, not ignorant of the signs of drug use. Finally she spoke.

"Mama, we got to get you clean."

Her mother looked up. "Not without a clinic, we don't. I can't go cold turkey on my own, I wouldn't be able to do it. Besides, we got to get out of here first."

Tess acknowledged that truth with silence.

"Also," said Rose. She paused and took a big breath in. "There's another hard truth you have to know, and sooner is better than later." Tess looked up. "Antwon makes me have relations with him many a night. I despise it, but I have to pretend that I like it, or he gets real rough."

Tess couldn't speak. After a full minute, she said, "You mean, he rapes you."

Rose closed her eyes and bowed her head. When she spoke, it was from a place deep in her chest.

"You need to stay in the farthest corner that you can if it happens. Maybe the bathroom, where else is there to go? Don't make a sound or draw attention to yourself in any way. Because if he ever comes after you, I swear I'll try to kill him. And I will surely fail, and then you and I will both die."

Tess sat still with tears streaming down her face.

Antwon didn't show up with their dinner on Monday evening. Rose had saved half of a sandwich and some grapes from the lunch that he'd left for them earlier in the day, and she shared the food with Tess.

"Baby," she said, "meals are hit or miss with him. I always tuck bits of what he brings into a drawer, wrapped in napkins, to tide me over when he doesn't show up." Tess was shocked, but Rose just shrugged. "That's what life with a drug addict is like. You never know."

As they sat sharing the morsels of food, Tess asked her mother how she'd been able to cope with being locked up for so long. Rose sat in silence, toying with a grape, until Tess started to wish she hadn't asked. Mama seemed so fragile, nothing like the strong, confident Rose that she remembered. At last her mother spoke.

"At first when he wouldn't show up with a meal, I was terrified that he was going to let me starve. The hunger and fear kept me awake at night until I learned to set part of it aside each time he did bring something. But he always appeared in the morning with some food and my fix. And then after my fix, I felt okay again for a while.

"The other thing that nearly drove me crazy in the beginning was the silence. I screamed and hollered and pounded on the door until my fists were bloody, but no one came. When I realized that I was living in total silence – no traffic noise, no barking dogs, no parents calling their children, not even the wail of a siren penetrated these walls – that was the second time I gave up hope."

A television sat in a corner, and the two of them filled their evening with whatever they could find to watch. The local news didn't mention any missing girls, nor had Tess expected that it would. Missing girls were a daily fact of life in a city the size of Pittsburgh. Only the daughters of money or power, or at the very least the white citizenry, drew the attention of the media – certainly no one like Tess.

The two of them slept more or less peacefully for most of that night. They had each other, they were safe for the moment, and sleep offered a blessed reprieve from the constant worry of how to escape. They curled up together like kittens, drawing warmth and strength from each other's presence.

In the early hours, Tess awoke to find her mother bathed in sweat and twitching. She was smacking her mouth and scratching herself, and her legs were spasming enough to kick Tess a couple of times. Was Rose sick? Tess didn't know what to do, but her mother didn't seem to be awake. She took the blanket off the bed and rolled up in it on the floor, waiting for daylight.

Chapter 27

Sunday night at the hospital melted into Monday morning without a noticeable difference. Irv was awakened at regular intervals to be poked, measured and medicated. Sometimes he looked at the clock on the wall, but it didn't mean much to him. When food came, he picked at it with his right hand and ate just a few bites. The faces around him changed with the work shifts. They all wore the same pale green uniforms, though, and they might as well have been just one person. He mostly stopped thinking about the outside world as he drifted along in the timelessness of the hospital room.

When Joseph walked into the room right after a nurse had cleared his lunch tray, Irv was startled. He had actually forgotten about his son, and that realization frightened him.

"Hi, Dad," said Joseph with a careful smile. "How are you feeling today?"

Irv tried to speak, then cleared his throat and swallowed some phlegm. In a gravelly voice, he finally managed to say, "Okay." It was just one word, but it felt like a major victory. He started to cough. Joseph picked up a nearby water glass with a bent straw in it and held it to his father's lips. With a sour face, Irv took a few sips.

Joseph set the glass down and looked at his father. "You had me pretty worried there, Pops, but the doctor says it was a minor stroke. You should be able to check out of here in a day or two."

"I wan' tell Tesh I'h okay."

"Who's that, Dad? Oh, is that the young girl you've got doing odd jobs? I doubt if she's going anywhere. There'll be time enough to tell her you won't be needing her anymore."

Irv was trying to speak when yet another nurse came into the room and adjusted his drip bag again. "Would you like to take your father for a walk?" she asked. "Just up and down the hallway for a bit. It's very good therapy."

"How about it, Dad?" Joseph looked hopeful.

Irv grunted as he tried to swing his legs over the side of the bed. Immediately the nurse was there to help, sitting him upright and adjusting his IV pole. Joseph and the nurse got him to his feet and steered him toward the door.

Joseph and his father shuffled slowly up and down the short hallway in the ward, Irv clinging to his son's arm while Joseph steered the IV pole. Irv's color gradually began to look better.

"Ih's uh damn bore tah stay i' beh all da ti'."

"I know, Dad."

"I wah go home."

"I know you do, Dad."

"Wheh' cah' I go?"

"Maybe tomorrow. We'll see what the doctor says about it."

After traversing the hallway a couple of times, they arrived back at Irv's room where Joseph sat him down on the edge of the bed. A nurse's aide was there to see whether Irv needed to use the bathroom. Irv's face lit up at the thought of using an actual toilet, and he nodded. At that point, Joseph gracefully departed.

"See you tomorrow, Dad," he said before leaving. He walked to the hallway and looked back. "I love you," he said as he closed the door.

+++

Monday night passed for Irv as unnaturally as had the night before, with one notable exception. His roommate had been checked out during the day, and Irv definitely didn't miss hearing the old coot snore and gasp all night. Green-uniformed staff woke him periodically to perform whatever tasks their checklists told them to do. He was allowed to use the toilet in his room, dragging his infusion pole beside him on its long cord as though it were some sort of guide dog. He was tempted to give it a name.

In the morning, he had a pleasant surprise. A nurse came in and, without explanation, removed the lines that had been connecting him to various bags hanging from his IV pole. When she was finished, he asked her whether this meant that he could check out. Winking at him as though he were a schoolboy, she said, "Well now, that's up to Doctor, isn't it?" He had an urge to throttle her, but he lacked the strength.

When at last Dr. Ashwan showed up on his rounds, he examined Irv's chart closely before speaking. He asked Irv who the President of the United States was, made him count backwards from ten, asked what the current year was, asked what his son's name was, and then pronounced him ready to go home with a designated caregiver.

Irv struggled back into the clothing that he'd worn on the way to the hospital. When he was dressed, an orderly helped him into a wheelchair and onto the elevator. Joseph met them at the admissions desk on the first floor. He filled out the paperwork to check his father out of the hospital, putting his own address in Millvale as the location where Irv could be reached. Irv was asked to sign, and he kicked up a fuss when he read the paperwork.

"I'm goi' to my *ow'h house*," he said loudly.

"Dad," said Joseph pleadingly, "Please come on out to Millvale. It's a nice little town, it's just across the river, it's not like those soulless suburbs that you love to hate. We have an extra bedroom for you, and we can even convert the exercise room into your very own office. I don't want to leave you on your own."

Irv sat with his arms folded across his chest. He refused to move, and the orderly holding the wheelchair looked confused.

Joseph was forced to step aside and hold an angry, whispered conversation with Irv as the admissions nurse watched the exchange with a bored expression, snapping her chewing gum while the scene unrolled. Joseph gestured urgently. Irv closed his eyes and shook his head. Joseph held out his hands in a pleading gesture. Irv turned his face away. Finally, Joseph stamped his foot and threw his arms in the air. Irv exhibited a lopsided smile, clearly savoring his position as victor and elder statesman.

"So, what address should I put on this form?" the nurse asked when Joseph stood in front of her again. He recited Irv's address through clenched teeth and asked her to call for a cab.

Joseph maneuvered his father into the cab and slid in next to him. "I hope you know what you're doing," he said fiercely as he buckled Irv into a seat belt.

"Mrs. Hollander ca' take care o' me," Irv said with his arms folded in front of him.

"Mrs. Hollander is your cleaning lady," Joseph shot back angrily. "I don't feel right about this at all. What do we know about her?"

"You don' need to know all about everything. I be alright an' call you every day."

"I don't like it."

"You doh' like it but is my life not yours."

Joseph sat glowering. After fuming for a couple of minutes, he took an alarm token on a tether out of his pocket and placed it around his father's neck.

"You need to wear this all of the time. If you press this button," and he pointed to the device, "help will be on its way. Promise me that you will wear it all of the time."

"Sure, sure," said Irv. "Son, don' worry about me. I'h good."

The cab drew up to Irv's front door, and Joseph helped his father out of the car and up the porch stairs. He used Irv's key to let them both in. George and Dickens came running, winding themselves around both of the men's legs and mewling loudly.

"We got to feed these cats," Irv said without a hitch in his speech. He headed off to the kitchen, leaning on his cane. Joseph trailed along behind his father, texting on his phone all the way. When they got there, Irv pointed to the kibbles bag and waited while Joseph dished out their dinner. The water bowl was dry, and Irv pointed to that as well, indicating that his son should fill it. Satisfied at last, Irv turned back toward the living room and his recliner. He settled himself into his chair with a sigh.

"You go on home," he said to his son. "Let me rest."

Joseph let himself out, and the quiet of the house settled around Irv like a comforting blanket. After a while, he wondered where Tess might be now. She'd been living on the streets before she took shelter in his home, so he wasn't too worried about her ability to get along without him. Still, the unfed cats and their empty water bowl were an unusual situation. Tess was always very attentive to the cats.

He was pretty sure she'd be back soon, but his eyes wandered to the slip of paper next to his chair. She had left her cell number in case he wanted to reach her. Picking up the house phone, he carefully dialed the number she had left. A recorded message told him that the number was not available. That seemed curious. He started to worry a little bit more.

Pawing through the papers on his side table, he searched for another number. Finding what he wanted, he dialed with some effort and reached Grace's voicemail. After the greeting and the beep, he left his message.

"Grace. It's Irv. I need help. Please come."

Dickens climbed into his lap and commenced to purr. Stroking the cat sent Irv into his normal afternoon nap, all the sweeter for being back in his own home. He was awakened much later by a loud knocking, followed by a voice declaring, "It's Grace. Open the damn door."

When he managed to open the front door, Grace burst in like a force of nature.

"What happened to you?" she asked, eyeing him closely. "You look all catawampus."

"I had a lil' stroke," he said as he made his way unsteadily back to the recliner and sat.

"A little stroke? What's a little stroke? Looks to me like you can walk and talk, after a fashion. What kind of help you need? I'm here." She sat on the couch.

Irv played with the buttons on his sweater before answering.

"I tol' my son . . . I could hire you as my helper," he said as he stared down at his buttons. A stretch of silence followed.

"Did you think about asking me first?" she asked after a moment.

"I jus' tol' him that so he wouldn' make me go home wi' him. Tess can help me."

Grace continued to look at him silently.

"On'y I don' know where she is," he admitted finally. "So I called you."

At that, she straightened up and leaned forward.

"Does she know you had a stroke?" she asked. "When did you last see her?"

Irv explained haltingly what he could remember. Joseph had found him and taken him to the hospital. He thought that had been a couple of days ago, but he wasn't sure. When he was released from the stroke ward, he had insisted that he would not go to Joseph's house in Millvale, telling his son that he could go home and ask Grace for help. He did not mention Tess to Joseph. When he got home, Tess wasn't around, and the cats had not been fed nor watered. Plus, her cell phone didn't seem to work anymore. He was worried.

As his agitation grew during his struggle to get the story out, Grace seemed to realize that he was in a fragile state of health. She tried to soothe him, telling him that Tess was a strong, resilient girl who'd survived tough times on her own

255

and had probably done just fine in Irv's absence. She insisted the girl was bound to be home by nightfall.

"I'll go see about something for us to eat, and we'll figure this out," she said.

When she returned from the kitchen, she had some bowls of heated-up canned soup and sliced toast on a tray alongside two cups of tea. The fragrant mix of soup and chai smelled to Irv a lot like home had when Helen ruled it, and he had a disembodied moment. His hunger brought him back to the present, though, and he was ready for some food.

The two of them shared the meal together as the afternoon faded to a golden evening. Irv needed some help with his soup, but Grace didn't fuss around too much, and he appreciated her discretion. She cleaned Irv's face and hands with a wet towel, then helped him to the bathroom, where he managed on his own. As he made his way to his bedroom, she stood to one side, obviously waiting to be asked for assistance. But he insisted that he would sleep just fine in the clothes that he had on, so she helped him off with his shoes and settled him into his bed. She promised to return in the morning.

The summer evening's light was fading. Tess had not yet come home, but Grace had reassured him that she'd probably be back by dark. He felt comforted that she knew her way around town on her bicycle, until the thought occurred to him that the bike didn't have a light on it. He pushed that idea away, realizing that he couldn't do anything about it. It was just an old grandpa worry.

Lying in bed as the sun set, he listened while Grace called for a cab. He heard the front door latch close behind her as she went out to stand on the porch. He could have gone to the front room to double-lock the door as usual, but tonight it didn't seem worth the effort. He heard a car pass the house, then return the other way, slowing each time as it went by. That didn't surprise him. Tess was almost old enough, and certainly pretty enough, to attract some attention from boys.

A lace curtain fluttered softly in the breeze of a half-open window that let in the quiet coo of a mourning dove. Mothers were starting to call their children in for the night. A few dogs barked in scattered locations, but the street was quiet by the time he heard Grace's cab pull up. Irv listened to the cab depart and felt himself relax. All would be well in the morning, he thought, as he drifted off to sleep.

Chapter 28

On Tuesday morning, the fear and anxiety returned full force the minute Tess opened her eyes and looked around at their padded prison. She needed to figure out a plan, and she knew that her mother, impaired as she was, could not help Tess carry it out. She rose and dressed, trying not to wake Rose, but her stirrings roused her mother anyway.

"Tess? 'Zat you?" were her mother's first words. "Where's Antwon? I want my food an' stuff." She rolled over. "Tess, you go get me a cuppa tea. Put some sugar in it."

Tess looked at Rose's half-closed eyes and saw that she was disoriented and groggy. She decided to go along with her mother's dream state. "Okay, Mama, I'll take care of it," she said, as though that were something she could actually do.

A rattling of keys and locks alerted them that Antwon had arrived with the morning tray. Breakfast was one meal that Rose had said he never failed to provide, since it was accompanied by her daily dose of heroin. Sure enough, he'd brought the same provisions as the day before, including the loaded needle.

They all followed the same routine as they had on Monday morning, except that Rose seemed a bit more on her guard and well-behaved now that she had her daughter there as witness and protector. She ate the food that was offered and then succumbed to the needle, all without the groveling performance that she had put on the day before. It was hard to say whether Antwon noticed any difference, since he was fidgety all on his own. He was eager to get out of there, more so than usual, which aroused Rose's suspicion. She reached for her daughter as if to embrace her, putting her mouth to Tess's ear.

"There's some kinda deal goin' down. He's worried," she whispered to Tess before sinking back onto the mattress. The discomfort that Tess felt upon seeing her mother collapse under the drug's effects was almost as intense as it had been the day before.

Tess turned around to see Antwon standing close behind her. He grabbed her arm and pushed her back against the doorframe. Pressing up against her, his hands traveled over her T-shirt in a way that made her cringe with fear and disgust.

"Now, what am I gonna do with you?" he said, leering at her. Tess stared straight into his eyes and then spat at him. He wiped his face and slapped her hard across the jaw. "That didn't help your case none. I won't forget it."

Releasing her, he took up the tray of dishes and left. The door closed, and the clatter of metallic noise reminded her again that she and Rose were securely locked in and soundproofed against the world. Rubbing her jaw, Tess boiled with both fear and anger.

She looked around the room, taking careful note of every detail that she might have missed during the fear and emotion of the previous day. She examined the windows up close, then peered at the skylight, considering what furniture she might pile up to boost her to a height where she could reach it. She knew that her mother might have considered all of the same possibilities – Rose was a fighter, after all – except that she had been kept in a drugged state during all of her captivity.

259

As she thought about gaining access to the skylight, she doubted that she would have the proper leverage behind her to breach the strong glass with just her feet. Antwon had taken any tools that she could have used. She looked again at the windows. Glass could be broken, but the securely nailed plywood covering it was a strong deterrent against any leg kicks than her 105 pounds of weight could manage. It looked like she and Rose were trapped.

Tess was not ready to give up, though. Busting their way out of the garage looked problematic, if not downright impossible. Instead, they would have to stage an event that would cause Antwon to leave the door open long enough for one or both of them to bolt to freedom.

She had all day to think about various scenarios, since Rose was zoned out and mumbling most of the time. She paced the room like a caged tiger, staring at their shared confines while she plotted. Her rage against Antwon inspired her to take greater mental risks in her planning. As her fear and anger grew, she realized that she would prefer to die rather than remain captive. Her thoughts, while scary, felt empowering – a little like writing a story, with her as the protagonist, and deciding what the end would be.

Lunch did not appear that day. Tess realized that her mother was usually in a drugged stupor for a few hours after breakfast, so it was quite possible that she couldn't rely on a mid-day meal. She decided to follow her mother's example and put some scraps aside the next time they were fed.

The afternoon stretched on as Tess tried to imagine the scene that she could create to distract Antwon long enough to leave the door open. After a while, Rose came out of her fog and sat cross-legged on the bed, singing softly to herself and doodling in a pad of paper with a pencil.

Antwon finally returned, bringing a take-out box of fried chicken, biscuits, mashed potatoes and coleslaw.

"Here you go, ladies," he said, glancing around the room with a surveying eye. Tess noticed his attention lingering on the wooden crate that she now saw was supporting the TV set. "Don't y'all be up to no tricks in here. I'll be keepin' a careful watch on what you're up to."

He tossed the box of take-out on the table, looked around the room once more, and then left again, securing the locks behind him. Rose and Tess launched into the food without speaking, eating rapidly, although each of them carefully wrapped a piece of chicken and a biscuit in their napkins for later.

As they settled into their evening of television and boredom, Tess began to share her thoughts with her mother. Tess discussed ideas, devised plans, argued the pros and cons of each, came up with variations, and at last proposed a course of action. Rose was doing most of the arguing; she insisted that none of the plans would work. She whined about the risk, saying she was doing okay the way things were and why didn't Tess just concentrate on saving herself.

"The way I see it, Mama, this is our one chance," said Tess, looking at Rose with her jaw set. "We got to make it work." She was rightfully worried about her mother's ability to carry out her end of the plan. Could Rose fake the drug injection in the morning, leaving her clear-headed enough to get out?

"Listen. I know you've got to have your daily hit or you get sick. I understand. But just for tomorrow, just this once, shoot it into your sleeve while I distract him. I promise I'll get you what you need after we're out of here."

"Oh, no, no. Baby, I don't think I can do that," said Rose. "I need that drug a most powerful lot."

"Mama, it's that or die. And I'll die with you. Now which do you want?"

Rose didn't answer, but she bit her lip hard.

Mother and daughter spooned up together on their mattress that night, holding each other without speaking. Eventually their bodies relaxed, and their breathing slowed as they rested together, like aspens sharing their roots for strength. Even Rose's early morning struggles failed to dislodge Tess from their shared bed.

+++

Irv woke up Wednesday at dawn with one cat tucked in closely on each side of him. He dozed for another hour or more, hemmed in comfortably by warm, vibrating companions. After a while, however, the cats began pushing at his ribs, poking their faces into his nose, and otherwise making it known that they were not being attended to.

Sitting up with some difficulty, he wondered why Tess wasn't taking care of them. He moved slowly toward the kitchen, using the walker that he had been given when he checked out of the hospital. He managed to scoop out some kibbles for each of them while trying not to fall. He then checked to see whether Tess might have gone out before he got up, but the door was locked, and the key was hanging from its cup hook.

Something seemed very wrong about the situation. Tess was supposed to take care of the cats – it was part of their deal. Not only that, she was fond of the cats. It was not like her to neglect them. Crossing the front room, he came to Tess's closed bedroom door. He knocked, but there was no reply. When he opened the door, the room was empty. He checked her window and found it closed and latched.

His heartbeat ratcheted up. Where was she? How long had she been gone? And how could she have disappeared without leaving any doors or windows unlocked? A wave of panic washed over him as he realized that he had been missing from the scene over the last several days. For God's sake, he'd been a fool to imagine that he was fit to take a minor into his home and protect her.

He stumbled over to the phone and called Grace. She answered on the second ring.

"What is it, Irv? Are you alright?"

"No. I mean yes, I'm okay. But Tess is missing."

"Missing? What do you mean?"

"I mean she didn't come home last night. I don't know where she is. I don't even know how long she's been gone." He paused, out of breath, and gasped in some air. "Please help."

"Let me call a cab, and I'll be on my way."

+++

Irv clutched his teacup in his shaky right hand, trying not to let the liquid slosh. Rising now above his panic was a good dose of anger, mostly with himself for getting involved in something as clandestine as harboring a minor fugitive in his home. Grace had been arguing steadily that he needed to call the police, and he was resisting.

"If the police were to come in here, they'd be sure to arrest me on some kind of morals charge," he groused. "This whole arrangement was illegal from the get-go. It's just as likely as not she's run off again, the same as she's done several times before. She has a history of it."

"Don't be silly. Why would she run away from you?" asked Grace. "She has free room and board, nobody bothering her, a weekly allowance just for doing some chores — it doesn't make any sense. Besides, where would she run off to?"

"Why do alley cats run away? Somebody else has better food, simple as that."

"You don't believe any such thing. You know her better than that. The poor girl just wants to find out what happened to her mother. Now why don't you tell me what you know about that situation?"

Irv shifted uncomfortably and rubbed his chin.

"Fess up, Irv. You know more about her than she thinks you do."

"Alright," he grumbled. "I promised her that I wouldn't go into her room, but afterward I realized that I didn't know anything about her, except that she said her mother had disappeared. I became rather nervous about my lack of knowledge, as I'm sure you can understand. What if she was planning to rob me?"

Grace raised her eyebrows but said nothing.

"Anyway," he continued, "One day when she was out — or maybe it was a couple of times, I forget — I went in there and read parts of her journal."

"Irving Gladstone!"

"Yes, well… The story is that she woke up in a hospital bed with a head injury and no memory of how she'd ended up there. No one came to claim her, and she was turned over to the foster system. She's been looking for her mother ever since. "

"Has she remembered anything since then?" asked Grace.

"Memories of the day of her mother's disappearance have been coming back to her in bits and pieces. Those memories led her to pursue Antwon, and you've already seen what that cost her."

"I was appalled that he would beat her, but I didn't understand why she didn't call the police at the time. Now, maybe I understand a bit more."

"She had it rough in those foster homes, that's no joke. She kept running away, but the police kept bringing her back. Until she showed up here." He sighed. "Now she's gone again, and if the police find her, they'll just repeat the whole scenario."

Grace sat quietly for a few moments with her head in her hands. Then she got up and headed for the kitchen, promising to fix them both some lunch.

While Grace was in the kitchen, someone knocked on the front door. Irv stood with his walker and shuffled over to look out the peephole. He saw the same young man who'd been threatening Tess in the back yard, the one over whose head he'd let loose a shotgun blast.

"Grace!" He tried to shout, but her name came out as more of a squawk. "Grace, I need you to come in here!"

She didn't hear him over the noise she was making with the electric can opener. Irv turned his walker and headed her way as the caller began to ring the doorbell. Grace came out of the kitchen, meeting Irv half-way as she dried her hands on a towel.

"Who's that at the door, Irv?" she asked.

"It's the very same hooligan that I had to chase off a week or so ago, when he was scaring Tess. I cannot believe he has the nerve to show up at my front door. Get me my shotgun from the closet."

"I will do no such thing. Let me talk to the fellow." She walked over to the front door, opening it with the chain still in place. "What can we do for you?" she asked.

SloMo stood there with a surprised look on his face.

"Who are you?" he asked.

"That, young man, is not the question to ask. I would like to know why you are here standing on the front porch," she answered evenly.

"I come to find out if Tess is at home," he answered formally.

"No, she is not home at present," said Grace. "Is there something else?"

SloMo relaxed his stance.

"Yeah, the thing is, that's just it. Do y'all know where she's at?"

Grace looked at him through narrowed eyes.

"'Cuz I think I know where she might be," he said, "and I figured you might want to know, too." A stunned silence followed this information.

"You'd better come in," Grace said finally across the chained entryway.

"Not if that old dude's gonna shoot at me again," said the youth.

"I'll take care of that. My name is Grace. And you are?"

"I go by SloMo," he mumbled.

"If you have a gun with you, SloMo, you'd better leave it on the porch. You can put it in that empty flowerpot over there," she said with a wave of her hand.

He looked surprised.

"I am a law-abiding citizen," she said firmly. "I also know the neighborhood. Now do as I say, or you don't come in." He stared at her for a moment, then slouched over to the flowerpot and deposited his weapon as she unchained the door.

Disarmed and on his guard, SloMo wound up sitting on Irv's couch. His foot tapped incessantly.

"Mind if I smoke?" he asked.

"Don't even think about it," Irv growled from his recliner. SloMo slumped back with a sigh.

"So here's the thing," said SloMo. "I ain't involved in none of this, no way, but Tess, she told me she wanted to find out more about this Antwon Jackson dude - where he lives an' shit like that."

"She came to you for assistance? After what I saw in my own back yard?" Irv wasn't buying it.

"Oh, yeah, me and Tess, we go way back."

Irv remembered the pages in Tess's journal and itched to throw the guy out. He shot an angry glance at Grace, who pushed her hand down below her chair arm, signaling to him to slow down and be quiet.

"Anyways," he continued, "she wanted to go pokin' around his house. I told her I didn't think it was such a good idea, but she wouldn't let go of it. So I gave her a ride over there, told her I'd be back in an hour to get her. Then she didn't show up on the street, so I called. This Antwon guy, he

267

answered her phone. He got up in my face, and then the phone went dead. That's all I know."

"When was this? When did you take her over there?" asked Grace.

"Must'a been Sunday night," he replied.

"And you didn't think to look for her until now?" Irv shouted. "What is wrong with you?"

"Ain't nothin' wrong wit' me, dude," SloMo said angrily. "I been drivin' by this house from time to time, wondering about it, but I never saw her around. So today I decided to tell y'all what I know. That's all."

"How do you know where this Antwon fellow lives, anyway?" asked Irv with an edge in his voice.

SloMo took a minute to answer while he crossed and uncrossed his legs, yanked his shirt sleeves down, and cleared his throat.

"Well, see, him and me are sort of what you could call business associates," he finally answered.

"And what kind of business is that?" Irv persisted.

"Look, ol' man, I come over here to tell you where Tess is," he said as his voice rose again. "You wanna know or don't you?"

Grace took action to diffuse the situation.

"Thank you, SloMo, for coming here with your information," she said calmly, sending a warning look toward Irv. "And now I think you'd better call the police and tell them what you suspect."

Chapter 29

When Antwon delivered the breakfast tray on Wednesday, Tess confronted him. "Listen here, Antwon, my mama's not feeling too good today. I'm pretty worried about her."

"She just needs her daily dose of medicine. She gonna be fine after that."

"No, it's something different. Her head ached all night, and she had a fever and the sweats. I don't know what's wrong with her."

He walked over to the bed where Rose lay shivering under the piled-up blankets and put his hand on her forehead.

"What's the matter, Rosie? You got a fever? C'mon over here and I'll fix you right up," he said.

She pulled the blankets tighter around herself and moaned.

"This is just pure need of medicine, that's all. Could be, I should up your dose. I got today's needle ready, but tomorrow I'll add some. Now gimme your arm." He pulled her arm out from under the blankets and wrapped the elastic around it. "Girl, bring that needle over here."

Tess did as he told her and gave the needle to him, but Rose grabbed it away.

'I think she wants to do it herself," said Tess.

Antwon turned to her and scowled. "Shut your mouth, girl" he said. "What do you know about this anyways?"

She glared back and made as if she was going toward the door.

"You ain't going nowhere, girl," he said, grabbing her and hauling her back.

Turning back to Rose, he saw that she held the empty needle out to him. He stood and told Tess to try to get her mother to eat something. Leaving the tray, he went out and locked up after himself.

They waited a few minutes to be sure he was gone, then Rose threw the covers off herself.

"You did good, Mama," said Tess.

"I thought I was gonna cook to death under all those blankets," she said with a chuckle. Then her face turned desperate. "But you better make good on getting me a hit today. I'm relying on you, Tess. I need it bad."

"I know you don't feel so good right now," Tess said, "but please just eat this one little ol' boiled egg. You got to be strong when the time comes." She coaxed her mother, supporting her shoulders so that she could get the egg down, then laid her gently back on the pillows. "You're gonna be clean and healthy before long, Mama. I promise."

Rose sighed and made a sour face. "What'm I supposed to do again? I forget."

"You're gonna act even sicker when he comes back, that's what. You're gonna throw a mighty fit. And then we're gonna get out of here and I'll get you what you need. But out there, you won't have to be a *slave* to get help."

Her mother winced at the word and lay back down.

Tess was on edge all morning. She couldn't predict when or if Antwon might show up. Would he yank her out of the garage and haul her off to sell her to some pimp? He had as good as threatened that very thing. Or would he ignore his prisoners and leave them unfed, as he'd done before?

If he didn't show up at all, she'd have to think of a whole new plan. She rubbed her shoulders as she paced the small room. Casting her eyes around the cramped space they were in, her attention settled on the wooden crate supporting the television set. She was sure she'd seen Antwon focus on it. She had felt at the time as though he had been checking to make sure it hadn't been tampered with.

"Mama," she said, "help me get the TV down off this crate."

"What? No, just leave it alone, for God's sake. I'm resting. And I'm not feelin' too good, neither. You better get us out of here and get me what I need, or you can just go on out of here on your own." Rose was clearly not doing well, having missed her morning dose. She was fidgeting, irritable, and scratching herself even more than usual. Tess was plenty worried that her mother wouldn't carry through on their plan.

"Okay," she said, "but you gotta be ready for when Antwon comes. Remember what to do? You got your toothbrush ready?"

"Yeah, yeah. Whatever. I don't like this. It isn't gonna work, and then we'll be in worse trouble than we already are."

"Mama. We discussed this. We agreed. Don't you dare back out on me now, I'm counting on you to do your part."

Rose mumbled something, sniffed a few times, and flopped over on the mattress with a sigh.

Tess looked again at the old TV in its bulky frame and decided she could just about manage to get it off the crate by herself. She tried to lift it, but it was a whole lot heavier than the new thin TV's. She managed to move it to the back edge of the crate, where it teetered slowly and fell to the floor, landing screen side up with a thud. Antwon would surely notice, and she trembled to think what he might do to punish her.

She got down on her knees and pried at the lid of the crate. It wasn't too hard to get the top off. A pile of file folders was stacked vertically inside, with dates written on the tabs. She plucked one out of the collection at random and opened it. What she saw froze her with horror. Photos of tortured women slid out, bodies hung by their wrists, naked, clearly violated. She clapped her hand over her mouth to stifle a scream. Was this some kind of sadistic treasure chest?

In a panic, her pulse racing, she flipped to the first file in the stack. The page on top was a receipt for an invoice. "Dear Mr. Jackson," she read. "Thank you for your subscription to 'Babes in Bondage'. Your subscription entitles you to high-quality photographs of bondage poses, which will be mailed to you on a monthly basis. Please know that these photographs are copyrighted set pieces. Any reproductions or unauthorized publications are strictly prohibited, per the terms of your subscription, and are punishable by law." The text ran on, but Tess was too stunned to read further.

Antwon was definitely more twisted than she had even imagined him to be. What the hell was he doing with this stuff? Was he sitting in here looking at these pictures while Rose was cruising on her fix? What had he done to Rose? And what would he do to Tess? She couldn't even think about it. She had to get her mother and herself out of here, no matter whether they lived or died.

She put the lid back on the crate and, with tremendous effort, managed to lift the television set back on top of it. She was desperate. Her plan had to work. It was their last chance. But would her mother go along with it?

Shaking both from the physical effort and from the impact of what she'd seen, she sank down in a corner. Taking deep breaths, she managed to calm herself enough to get back on watch. It was after two o'clock, and Antwon could be coming with food any time now. She knew that she wouldn't be able to hear him approach, due to the garage's soundproofing, but she kept her ears trained on the door as the long minutes passed.

The moment she heard him working the locks, she ran to her mother and grabbed her by the shoulder. Rose already looked pretty out of it in her current state, but Tess jammed a sudsy toothbrush into her mother's mouth and rubbed it around. She whispered to her mother to let the foam leak out the corners. Then she pushed the brush under a pillow and started screaming.

"Mama! Mama, what's wrong with you? Talk to me, Mama!" She punctuated her cries with shrill, piercing wails while she shook her mother roughly.

Antwon burst in, dropping the take-out bag he was carrying. He grabbed Tess around the waist and clapped his hand over her mouth. She struggled wildly, kicking his shins and trying to bite his hand.

"Shut up, girl! I'm gonna knock your head in if you don't shut up!"

While he was struggling with her, he looked up to see Rose writhing on the bed. She was shaking violently all over, her head thrown back and her eyes rolled into her head, white foam leaking out of the corners of her mouth.

He dropped his hand from Tess's mouth in shock.

"She's having a seizure! Do something, Antwon!" Tess yelled. Caught off guard, he loosened his grip. As soon as she could wrest herself free, she darted out the open door and ran. Antwon spun around and took after her, leaving Rose behind. Tess was terrified, hoping someone would be there to see her run, hoping someone would care enough to get involved. No one appeared from the houses on either side.

Tess ran down the driveway to the sidewalk, screaming for help. When she reached the row of bushes separating Antwon's house from the neighbor's, she crouched down and searched the street in both directions. There was no one in sight - not a car, not a pedestrian, not even a stray dog. Someone in a house across the street pulled a curtain shut, and she heard a lock click into place. She sprang up and kept running. She was fast, but Antwon was getting closer. By the time she reached the end of the block, she could hear his shoes slamming on the pavement behind her.

When she thought that her lungs were about to burst, she suddenly tripped and skidded along the sidewalk on one bare knee, scraping the flesh off down to the bone. Shrieking with pain, she staggered to her feet. Although she was barely able to stand, she stumbled along until Antwon caught up, grabbing her by her braid and yanking her backwards. He twisted her arm behind her back at an agonizing angle and hissed out a stream of curses through clenched teeth. Sweat dripped off his face and landed on her shirt. His foul breath came in ragged gasps, sickening her as he pinned her close. Blood streamed down her leg and pooled at both of their feet until they were slipping in it.

He dragged her backwards toward the driveway. She bit his arm, and when he reacted, she jabbed her fingers toward his eyes. Enraged, he dodged her and threw his arm around her throat, cutting off her air supply. Choking and pulling ineffectually on his arm, her eyes widened as she began to suffocate. She was terrified that he would snap her neck right there.

Suddenly, police cars were speeding toward them from both directions, sirens wailing. Officers jumped from their cars and crouched behind their doors, guns drawn. Antwon pulled a revolver from his waist and held it to Tess's head, shielding himself with her body. Someone in a captain's uniform ordered the police to stand back and wait.

"You want this girl to stay alive? Then you better let me walk away," Antwon shouted.

Police squatted warily in place with guns trained on Antwon, but no one fired a shot. An uneasy silence hung in the air. Three minutes later, an unmarked sedan drove up and stopped half a block down the street. A plainclothes detective climbed out of it and began to speak through a bullhorn.

"Think carefully, Mr. Jackson. We already have a warrant against you for dealing in heroin and methamphetamines. You may also be facing kidnapping charges."

"You gotta catch me first," Antwon yelled.

"I promise you, we are not going to lose track of you, whether or not you harm this girl. Do you want to add murder to your list of indictments?"

At that moment, Rose stepped out from behind the corner of the house, holding her arms out in front of her. The detective ordered her to drop to her knees, and she did so.

"Antwon, babe, let go of Tess," she said in a coaxing voice. "Please, honey. We can all be a family again if you just do what the police tell you."

"Shut up, Rose," he answered without turning his head.

"You don't want to do this," she begged.

"Shut your mouth!" he roared.

Rose's interruption distracted him enough to allow Tess a split second to fight back. She slammed her free left elbow into his crotch as hard as she could, then pivoted and fell to the ground, her pinned right shoulder making a loud popping sound as it dislocated. Immediately, several shots rang out as police fired, hitting Antwon in the head. Bits of brain, blood and bone showered down on her as she screamed in pain.

Rose started running toward Tess, but an officer grabbed her arm and restrained her.

"Let me go, I'm her mother!" she yelled, breaking free to run to her daughter.

Other uniforms circled in on Antwon, guns drawn, to ensure the obvious fact that he was dead. Tess lay white-faced and shivering in the puddle of blood and gore that was growing around her. An officer covered her with a blanket and took her pulse. He shouted to his partner to call an ambulance. Radios crackled in the background as officers started to secure the area with yellow tape. The detective walked up and searched Antwon's pockets with gloved hands, dropping everything he found into a clear plastic bag.

Tess watched him wordlessly before sinking into unconsciousness.

Chapter 30

Their tea grew cold as Grace and Irv sat waiting - for what, they didn't exactly know. The ticking clocks seemed to Irv to be a countdown of sorts. They had allowed SloMo to alert the police about a situation that might or might not involve Tess. He was desperate to know where she really was and powerless to do anything about it. He didn't know what exactly was happening, but he sensed that it was happening right about now.

"What have we done?" he asked nobody. "We took the word of a hooligan, and it could all have been just a set-up."

"Oh, Irv," said Grace. "What do you know about a set-up, anyways? This fellow was shady, that's for sure, but he knew where to find Antwon, and that's all we had to go on."

"At least we got him to call the police with his 'anonymous' tip," he said. "If the police knew what I've been up to here, they'd haul me off to prison."

"This SloMo fellow wanted Antwon caught. If his problems with Antwon saved our Tess, well then, good enough," she said. "Anyways, the police can trace your phone, so they'll know where to follow up."

They continued their conversation, discussing Tess's future situation and what might be done about it. Neither of them dared to bring up the subject of the imminent danger that Tess might be in. The afternoon crept on as their talk moved to other topics until they were chatting almost like old friends. They both jumped when the doorbell brought them sharply back to the present.

"Police," said a female voice.

Grace looked at Irv, and he nodded. She went to the door and cracked it open with the chain in place. She waited for the officer to show her badge, then slipped off the chain and widened the door so that the officer could come in.

"Ma'am, I am Officer Winslow. We received a call which originated here about a possible abduction. May I speak to you about that?"

"Yes, of course."

"Can you tell me what happened?"

Irv and Grace had discussed their story, and they were both ready, having agreed to keep Grace out of the situation.

"A man came to the door asking whether he could use my phone to report an emergency," said Irv. "I asked what kind of emergency it might be, and he told me it was a kidnapping. So, of course, I said yes."

"And are you the primary resident here, sir? What is your name, please?"

"I am Dr. Gladstone, Professor Emeritus of the University of Pittsburgh. I am the only resident. I have owned this house for fifty years," he said. "I am widowed, and my son is now grown and lives elsewhere."

"And you, ma'am?"

"This is my monthly housekeeper, Mrs. Hollander," said Irv. "She does not reside here."

"How do, ma'am," said the officer with a nod. "And how did you come to be here at the time of the man's request to use the phone?"

"Well, I was doing my cleaning," said Grace, "and after this stranger showed up, Dr. Gladstone was kinda nervous like, and he asked me to stay on a bit."

"I see. May I ask you both for your first names?"

They both responded, and the officer made an entry in her notepad.

Tucking the pad in her front pocket, she continued. "Are either of you acquainted with a young girl named La'Teesha Baxter?"

They both looked blank and shook their heads.

"Well, that's interesting. Because someone of that name has been asking particularly after a man named Irv from her hospital bed."

+++

Irv and Grace had been briefed by the police about the entire situation. Now they walked hesitantly into the hospital room assigned to La'Teesha Baxter. Stepping around the curtain separating her from the other occupant, they found her resting back on her pillow with her right arm in a sling, a brace around her shoulder, her right leg elevated and heavily bandaged. She was awake, but just barely.

"Hey, y'all," she said quietly. "They got me on some good pain-killer here, so I'm gonna check out pretty soon. But I wanted to see you first."

"I'm very proud of you, Tess. You are a brave girl," said Irv.

"How's your mother?" asked Grace.

"Not so good. She's been through a lot, and she's pretty shook up. Also, she gotta come off the drugs that Antwon been shootin' into her, and it's a struggle. I can hear her hollerin' clear down the hall. But she's a fighter, my Mama. She'll be okay."

"Why did you try to do this all by yourself, Sugar?" Grace was leaning close, holding Tess's hand.

"I didn't trust anybody to help. That's the simple reason. Also, I figured that any grown-ups who knew would just try to stop me." She paused. "Or maybe get hurt themselves. And I was hell-bent to find my mother."

"You were strong, Tess. Do you know why Irv wasn't home on Sunday and why he didn't come looking for you right away?" asked Grace.

"A nurse told me he was right here in this hospital." She yawned. "Imagine that. Glad to see you up and about again, Irv."

Irv gazed down at her for a moment. "I love you, dear girl," he finally said with a knot in his throat.

"Love you, too, Irv, you old rascal," she said as she nodded off.

+++

Grace entered her dining room holding aloft a cake illuminated with fourteen candles. Everyone seated around the table held their breath.

"Happy birthday!" cried the small gathering in unison. Tess looked around to see Irv beaming with pride and her mother clamping her mouth closed in a tight line, trying not to let her lips tremble. Tess blew out the flames with one long whoosh, and everyone clapped.

"What did you wish for?" asked Grace.

"I can't tell you, or it won't come true," Tess argued.

"No, Baby, you blew out all of the candles, so it's bound to come true," said Rose, using her napkin to wipe at her eyes. "We're blessed enough to be here, so your wish must have been mighty beyond that. But you don't have to tell us."

"I already got my big wish, obviously," she said, looking around the table. "I'm just so happy that Mama and I are together, and that we can live here with Auntie Grace. This was just a little wish."

"She doesn't have to say if she doesn't want to," said Irv with a wink.

"Could it have anything to do with this Rasheed who walked you home from the bus stop three times last week?" asked Grace. "He's very nice-looking."

"Auntie Grace, please!" Tess rolled her eyes and threw her napkin over her head. The assembled members of this put-together family pretended not to notice the display of adolescent embarrassment and went on with their celebration.

"Tell me how you're getting along, young lady," said Irv, looking directly at Tess.

"Well. High school is different. We've got more say about things like what we study and when. I like that," she said. "But we also have to think about what we want to do after high school, so that we can choose our courses. I like that, too."

"And what do you think you want to do?" asked Irv.

"I'm not sure yet. I love history, but I also joined the school paper because I love to write," she said. "I like real stories about real people." Irv beamed at her, then turned toward her mother.

"How about you, Rose?" he asked. "How is your health these days?"

"Kind of you to ask, Irv. I'm still in recovery, will be for a long time. But there is no part of me that longs for the drugs, my mind is set about that. So it's really a matter of healing my body and my spirit."

"You have a lot to heal from," he said, looking gravely at her.

"I do, indeed. But I've got my Tess here, and that is a healing balm on its own."

After cake and tea were finished, Irv stood with the help of his cane.

"Thank you, all. This has been a most felicitous evening," he said. "And, so that the three of you may continue your celebration in peace, I shall now call a taxi to come and transport me home."

"Why don't you just ask your son to fetch you?" asked Grace.

"My dear Grace," he said, "Although my son now shares my residence, the less that I must depend on him, the better my quality of life shall be. No, I will arrange my own transportation for as long as I am able."

Grace smiled and bowed her head. Tess got up from her chair and gave him a big hug.

"Like I thought from the start, Irv, you're a stubborn old guy," she said. "Good thing for me, huh?"

A CONVERSATION
WITH JENIFER ROWE

Where did the idea for Unexpected Findings start?

The story began as a prize-winning 700-word flash fiction piece, in which I tried to envision a modern-day "odd couple" — two people from very different backgrounds who are thrown together and find they can be of help to each other. Readers kept asking me what happens next, so I turned it into a novel.

The premise starts out with each individual trying to see what they can get from the other party. Gradually, the relationship grows into one of symbiosis, where each of them sustains the other for mutual benefit. I am a biologist by education, and I wanted to explore how a functional agreement between two people (as with any two organisms) could develop into something more resembling a family structure.

Why do these two people — Tess and Irv — seem to fall so easily into their situation with each other?

They are both outsiders, isolated from the normal workings of society and cut off from the community support systems that most people rely on. Tess has no parent and no other family. Irv has, with the exception of his partially estranged son, shut himself off from the world through his own choices. Their temporary agreement serves both of them and seems to be 'low risk' in the beginning. They each have to re-evaluate the situation as they grow closer and the stakes rise.

How do you envision Tess?

Tess is a smart and scrappy girl. She was raised by a strong woman who fell prey to economic frailty, and who may have made some bad decisions. Tess is determined to survive, and she's not going to give up easily.

What are you working on next?

I will say that it is another family drama with some high tension involved, set in another time and place.

CPSIA information can be obtained
at www.ICGtesting.com
Printed in the USA
LVHW091126241220
674783LV00001BA/140